The rain drilled relentlessly on the roof of Warren Chambers's four-year-old dark gray Ford. Ideal car for a private eye. Shabby, fading, perfectly camouflaged at night, hardly noticeable during the day, no flashy Corvette or Alfa Romeo, not in this profession, man, even if you could afford one.

It was now three in the afternoon and Warren was watching the front plate-glass window of what had once been a beachwear shop but was now an aerobics studio. The plate-glass window was painted over red and the words The Body Works were lettered onto it in pink. Leona Summerville, carrying a black umbrella and wearing yellow tights, a black leotard, and black aerobics shoes, had gone into The Body Works at one forty-five. He had watched her running across the mall from where she'd parked her green Jaguar, dodging puddles, the black leotard riding high on the yellow tights and showing a lot of ass, and he had thought she didn't look at all like a woman in need of any body work, but perhaps she'd been a three-hundred-pound midget *before* she started coming here.

Axiom of the trade: If a fat married woman suddenly starts losing weight, she is having an affair.

THE HOUSE THAT JACK BUILT

Ed McBain

A *Warner* Book

First published in the USA by Henry Holt
and Company Inc. 1988
First published in Great Britain by Hamish Hamilton Ltd 1988
Published by Sphere Books Ltd 1990
Published by Warner Books 1994
Reprinted 1995

Printed in England by Clays Ltd, St Ives plc

ISBN 0 7515 1305 9

Warner Books
A Division of
Little, Brown and Company (UK)
Brettenham House
Lancaster Place
London WC2E 7EN

This is for Nancy and Bo Hagan

1

This is the farmer that sowed the corn that kept the cock that crowed in the morn . . .

Matthew wondered what he was doing here.

I'm an *attorney,* he thought. Why am I lying here in the rain?

"Listen," Warren whispered.

Matthew listened. He could hear the sound of angry waves pounding in against the beach. He could hear the rattling of palm fronds on the sharp wind. He could hear the rustle of sea oats along the shore.

Nothing else.

"Didn't you hear something?" Warren whispered.

"No," Matthew whispered.

They kept watching the house.

They were lying behind a huge sea grape on the side of the house facing the water. A cold drizzle pattered onto the broad leaves of the plant. The sand under them was cold and wet. The wind kept blowing in fiercely off the water. This was the third day of February. It had begun raining on the morning of the murder. It had been raining steadily for the past five days.

Words.

You listened to words and they didn't mean anything until the pictures began to form. In the beginning, Matthew hadn't conjured any images, he had heard only the string of words coming from Ralph Parrish's mouth. Parrish had come down to Florida to see his brother. Drove down from Indiana a week ago; Wander Indiana, his license plate had read. Came down here for his brother's fortieth brithday. Parrish's brother was gay. Parrish knew that. But he hadn't been prepared for his brother's party, here in the house on the beach. Men wearing dresses. Men dancing with each other. Kissing other men. Parrish had gone up to his room at ten minutes to midnight. At a few minutes before seven in the morning, Parrish heard his brother screaming. He ran downstairs.

Fifty-two or -three years old, Matthew thought when first he met the man. Hair graying at the temples, a somewhat bulbous nose, a thin-lipped mouth. Broad shoulders that made the denim jailhouse clothing appear far too tight. An Indiana farmer who should have felt right at home here in Calusa, where so many Midwesterners now made their homes. But he'd been arrested for killing his younger brother.

Words.

Jonathan—the brother—greeting his Friday-night party guests. Despite the chilly weather, he is wearing pleated linen slacks and a designer silk shirt unbuttoned to the waist. Ornate gold crucifix on a thick gold chain nesting in the wiry hair on his chest. A gift from a former lover. A memento of Jonathan's "Italian Sojourn," as he calls it when he is in his bitch mode. Parrish uses exactly those words: his brother's bitch mode. Matthew suddenly wonders if he, too, is gay.

Words.

But some images are beginning to form.

The crucifix is a little bauble from a Chicago dentist fresh out of the closet and summering in Venice. *Bruce* Something, would you believe it? Jonathan all sleek and slender and blond and pale and blue-eyed, with Bruce's long-ago crucifix on his chest and the bells of St. Benedict down the road tolling the hour as the guests arrive, bong, bong, bong and so on, seven o'clock sharp. In Calusa, Florida, everyone always shows up on time, no chic half-hour, forty-five-minute tardiness here, oh, no, mustn't miss any of the festivities. Middle West morality, Middle West manners transported due south to the Gulf of Mexico.

"Jonathan, this is heavenly!"

This from a splendidly bejeweled old queen wearing a mink stole over a Pierre Cardin knock-off. One of Jonathan's friends. Standing there on the deck of the old Whisper Key beach house, the air redolent of *Poison* and *Shalimar* and *Tea Rose* and God only knew what other mingled fragrances, half the men in drag, the others looking blissfully Blass, all of them ooohing and ahhhing as the sun sets over the Gulf, the last sunset anyone will see for the next five days because it will begin raining at a quarter to five in the morning.

Jonathan says, "My brother's a gentleman farmer, you know."

A biker look-alike in black leather—the only rough trade in evidence—says, "And do gentlemen farmers plow deep?"

And the perfumed queen in the mink stole says, "Naughty, naughty," and taps him with a Japanese fan.

Pictures forming.

Scents.

Sounds.

Jonathan puts on the new CD someone brought as a birthday gift, and someone else remarks on how cold and crisp and scintillatingly sharp are the sounds blasting from the speakers. A couple begins slow-dancing close, and before anyone can breathe the word AIDS, everyone else is dancing, and it is just like old times, ah, those dear, dead times, hands on buns, fingers widespread at the napes of necks, sock it to me, darling. Ralph Parrish is watching a road-show production of *The Boys in the Band*, and it turns his stomach. He tells this to his brother in no uncertain terms. The two argue violently, and Parrish stomps upstairs to his room on the second floor of the house.

Downstairs, he can hear laughter, they are laughing at him.

And music again.

He drifts off into a troubled sleep. He dreams of acres and acres of sunwashed corn, his cash crop back home, but behind each withered stalk there are fornicating fags.

The faintest hint of light on the drawn window shade.

The sound of rain pelting the deck below.

Voices raised in argument.

And his brother screaming.

And now words erupt into fullblown images, Parrish throwing back the sodden sheets, his bare feet touching a wooden floor sticky with salt, his brother still screaming, the scream a blood-red splash on the pale gray dawn, and then words again, "I don't *have* them! I don't know where they are!"—his brother—and another scream.

And silence.

Parrish races downstairs.

A door slams.

Through the window, he sees someone running northward up the beach.

Running through the rain.

Wearing black.

On the floor, his brother is wearing red.

The pale linen slacks are stained red, the open silk blouse is stained red, his brother is red with the blood that seeps from a half-dozen cuts on his hands, blood that seeps in agonizing slow motion from the wound sucking the blade of the knife plunged into his chest.

Jonathan looks up at him.

His eyes are brimming with terror and pain.

Parrish's first instinct is to pull the knife from his brother's chest.

He tells this to Matthew later.

"I thought I could relieve his suffering if I pulled out the knife."

His words to Matthew.

He pulls out the knife.

And blood spurts up onto his hands and his face.

"So much blood," he later tells Matthew.

Words.

Remembered words in the falling rain.

Images of blood.

The Indiana farmer still maintained that the man in black was either the murderer or a witness to the murder. If the murderer, he would almost certainly come back to the house to get what he was looking for the first time around. The Calusa cops had finished their work here early this afternoon. Now Matthew and Warren lay on their bellies in the rain, waiting for the possible appearance of the stranger in black, who'd run off into a gray, wet dawn on the morning of January thirtieth.

"Don't you hear it?" Warren whispered.

"No," Matthew whispered back. "What?"

"There's definitely somebody in that house," Warren said.

And got to his feet.

Thirty-four years old, black and tall and slender, a former St. Louis cop, now working as a private eye here in Calusa. A .38-caliber Smith & Wesson came out of a holster clipped to his belt. He stepped around the sea grape. Matthew wished he was home in bed. But he followed Warren up the path to the steps rising to the deck, and climbed the steps behind Warren, onto the deck, the deck slippery with rainslick, dark clouds scudding across the sky, no moon at all, what a lark. A Sheriff's Department CRIME SCENE sign was still tacked to the French doors at the back of the house.

Warren listened at the doors.

And nodded affirmation.

Someone was in there.

Matthew could hear the sounds, too.

Someone rattling around in there.

Searching?

For what?

The doors were locked. It took Warren twelve seconds to loid the Mickey Mouse lock with an American Express credit card.

No one in the living room. Dim shapes taking form in the darkness. A sofa. Several rattan easy chairs. A bookcase. A coal scuttle. A desk against one wall. A blacker rectangle, a doorframe. Beyond the doorframe a sound again. Warren put his hand on Matthew's arm, cautioning him. They waited.

A kitchen beyond the door.

Silence now.

An open window. A curtain flapping on the wet sea wind.

Another sound.

Their eyes adjusted to the darkness.

A refrigerator. A sink. A counter. A table. On one of the chairs—

Eyes.

A mask.

"Freeze!" Warren shouted, and crouched, and thrust the gun forward in a two-handed policeman's grip.

"It's . . ." Matthew started, too late.

Warren had already blown away the raccoon.

In Florida, raccoons look like hyenas. They are not soft and cuddly and cute the way they are in northern climes. They do not need as much fur down in the Sun Belt. You never feel like hugging them or petting them. They are not adorable. They do not waddle out of the canals and waterways, they slink. Their sparse wet fur clings to their skinny bodies, and they move with a swift, hyenalike gait as they forage for food. They can open garbage cans as deftly and as effortlessly as a burglar or a cop opening a locked door. If they get inside your house, they will wreak havoc there. Better a hurricane than a raccoon.

Warren Chambers was happy he'd shot the raccoon.

"They carry rabies," he said.

Frank Summerville was not happy that Matthew and Warren had broken into the Parrish house and killed the raccoon.

"You're not a private eye," he said.

"I know," Matthew said. "I'm an attorney. Warren's the private eye."

"Be that as it may," Frank said, "you had no right breaking into the Parrish house."

They were in Frank's office. Summerville & Hope on Heron Street. The street name conjured a big Florida bird preening in Florida sunshine—but it was still raining. Frank's description of Hell was rain in Florida. A displaced New Yorker, forty years old, five feet nine and a half inches tall, with a round face, dark hair, and brown eyes. Constantly talking about the Big Apple. He called Calusa the Little Orange. He called Miami the Big Tamale, a slur on its Hispanic population. He hated Florida. Matthew kept wondering why he didn't simply move back to New York. And hoping he wouldn't. He was a good friend and a good partner.

And something was troubling him today.

Something more than the interminable rain and the dead raccoon.

He knew his partner well.

Something in those eyes.

"What is it?" he asked.

"What *is* it? You break into a house ten minutes after the police are done there . . ."

"Parrish is sure the killer's coming back."

"That's exactly what *I* would say if *I* was the killer and I wanted my attorney to think I *wasn't* the killer."

"Frank . . . he's innocent."

"So he says."

"I wouldn't have taken the case if I thought . . ."

"Yeah, yeah, I know your code."

Silence.

Matthew looked into those eyes again.

"You want to tell me about it, Frank?"

"Your code? Sure. You think . . ."

"No, not my code."

"You think the world is full of either good guys or bad guys. The good guys don't commit murder."

"That's my code, huh?"

"On the evidence," Frank said, and nodded curtly.

Another silence.

"Tell me," Matthew said.

"Tell you what?"

"Whatever it is."

"Come on, it's nothing."

"What is it?"

"Come on, you don't want to hear this shit."

"I do."

Frank looked at him. He sighed heavily. He turned away, facing the window. Rain riddled the panes.

"Leona," he said.

Leona Summerville, his wife. Two or three years younger than Frank. An inch shorter than he was. Wore her black hair cut in a Dutch bob these days. Narrow, pretty face and high cheekbones. Tip-tilted nose. Generous mouth and a dazzling smile. Wasp waist, flaring hips, long legs, and exuberant breasts. On the League to Protect Florida Wildlife, went to meetings once a week. Which was maybe why Frank was upset about the raccoon.

"What about her?" Matthew asked.

Frank turned from the window. Behind him, rainsnakes slithered.

He did not say anything for a very long time. Matthew waited.

"I think she's playing around," Frank said.

Words.

No pictures yet.

Well, yes, the immediate picture of Leona fiercely naked in a faceless stranger's embrace. An erotic video shot. Snapped off instantly and willfully, gone in an immediate electronic flurry; Matthew did not want to see it.

But the words kept coming.

Leona's inadequately explained absences and lame excuses over the past few months. I'm going to a movie with Sally. I have to get my nails done, the manicurist moonlights at home at night. The girls are going out for dinner Monday night, we thought Marina Lou's. I have to shop for my sister's anniversary present, the stores are open late tonight. I'll be gone all day Saturday, I'm tagging plants for the church sale. And the phone calls. Hangups whenever Frank picked up. Hello? And a hangup. Or, more recently, men—they sounded like different men each time—asking for Betty or Jean or Alice or Fran and then apologizing for having dialed the wrong number. The underwear hidden in the back of her dresser drawer. Crotchless panties he'd never seen her wear. Garter belts and seamed stockings. Bras with nipple-holes. The new haircut. A new perfume. A different brand of cigarettes. And last night . . .

"This gets personal," Frank said.

"Let me hear it."

"She was with the wildlife people . . . that's what she told me. Went to the meeting after dinner, got home at a little before midnight. The meetings usually break up around eleven-thirty."

He hesitated.

"Matthew, I don't want to believe this."

"Neither do I."

He seemed on the edge of tears.

"She . . . you know, she . . . she wears a diaphragm. When we . . . before we make love, she . . . she goes into the bathroom and . . . and puts it on. Inserts it, whatever."

He turned to face the window again. It was still raining.

"I was in bed when she got home. I watched her undress. And I

. . . I wanted to make love, you know, so when she got into bed beside me, I started . . . you know . . . kissing her and . . . and touching her . . . and . . ."

Pictures again.

Both of them naked in bed. Frank outrageously erect, Leona accepting his wild caresses. His hands wander her breasts, her belly, and at last search her out below, fingers exploring. She moves to get out of bed, "I don't have anything on," she says quickly, and tries to roll away from him, but she is too late, his fingers are already inside her.

"She was wearing the diaphragm," Frank said.

Silence except for the rain.

"She was wearing it when she left the house, Matthew."

The steady drilling of the rain on the leaves of the palm outside his window.

"She . . . she said she was *hoping* we'd make love, *planning* on it. But that . . . that isn't Leona. She never . . . I mean . . . it's always been a spontaneous thing with her."

Matthew nodded.

"Did you call any of these people?" he asked. "The wildlife people? To see if there really *was* a meeting last . . . ?"

"There was a meeting, I know that. She isn't stupid."

"Was she *at* the meeting?"

"There are fifty, sixty people in the group, no one keeps track of who's there, or who leaves early, or . . ."

"Except you. Clocking her comings and goings, checking out her perfume and her cigarettes and her underwear . . ."

"Yes. That's what I've been doing."

"Has it occurred to you that she may be telling the truth?"

"One of the good guys, huh?"

"I've always thought so, Frank."

"I know she was lying about the diaphragm."

"You don't know that for a fact. Maybe she *did* plan on . . ."

"Then why'd she say, 'I don't have anything on'? When she was already *wearing* the damn thing!"

"Maybe you misunderstood her. Maybe . . ."

"No."

"Maybe she meant . . ."

"No."

"Why don't you ask her what she meant, Frank? Talk to her. For Christ sake, she's your *wife*!"

"Is she?"

Their eyes met.

"How busy is Warren?" Frank asked.

"Very. Why?"

"I want to put him on her."

"I don't think you should do that, Frank."

"I have to know. One way or the other, I have to know."

Matthew sighed.

"Could . . . could you talk to him?" Frank said.

"If you really want me to."

"Please."

"I'll have to tell him, you realize . . ."

"Yes, who she is. Yes. Of course."

Matthew sighed again.

"I'll put him to work," he said.

"Thank you."

"I hope you're wrong about this."

"I hope so, too," Frank said.

First things first, Warren thought. If the lady's running around, she'll still be doing it tomorrow or a week from tomorrow. No hurry when it came to cheaters. Important thing now was to talk to the man in black.

Warren was sitting at a table nursing his fourth beer. He wondered if you could catch AIDS in a joint like this. The state of Florida ranked third in gay population after New York and California, but so far only seventy-five AIDS or AIDS-related cases had been reported in Calusa. On Warren's block, that was seventy-five too many. Especially if you could get it from a beer mug.

The bartender had told him he would point out Ishtar Kabul the moment he walked in. Ishtar Kabul. The family name undoubtedly appropriated from the city in Afghanistan, the surname from the motion picture. Someone had told Warren that *Ishtar* in Arabic meant *Howard the Duck*.

Ever since he'd begun working this case—and except for last night when he'd shot the raccoon—Warren had been tracking down the witnesses the State Attorney intended to call. Twelve good men and true. Just like the jury who would hear them testify that Ralph Parrish and his brother had argued violently on the night before the murder.

He had located most of them at the addresses the State Attorney had supplied, and then had started looking for the rest of them in the city's gay bars. There were only three such bars in all Calusa: Scandal's, above the Greek restaurant in Michael's Mews; Popularity, across from the airport on Route 41; and The Lobster Pot, here on the corner of Tenth and Citrus. The Lobster Pot was the oldest and sleaziest gay bar in town. The gay community called it The Shit Pot. It was Christopher Summers who'd told him that.

He had finally found Summers late this afternoon, in the public park across from Marina Lou's, one of Calusa's known homosexual cruising areas. Summers did not look at all like the drag queen Parrish had described. No mink stole or pearls or Japanese fan. Sitting on a bench in the rain, big blue-and-white WUSF public-radio umbrella over his head, wearing a tan tropical suit, looked like a respectable banker, which for all Warren knew he maybe was. Warren had taken a seat on the bench. In thirty seconds flat, Summers asked him if he wouldn't care to run over to his place for a drink. Warren told him No, thanks, he was hoping instead to talk about the party at Jonathan Parrish's house last Friday night.

Summers said, "Oh."

So they'd talked.

Sat in the rain and talked. Both of them huddled like lovers under the big blue-and-white umbrella. Pitter-patter went the rain.

"Yes," Summers said. "There *was* a man dressed in basic black at Jonathan's party—black leather as I recall—a man named Ishtar Kabul."

Warren asked if Kabul was himself of the black persuasion, a name like that.

Summers said, "Oh, no, he's as white as you or I," and then realized he was speaking only for himself, Kemosabe. But, yes, Kabul was in fact white, and in his twenties, and of course gay. Before the night of the party, Summers had run into him only once before, Kabul coming out of The Lobster Pot, Summers idly strolling past. "Are you sure," he asked, "that you wouldn't like to come up to my place for a drink? I can make a little fire, this dreadful rain. You certainly don't intend to go to *that* place, do you?" Which was when he mentioned that the gays in Calusa called it The *Shit* Pot, because of its somewhat less than elegant appearance and reputation.

Somewhat less than elegant was definitely what you might call The Lobster Pot. Obligatory fishnets hanging on all the walls, dead red lobsters trying to claw their way free of them. Tables fashioned from hatch covers, the brass so tarnished you could almost taste it. Lighting out of *Casablanca*, dim and smoky. A long, scarred bar lined entirely with men. A jukebox blaring rock.

Ishtar Kabul came in at a quarter to eleven, his arrival noted by a discreet nod from the bartender.

Still wearing black, the guy had nerve, Warren had to say that for him. If indeed he was the cat who'd juked Jonathan Parrish and then run off into the rain, you'd think he'd have switched to shocking pink by now.

But no, black it was.

Furling a big black umbrella, shaking water all over the floor. Black hair and black jeans and a black V-necked sweater, sleeves shoved up to the elbows. Black boots. Black leather wrist band on his right wrist, black-strapped Seiko digital watch on his left. Big silver-and-turquoise necklace hanging on his chest. Little silver-and-turquoise earring in his left ear. Blue eyes to match. Flashing. Checking out the meat rack.

Warren raised his hand.

"Ishtar!" he called. "Here!"

Kabul turned, squinted into the near-darkness.

"Here!" Warren called again, and waggled the fingers on his right hand.

Kabul came over to the table.

"Do I know you?" he asked.

"Now you do," Warren said, and flashed a big watermelon-eating grin. "Sit down, Ish. We got some talking to do."

"Nobody calls me Ish," Kabul said, and started to walk away.

"What did Jonathan Parrish call you?" Warren said to his back.

Kabul stopped dead in his tracks. Black jeans tight across the buns he was advertising. Slowly he turned, like a man in a vaudeville routine.

"*Who?*" he said.

"Jonathan Parrish," Warren said. "Sit down."

Kabul hesitated.

"Sit, darling, I won't bite you," Warren said, and flashed the Sambo grin again.

Kabul looked him over, blue eyes intense, wondering.

And finally sat.

He looped the handle of the black umbrella over the back of his chair.

He looked across the table at Warren.

"So?" he said.

"So where've you been all my life?" Warren said. "Or at least since last Saturday?"

"What are you?" Kabul asked. "Fuzz?"

"Semi," Warren said.

"Meaning?"

"I'm a private investigator."

"But you're kidding! Are there *really* such things?"

"In person," Warren said.

"Will wonders never?" Kabul said, and shook his head.

"So, Ish," Warren said, "you favor black, huh?"

"Occasionally," Kabul said. "Your place or mine?"

"Naughty, naughty," Warren said, repeating the words Summers had said to Kabul on the night of the party, courtesy of Ralph Parrish, now languishing in jail for the murder of his brother. The words did not seem to ring a bell. Kabul's eyes were wandering the room now, searching for a likely partner. He seemed bored with what was going down at the table here.

"You were wearing black the night of the party, weren't you?" Warren said.

"What party?" Kabul asked. Still bored with all this shit.

"Here it is," Warren said. "Straight. You were wearing black on the night *before* the murder. Parrish's brother saw someone in black running away from the house on the morning *of* the murder. I want to know where you were at seven A.M. that morning, while Parrish was getting himself stabbed."

"Home in bed."

"Alone?"

"Don't be ridiculous."

"Who with?"

"A lady named Christie Hewes."

"A lady?"

"A lady, yes."

"You're a switch-hitter, Ish?"

"I'd make it with an alligator if it didn't have such sharp teeth."

"Do the police know about this lady?"

"The police know about her. They've talked to her, they know I was with her. Anyway, what is this? The police already have their killer."

"We don't think so, Ish."

"Who's we?"

"*Me*," Warren said. "You're sure about this lady, huh?"

"I'm sure." Kabul smiled. "What's your name?" he asked.

"Warren Chambers."

"Should I call you Warr?"

"No."

"Then don't call me Ish."

"What's your square handle, Ish?"

"You're impossible," Kabul said, and rolled his eyes.

"Herman? Archibald? Rodney? If you picked Ishtar, it must've been a lulu."

"What's *your* square handle?" Kabul said. "Leroy?"

"That's getting racist, right?" Warren said.

"No, *Amos* would be racist."

He was beginning to enjoy all this. He didn't think this was serious here. He figured the cops had already been to see him, so why should he tell anything to a two-bit private eye? It was time for a little dog-and-pony act, time to lay a little bullshit on the man.

"Let me 'splain something, Sapphire," Warren said. "We have a client who is facing the electric chair, dig? Now let's suppose we ask the State Attorney to run a little lineup, and let's say our man identifies you as the cat he saw running off up the beach . . ."

"Why would he do that? I was home in bed. That would be perjury."

"Why, gosh, I suppose it would. But maybe he'll think perjury's better than the electric chair, huh? Are you getting the drift, Ish?"

"Don't call me Ish."

"Ishtar, excuse me. Is it beginning to penetrate, Ishtar?"

"I love the words you use," Kabul said. "Penetrate."

"Could you please cut the tutti-frutti?" Warren said. "What do you want me to do, Ishtar? Open this can of worms for the State Attorney, or keep it all in the family?" Still bullshitting. The S.A. already had his case, and he wasn't about to run a lineup. "Decide, okay?"

"I was in bed with a lady named Christie Hewes."

"That's your story, huh?"

"The police checked with her, they . . ."

"I'll be checking with her, too," Warren said.

"So check."

"I will. And I'm a lot better than the police. You'd better be damn sure you were with her. Otherwise, when our man identifies you . . ."

"You're not frightening me."

"Good, I don't mean to frighten you. I'll be running along now," Warren said, and rose, and shoved back his chair. "Nice talking to you," he said, "I'll give Christie your regards."

"Wait a minute," Kabul said. "Sit down."

Warren kept standing.

"She's scared enough as it is," Kabul said. "Leave her alone, okay?"

"Scared of what?"

"Shit, man, this is a *murder* case!"

"Really? Gee."

"Your guy gives the cops a bunch of shit about a man in black . . ."

"You," Warren said.

"No, damn it, not me! Somebody he made up. To save his ass."

"You're beginning to catch on," Warren said. "The minute he makes positive identification . . ."

"Leave Christie alone, okay?"

"Why?"

"I don't want the police visiting her again. She already signed a statement."

"Uh-huh."
"You go there and scare her . . ."
"Me?"
"You get her to change her story . . ."
"Oh? Was she lying, Ishtar?"
"I'm not saying she was lying. But if she changes her story . . ."
"That means she was lying."
"And if then your guy says *I'm* the one he saw on the beach . . ."
"Which is just what he will say, I promise you."
"Then we're *both* in trouble."
"You more than the lady. Scare her how, Ishtar?"
"Into saying I wasn't really with her."
"But you were, weren't you? That's what you told the police. That's what Christie swore to."
"Yes."
"Then what are you worried about?"
"I'm not worried."
"Good. Then I'll just go talk to her."
"No. Wait."
Warren waited.
"I don't want to get anyone in trouble," Kabul said.
"Who don't you want to get in trouble?"
"I can't tell you that."
"Were you with someone else?"
Silence.
"Not Christie, huh?"
The silence lengthened.
"And not an alligator either, I'll bet."
"Look . . ."
"Who was it, Ishtar?"
"He's married," Kabul said. "The man I was with."
"Ah," Warren said. "What's his name?"
"You'll only get him in trouble."
"No, I'll only talk to him. Privately. Discreetly."

"I'll bet."

"Or I'll dog your tracks for the next month until I catch you and him in bed together, and then the shit'll really hit the fan. Pictures, Ishtar. In living color. Speak."

Kabul was silent for a very long time.

"Listen," he said at last. "I really love this guy. I don't want to get him in trouble, really."

"Who? Tell me his name."

Another silence. Someone across the room laughed shrilly. Kabul looked toward the bar. Over his shoulder, almost in a whisper, as though reluctant to let the name escape his lips, he said, "Charles Henderson."

"Thank you. The address, please."

"He lives on Sabal Key."

Still watching the action at the bar.

"Where on Sabal?"

"Sabal Towers."

"Any address?"

"I don't know the address. It's the big condo there. Sabal Towers."

"Apartment number?"

"I've never been to his apartment."

He turned, looked up at Warren.

"Listen . . . please be careful," he said. "Charles is very shy, and very vulnerable . . ."

"And very married, I know," Warren said.

"Yes," Kabul said.

"He's got nothing to worry about," Warrren said. "And neither do you. *If* you were really with him that morning."

"I was."

"I hope so," Warren said.

He really didn't hope so. He hoped Kabul was lying in his teeth. That way it would be easy.

But he knew it never was.

2

This is the cock that crowed in the morn that waked the priest all shaven and shorn . . .

The body was in one of the refrigerator compartments at Good Samaritan's morgue. It had been transported by ambulance from Whisper Key to the hospital on the morning of January thirtieth, and the autopsy had been done that very day. This was now the fifth of February, but no one had yet claimed the body. The only person who might have wanted to claim the body was in jail, accused of having caused its present condition.

"Except for the defense cuts on the palms of the hands, it was a very neat stabbing," Bloom said. "Straight to the heart and goodbye, Charlie."

He seemed not to notice the stink in the morgue.

Matthew wished it would start raining here in the morgue. Wash away the stink. The stink was compounded of three parts bodily gasses to one part chemicals. Even here in the refrigerator room, the stink seeped through. Matthew wanted to hold a handkerchief to his nose, but he thought Bloom might consider that unprofessional.

"The knife matches the other ones on the kitchen rack, same set," Bloom said. "A chef's knife. Ten-inch blade, very effective."

A weapon of convenience. Which meant the killer had not gone to the house with the express purpose of committing murder. Which lent credence to Ralph Parrish's claim that the killer had gone there in search of something. But what? And why kill?

"Accused's fingerprints on the knife," Bloom said.

Reeling off the facts tonelessly. Big man with a nose broken more than once, hands of a street fighter, shambling gait, cadences of the Big Apple in his speech, New York City to Nassau County to Calusa, a policeman for half his life. Just the facts, ma'am.

"Victim's blood all over him, same type, no question about it. Tested positive for AIDS, by the way, did you know that?"

"No," Matthew said.

"The way it looks to the S.A., *and* the Sheriff's Department, *and* us, is Parrish was still pissed off the next morning, starting arguing with his brother all over again, stabbed him in anger. The best you can hope for, Matthew, is Murder Two. You can prove there was no premeditation, you got a shot at Murder Two. Otherwise, your man fries."

No emotion in his voice. Your man fries. The Indiana farmer fries. The farmer who, for the past God knew how many years had been supporting his only brother, keeping him in style down here where the sun always shone (except in February). Kept him in luxury in a house he himself had paid for, prime beachfront property on Whisper. Presumably accepted—or at least ignored—his brother's homosexuality until that night last week when he'd expressed revulsion for it. And killed him?

"I loved my brother," Ralph Parrish had told him.

And Matthew believed it.

The good guys and the bad guys.

Detective Morris Bloom was one of the good guys. On the wrong side this time, or at least on the opposing side, in that the Calusa P.D. was running routine witness checks for the S.A.'s office even though the crime had been committed outside the city limits. Whisper Key was Calusa County. The Sheriff's Department had responded. The Sheriff's Department had made the arrest.

"You take the wrong cases," Bloom said.

He looked sad saying it. Matthew was his friend.

"You know about the man in black," Matthew said. "Running off after Parrish came downstairs. Parrish mentioned him during the Q and . . ."

"Sure," Bloom said. Dismissal in a single word.

"And you surely know there was a man dressed in black at the party."

"We already talked to him."

"Ishtar Kabul?"

Warren had given him the name last night.

"His street name," Bloom said. "His square handle is Martin Fein. He's Jewish." He shook his head. He was wondering how a nice Jewish boy could have become homosexual. In Bloom's old neighborhood, nice Jewish boys didn't grow up to be fags. Not many of them grew up to be cops, either, but that was because in New York you had to be Irish to rise above the rank of captain. Or, nowadays, black. You were Jewish, it was better to aspire to the rabbinate. Or better yet, become an accountant.

"Matthew," Bloom said, "your man had the murder weapon in his hand . . ."

"He pulled it out of his brother's chest."

"Stupid thing to do, don't you think?"

"But he did it."

"So he says. Which is how the blood got all over his clothes."

"That's right."

"No, Matthew, that's wrong. *Nobody* is so stupid that he finds somebody on the floor with a knife in his chest and he pulls the knife out. Nobody. Unless he's been living on Mars and has never seen a movie or a television show. Your man argued with his brother the night before, there are twelve witnesses who are willing to swear they almost came to blows. The argument flared again the next . . ."

"One of those twelve witnesses was a man in black."

"What is this, a *mystery* story?" Bloom asked. "There are no mysteries in police work, Matthew, there are only crimes and the people who commit them. No strangers in black running up the beach into the swirling mists, no . . ."

"But there was."

"According to Parrish. Parrish is the only one who saw this mysterious man in black."

"Kabul was at the party. And he was wearing black."

"And he was also in bed with a lady . . ."

Bloom cut himself short.

"Okay, I gave you his alibi," he said. "You probably could've got it from the S.A., anyway, if you'd asked him. Kabul is clean, believe me. The lady swore up and down that she was with him at seven o'clock on the morning of the murder."

"A lady, huh?"

"A lady, yes. You never heard of bisexuals, Matthew?"

"Her name wouldn't be Christie Hewes, would it?"

Bloom blinked.

"You know this already, huh? The S.A. told you?"

"No, the S.A. didn't tell me."

I was in bed with a lady named Christie Hewes.

Kabul's initial alibi to Warren last night. Lied to the police and tried to lie to Warren as well. The only difference was that the police had been ready to accept the lie because they already had their killer. Warren hadn't been ready to accept *anything;* he was working to prove that Ralph Parrish had not committed murder.

"I assume you've got a statement from Miss Hewes," Matthew said.

"In a sworn deposition."

"Then I guess Kabul *is* clean," he said.

"Sure. You know what you've got here?" Bloom asked, and

looked down at the body on the stainless-steel drawer. "You've got a queer who was living high off the hog on his brother's money. A faggot cocksman. Brought charges of gay-bashing against one of his own lovers last September, a real sweetheart, Jonathan Parrish. You've got a straight brother from . . ."

"Tell me about the gay-bashing," Matthew said.

"Sure," Bloom said.

September seventh of last year. The Monday night ending the Labor Day weekend. Complaint call clocked in at a quarter to eleven. Calusa P.D. responded leisurely at eleven twenty-four. Scandal's, the gay bar over the Greek restaurant in Michael's Mews.

The responding uniformed cop—in Calusa, the blues rode solo—angled the car into the curb where a tall blond man stood at the gate to the Mews, holding the wrist of a sultry-looking woman wearing a purple dress, purple high-heeled ankle-strapped shoes, a purple leather shoulder bag, and a frizzied blonde wig. The blond man was bleeding from a cut over his left eye. The woman in the purple dress kept trying to pull away from him, but he held tightly to her wrist. It was a hot and humid night. The woman was sweating through her clingy purple dress. Big blotchy stains around the armpits. More stains between her abundant breasts. The police officer recorded the temperature as ninety-six degrees Fahrenheit, perhaps in corroboration of the woman's appearance.

At first, the blond man—who identified himself as Jonathan Parrish, the person who'd placed the call to the police—claimed only that the sultry, sweating woman in the purple dress had stolen his wallet. He told the police officer that he'd been "chatting her up at the bar" (Parrish's words) when the topic of conversation suddenly turned to sex. The woman in the purple dress told him she was a working girl who got a hundred bucks a throw, and Parrish took out his wallet and put it on the bar, and the next thing he knew the woman excused herself to go to the "loo" (Parrish's word again) and lo and behold, his wallet was gone. When she came back to the bar stool some five minutes later, he accused her of the theft. When she denied any knowledge of the missing wallet, Parrish immediately called the police. He now wanted the responding cop to search both the woman *and* the restroom, because if the wallet wasn't in her handbag or else tucked in her bra or her panties, then it was surely inside the toilet tank someplace.

The cop—whose name was Randolph Hasty—didn't know what to do at first. He knew he was not empowered to toss this lady unless circumstances reasonably indicated that she *had* committed, *was* committing, or was *about* to commit a violation of the criminal laws of the state. Hasty had only Parrish's word that a crime had actually taken place. But even if a crime *had* occurred, and he didn't yet know that for a fact, he was positive he'd be in very deep shit if he, as a male cop, went rummaging through this female's panties and bra. He wasn't even sure he could march into the ladies' room without a search warrant. It was all very puzzling. Hasty admitted this in his report. Well, sort of admitted it. What he wrote, actually, was: "The initial evidence at the scene was unclear as to 901.151." Which was Florida's Stop and Frisk statute.

It got even more puzzling in the next ten minutes.

The more Hasty kept looking at the lady with the blonde wig and the big tits, the more something seemed funny about her. Too much lipstick on her mouth, too much eye makeup. Voice a little husky. It occurred to him that perhaps she wasn't a woman at all.

In which case, maybe he *could* search her.

Him.

If a criminal offense had, in fact, already taken place.

At which point Parrish told him that the lady, or the gentleman as the case may have been, had struck him above the eye with his or her handbag, causing the bleeding cut which was positive evidence of the crime of Battery, a first-degree misdemeanor—*if* Parrish was telling the truth. Parrish went on to explain that he suspected the woman in the purple dress wasn't a woman at all, which conclusion Hasty had already reached, but was instead a man in drag cruising a known homosexual bar for the explicit purpose of gay-bashing.

"Are you accusing this person here of Battery?" Hasty asked.

"I am," Parrish said.

"Miss," Hasty said, "are you a male?"

The sultry blonde in the purple dress said nothing.

"If this person is a male," Hasty said to Parrish, "I think I can maybe search her."

"This person is a male," Parrish said.

"What is your name, Miss?" Hasty said.

The blonde still said nothing.

"His name is Mark Delassandro," Parrish said.

"Very well, Miss," Hasty said, and began his frisk.

With some embarrassment, he found a pair of foam-rubber breasts inside Delassandro's bra, and foam-rubber buttocks enhancers inside his panties. He did not find Parrish's wallet anywhere on Delassandro's person. Nor did he find it anywhere in the ladies' room, which he entered after a discreet knock on the door, and a brusque "Police officer!"

"I find no evidence of a crime having been committed," he told Parrish.

"How about him hitting me with his handbag?" Parrish asked. "Isn't that a crime?"

"Are you willing to make a sworn statement to that effect?" Hasty asked.

"I am," Parrish said.

At the police station—what was discreetly known as the Public Safety Building in staid Calusa—Bloom interviewed Mark Delassandro and learned that he and Parrish had been living together as lovers since the middle of July. He further learned that they had gone together to Scandal's that night (Delassandro in the dress and wig and shoes and padded lingerie Parrish had purchased for him at a Calusa boutique called Trash and Stuff) and that the cut above Parrish's eye had been precipitated by a quarrel that started at about ten-thirty that night.

The continuing gospel according to Mark maintained that the quarrel had begun because Parrish was flirting outrageously with a muscular twenty-year-old twit wearing a navy blue T-shirt and a dragon tattoo, who after two martinis began boasting to everyone at the bar that in New York City he had engorged organs larger than the one at Radio City Music Hall. Sitting there in drag all sexy and slinky while Mr. America flexed and boasted and Parrish adoringly batted his eyelashes, Delassandro had felt enormous discomfort, extreme jealousy, and something close to female helplessness. So he picked up his handbag and swung it at Parrish's head, hoping to knock his left eye out of its socket, but instead inflicting only a relatively minor cut over the eye.

The story about the wallet was sheer nonsense, Delassandro claimed. Parrish never even carried a wallet because it showed a bulge that spoiled the cut of his tailor-made trousers and detracted from the natural bulge he was flaunting. As for the so-called sexual solicitation, he and Parrish often played Hooker-John in public, for kicks, a sort of game that seemed exciting and theatrical. But yes, he had hit Parrish with his handbag. And yes, he had tried to put out his eye.

Battery, for sure, Matthew thought.

Attempted Aggravated Battery as a second charge.

"What'd you charge him with?" he asked.

"Nothing," Bloom said.

Matthew looked at him.

"Let me tell you something, Matthew," Bloom said. "On my block, this was a routine family dispute that should've been settled on the street by the responding blue. Okay, it wasn't. So there I was with an unsigned admission of Batt with a tack-on of attempted Agg-Batt in that Delassandro said he was trying to put out Parrish's eye, which was certainly intent to cause great bodily harm, permanent disability, or permanent disfigurement as defined in the statutes under 784.045, are you following me?"

"I'm following you," Matthew said.

"So. If I threw Delassandro in jail—he was only twenty-four years old—he'd be fish in ten seconds flat. If he got convicted after trial, he'd be facing a year in prison on the Batt charge and five more on the Agg-Batt attempt. So I asked myself a question. I asked myself, 'Morrie, is two fags having an argument a good enough reason to send this kid to prison, where they'll paint tits on his back and rape him day and night?' And you know the answer I got?"

"What answer did you get?"

"I got, 'Morrie, I think you better let him go with a warning.' You understand me?"

"Sure. You're softhearted."

"Bullshit," Bloom said. "Parrish wouldn't give us the statement he'd promised, and Delassandro refused to sign the confession, told me he'd made the whole thing up. A family dispute, plain and simple. So I asked myself, 'Morrie, do you have a case?' And you know the answer I got?"

"Morrie, you do not have a case."

"Correct. Morrie, you do not have a case."

"So you let Delassandro walk."

"I let him walk," Bloom said. "And you and me never had this conversation."

"Have you looked him up since the murder?"

"Delassandro? He's living in San Francisco. He did not kill Parrish, Matthew, if that's what you're thinking. He did not come back with his pocketbook to stab the man in the heart with it. As I was saying, Matthew, but you weren't listening . . ."

"I was listening."

"I was saying that what you've got here is a no-good fag prick who was kept in style by his straight brother from Kansas . . ."

"Indiana."

"Wherever, who suddenly can't take it any longer. He starts an argument with Parrish when he sees all those prancing queers . . ."

"Your star witnesses, Morrie."

"Sure, and don't think the S.A. isn't worried about that. But they heard and saw the argument, Matthew, that's all that matters. And then the brother wakes up even madder than when he went to bed. The priest next door hears the two of them screaming their heads . . ."

"What priest?" Matthew asked at once.

"You got your witness list, I'm sure he's on it."

"There's no priest on the list I got."

"Then maybe he's a new witness. Ask the S.A., he'll give you his name. He's the priest at St. Benedict's. He heard them yelling. They woke him up with their yelling."

"They woke him up."

"Yes."

"They were yelling loud enough to wake him up."

"Yes."

"Did he call the police?"

"No."

"He heard yelling, but he didn't call the police," Matthew said.

He was thinking priests wore black.

He was thinking maybe Ishtar Kabul *was* clean, *whoever* the hell he'd been sleeping with on the morning of the murder.

"Look, you'll get his name from the S.A.," Bloom said, "you can talk to him yourself. What I'm saying, I'm saying this is open and shut. A violent argument witnessed by twelve people. More screaming the next morning, only this time the guy who hears it is a *priest*, Matthew, try to discredit a *priest's* testimony. And here's your farmer client with bloody clothes and the murder weapon in his hand. Tell me something, will you please?"

"What?"
"Why did you take this case?"

The rain drilled relentlessly on the roof of Warren Chambers's four-year-old dark gray Ford. Ideal car for a private eye. Shabby, fading, perfectly camouflaged at night, hardly noticeable during the day, no flashy Corvette or Alfa Romeo, not in this profession, man, even if you could afford one.

His appointment with Charles Henderson—the man with whom Ishtar Kabul claimed to have been in bed on the morning of the murder—was for six o'clock tonight. On the phone, Warren had identified himself as Harold Long of the Prudential and had told Henderson that he'd been named as one of the beneficiaries in an insurance policy. There was not a man or woman on earth who would refuse to see someone coming around to give away money.

It was now three in the afternoon and Warren was watching the front plate-glass window of what had once been a beachwear shop but was now an aerobics studio. The plate-glass window was painted over red and the words The Body Works were lettered onto it in pink. Leona Summerville, carrying a black umbrella and wearing yellow tights, a black leotard, and black aerobics shoes, had gone into The Body Works at one forty-five. He had watched her running across the mall from where she'd parked her green Jaguar, dodging puddles, the black leotard riding high on the yellow tights and showing a lot of ass, and he had thought she didn't look at all like a woman in need of any body work, but perhaps she'd been a three-hundred-pound midget *before* she started coming here.

Axiom of the trade: If a fat married woman suddenly starts losing weight, she is having an affair.

He wondered how long she'd be jumping around in there.

He looked at his watch.

Two minutes past three.

My how the time did fly when you were having a good time.

After his phone call to Henderson at eleven, he had driven over to the address Matthew had given him, just to check out the Summerville house, get the feel of the place, see how many vehicles were usually parked outside, the gardener, the maid, the pool man, whoever, get some idea of who came and went legitimately. He'd been surprised on his second pass of the house when the lady herself backed out of the garage in the green Jag, there had to be a God. He followed her first to a beauty salon on Lucy's Circle where she spent an hour and a half in her exercise clothes and a blue smock getting her hair cut.

Second axiom of the trade: If a married woman suddenly changes her hair style, she is sucking some stranger's cock.

Leona Summerville drove next to a soup-and-sandwich shop on the mainland where, still in the exercise clothes, she took a table near the window and sat eating what looked like yogurt, staring out at the rain distractedly, her eyes sweeping the gray Ford once, and causing Warren to think he'd been made the first day on the job.

It was almost one-thirty when she finished eating.

Some men entering the shop turned to look at her as she came out.

Small wonder.

That high-cut leotard showing half her ass.

He thought he saw her smile.

Lots of married women, when they started having an affair, they began to think of themselves as infinitely more desirable. You saw a married woman flashing a lot of leg, or walking with a bouncy little wiggle, you knew she was thinking of herself as sexy and seductive, you knew she was thinking that if *one* stranger wanted to fuck her, then surely *all* strangers wanted to fuck her. Third axiom of the trade.

Warren was full of axioms today.

The work brought them out.

The moment she came out of the shop, she ran to a phone booth, didn't even bother opening the umbrella, just ran through the rain to the nearest phone booth, as if she'd been thinking about this call all the while she'd been eating her yogurt and staring at the rain.

When a married woman started making phone calls from a public booth, watch out, mister. Axiom number . . .

He watched her.

Turned her back to the traffic on the road.

Inserted a coin.

Dialed a number by heart.

Leaned in close to the mouthpiece.

Smiled.

Talked rapidly.

Nodded.

Hung up.

Came out into the rain again, no longer smiling, opened the umbrella this time, and ran to where she'd parked the Jag. Closed the umbrella, got into the car. Started it. Looked at her watch. Nodded again, and then drove to the mall and The Body Works.

She was still inside there.

Quarter past three now, how the hell long did these sessions take?

The door opened.

A flurry of women in leotards, tights, leg warmers.

Ooooo, it's still raining . . .

See you tomorrow, Betty . . .

Call me, Fran . . .

And Leona Summerville appeared in the doorframe in yellow and black, grimacing at the rain. Her umbrella snapped open like a spinnaker. She rushed for her car, long antelope strides, yellow legs flashing like streaks of sunshine in the pervading gloom.

Now we see who she called, Warren thought, and started the Ford.

"She went straight home," Warren told Matthew on the phone. "I stayed outside there till five-thirty, when Frank got home. She didn't budge from the house."

"Okay, good," Matthew said.

"You want me to pick up on her later tonight? I'm on my way now to see Charlie Henderson, find out who was doing what to whom while Parrish was getting himself juked. But if you can find out whether she plans to go out tonight, I can maybe be waiting when she leaves."

"I'll check with Frank," Matthew said.

"Does he *want* me to catch her?" Warren asked.

"He simply wants to know."

"An axiom of the trade . . ." Warren started, and caught himself.

"Yes, what?"

"A guy puts a detective on his wife, Matthew, he already *knows* she's fucking around. That's an axiom of the trade."

"Well . . . let's see," Matthew said.

"I'll call you when I finish with Henderson."

"I'll be home," Matthew said.

"Talk to you," Warren said, and hung up.

Charles Henderson was a stockbroker with the firm of Lloyd, Mallory, Forbes on Main Street in downtown Calusa. He was the only employee still there when Warren arrived at ten minutes to six. He explained to Warren that he himself usually went home at five-thirty; the exchange closed in New York at four, and the firm's switchboard shut down at five, so there was no sense hanging around.

"Unless, of course, someone has named me a beneficiary in his insurance policy," he said, and grinned.

He was a tall, thin man in his early forties, Warren guessed, prematurely white hair, blue eyes, a deep suntan. A framed photograph on his desk showed a woman and two little girls, presumably his wife and daughters. He was dressed as conservatively as a member of Parliament, and he had no speech or body mannerisms that would indicate he was homosexual. But Ishtar Kabul had said he was in bed with Henderson on the morning of January thirtieth.

"So," Henderson said, "who died?"

"Jonathan Parrish," Warren said, and watched his eyes.

Nothing flashed there. Not a glimmer of recognition.

"I don't know the name," he said. "Are you sure you've got the right beneficiary?"

"Do the name Ishtar Kabul ring a familiar note?" Warren said.

Instant spark in the eyes.

Then immediate recovery.

"Who?"

"Ishtar Kabul."

"I don't know that name, either," Henderson said. "What is this?"

"It's not insurance. And it's not blackmail, if that's what you think."

"No, what I think is I'd better call the police."

"I wouldn't."

"Who are you?"

"Warren Chambers."

"You said . . ."

"Only so I could talk to you."

"About what?"

"About where you were on the morning of January thirtieth."

"Why?"

"Why not?"

"I asked a question."

"So did I."

"This sounds like Pinter."

"Who's Pinter?" Warren said.

Henderson stared at him.

"Are you a policeman?"

Warren shook his head. "Private investigator," he said.

"Investigating what?"

"Investigating for a law firm."

"That doesn't answer the question."

"My grandfather always told me if I didn't like any particular question I should just answer a different question."

"I was in Savannah, Georgia," Henderson said.

"On the thirtieth?"

"No, on the seventh. I'm following your grandfather's advice."

"Oh? Didn't you like my particular question, Mr. Henderson?"

"What was the question?"

"The question was about the thirtieth of January. A Saturday morning. Seven o'clock last Saturday morning, the thirtieth of January. Where were you?"

"If that's the question, you're right. I don't like it. In fact, I don't like *any* of this. You come here under false pretenses . . ."

"Yes."

"Mention names of people I don't know . . ."

"You don't know Ishtar Kabul?"

"Never heard of him."

"Then how do you know he's a he? Ishtar could be a woman's name."

"Male, female, or three-eyed pig, I have no knowledge of anyone named Ishtar Kabul."

"Not even *carnal* knowledge?"

Watch the eyes.

Wary now.

"I'm a married man," Henderson said. "If you're suggesting . . ."

"I know you're married."

"How do you . . . ? Oh, of course, the photograph."

"No, Ishtar told me."

"I have two children . . ."

"Yes, I know."

"Ishtar again?"

"No, the photograph."

"Are we back to Pinter?"

"Who's Pinter?" Warren said again.

"What is this law firm looking for? The firm you represent?"

"A murderer," Warren said.

"Did this Kabul person murder someone?"

"Our client saw someone in black running from the scene of the crime."

"This Kabul person?"

"Ishtar was wearing black at a party on the night before the murder."

"Has he no other clothing, this Kabul person?"

"I'm going to level with you, Mr. Henderson. I gave Ishtar a lot of bullshit about our client maybe identifying him, but the truth is our client never saw the person's face and wouldn't know Ishtar from a hole in the ground."

"Then surely this Kabul person has nothing to worry about."

"Not so. We can take a sworn deposition from him. If he sticks to his alibi, and if you deny the alibi, then he's hiding something. And the State Attorney would be duty bound to find out *what* he's hiding."

"And what alibi is that, Mr. Chambers?"

"You tell me."

"I assume this Kabul person said he was with me."

"Why do you assume that?"

"You mentioned carnal knowledge . . ."

"I did."

"So I have to assume . . ."

"You assume correctly."

"This Kabul person said he was with me, is that it?"

"Yes, this *Kabul* person said you were in bed together on the morning of the thirtieth, is what this *Kabul* person said."

"And if I say we weren't?"

"We take it from there."

"To where?"

"To the deposition. Under oath."

"Then take it from there, Mr. Chambers. This Kabul person wasn't with me, and I wasn't with him. Neither of us was with each other, the man is lying, it was nice meeting you."

"You recognize . . ."

"Of course."

"His alibi . . ."

"I'm married."

"If he can't prove . . ."

"Entirely his problem."

"The State Attorney will . . ."

"Let him."

"He loves you."

"The State Attorney?"

"Are we doing Pinter again?" Warren asked.

"Who's Pinter?" Henderson said.

Silence.

"Gee," Warren said. "I forgot to tell you the next step."

"The next step is you get out of here."

"The next step, if Ishtar decides to save his own ass by naming you in his deposition, the next step is we go to the S.A. . . ."

"So go to him."

"I see you want to play hardball, huh?"

"What do you call this? Softball?"

"So far, it's just you and me. Your wife is home cooking dinner for you and your darling little daughters . . ."

"We have a housekeeper who prepares dinner."

"Terrific, but hear me out. We go to the S.A. and say here's a deposition in which Ishtar swears he was with you on the morning of the thirtieth. So now the S.A. calls in Ishtar who tells him, Yes, that's who I was with, and the S.A. comes to you to hear your side of it, just in case Ishtar is lying. Would you like to explain to your wife why the S.A. suddenly wants to talk to her straight-arrow husband? Would you like to explain why Ishtar Kabul thinks he was in bed with you that morning? It can get very messy, Mr. Henderson."

"How would it be any less messy if I tell you here and now that we were, in fact, together that morning?"

"It'd be less messy because the buck stops here."

"How do I know that?"

"Here's the way I figure this, Mr. Henderson. Kabul got Christie Hewes to alibi him . . ."

"*That* cunt," Henderson said, and rolled his eyes.

"Be that as it may, she's sworn to his whereabouts on the morning of the murder. So I have to figure Ishtar got her to lie for one of two reasons. One, he committed the murder. Two, he was protecting you. If he was, in fact, protecting you, then we've got no reason to pursue this any further. We're looking for whoever ran away from that house on the morning of the thirtieth. We're not looking to persecute two consenting adults doing their thing in private."

"How do you know *I* won't lie to protect him? The way Christie did."

"Because you'd have done it already, instead of my having to pull teeth here."

Henderson was silent for what seemed like a long time.

Then he said, "We were together."

"Good. From when to when?"

"Two in the morning to twelve noon. I was waiting for him when he left the party. My wife thought I was in Tampa on business."

"Where were you waiting?"

"A friend's house."

"His name, please."
"Her."
"Who?"
"Annie Lowell."
"Her address, please."
"1220 Beach Road."
"On Fatback Key?"
"Yes."
"I'll check this, you realize."
"I thought you told me the buck stopped here."
"I was lying," Warren said.

3

This is the priest all shaven and shorn that married the man all tattered and torn . . .

Warren's input:

Scratch Ishtar Kabul.

Annie Lowell was an eighty-two-year-old woman who lived in a luxurious house on Fatback Key. Annie was not a fag hag as the term was commonly understood in the trade. But Henderson was her stockbroker, and she had made a great deal of money through his kind and expert offices, and she saw no reason why she shouldn't allow him to use the guest house behind the main house every now and then, no questions asked.

Yes, she knew he sometimes used the guest house to entertain male acquaintances. Listen, Annie was eighty-two years old and she didn't care who did what to whom so long as it didn't frighten the horses. Annie could remember when there wasn't even television. Annie did not think that whatever Henderson and his male acquaintances did in the guest house could be any worse than what was on television these days.

Then the *big* question.

Yes, she knew the man Henderson had been with on the morning of the murder.

His name was Martin Fein.

Who, of course, was Ishtar Kabul.

Howard the Duck in Arabic.

Scratch Ishtar Kabul.

Warren's further input:

Leona Summerville had left her house on Peony Drive at eight o'clock last night, had driven in her green Jaguar to the home of a woman later identified as Mrs. Shirlee Horowitz (from letters in the mailbox Warren had perused this morning) where she remained for two and a half hours, going directly home from there to arrive on Peony Drive again at a quarter to eleven. Unless the lady was having a lesbian affair with Mrs. Horowitz—an unlikely possibility in that Warren had subsequently learned the woman was seventy-one years old, the wife of a retired gynecologist named Marc Horowitz, the mother of two children and grandmother to three, and the secretary of the League to Protect Florida Wildlife—Leona Summerville was so far clean.

All this from Warren at ten minutes past ten on a cold, bleak, wet Saturday morning.

In December of last year—when Matthew was still regularly dating his former wife, Susan—she'd asked if he thought Leona Summerville was having an affair.

"What?"

"Leona. I think she's having an affair."

"No."

"Or looking for one."

"No, I don't think so."

"She dresses like a woman sending out signals."

Pillow talk. Former husband, former wife renewing vows of undying love while wondering aloud about Leona's faithfulness. It had been raining that night. It was raining this morning, too. Maybe it always rained in Calusa. All water under the bridge anyway, rain down the gutters; he had not seen Susan since just before Christmas.

Another video.

Sudden.

Shocking in its clarity.

Leaping unbidden onto the screen of his mind.

Two or three years ago perhaps, one of Calusa's many charity balls. They are going in the Summervilles' car, they are on the way to pick up—had he been dating Dana O'Brien at the time? Had it been Dana? No matter. Leona is wearing a slinky green gown that matches exactly the color of her Jaguar. Frank, in dinner jacket and black tie, is driving. The windshield wipers snick at the rain, rain, go away. The tires hiss on wet black asphalt.

Leona has joined Matthew in the backseat, trying to help him with his tie as Frank negotiates the car around the twists and turns of the slippery road.

She looks stunning.

Green gown molding her body like a patina of tarnished brass.

Sculpted hair settled like a sleek black helmet on her head.

A green feather in her hair, over one ear.

Green eye shadow.

Dark lashes.

Brown eyes luminous under the Jag's courtesy light.

Brown eyes intent on his black silk tie and the hands working it.

Long red fingernails on those hands.

The light casting a pearly glow on the sloping tops of breasts scarcely contained in the gown's flimsy top.

Hands working.

Knees touching his.

The electric feel of silk over nylon.

Knees moving away at once.

"There," she says.

A Carly Simon mouth, widening over even white teeth.

He wonders who is fucking her.

The mouth widens, widens . . .

Click.

The time on the Ghia's dashboard clock was a quarter to eleven.

As he drove the car into the driveway of St. Benedict's church on Whisper Key, he suddenly wondered whether *all* marriages eventually ended in adultery.

He got out of the car, grumbling at the rain, and then ran through the pelting downpour toward the rectory, up a crushed-gravel pathway past a large wooden cross on a berm planted with rain-stooped hibiscus bushes. The church—built in the Spanish-style architecture favored at the turn of the century—was situated directly on the Gulf of Mexico, dominating a point of land beyond which was an ominous gray sky and a roiling gray sea. The Parrish house was located not a hundred yards north of the church, occupying a much smaller plot of land, but facing the same turbulent sea; Matthew could see the house from where he stood in the pouring rain and lifted the knocker on the thick wooden door to the rectory behind the church. He was fifteen minutes early. He hoped Father Ambrose would answer the door before he dissolved.

The priest looked as if he had wandered out of *The Name of the Rose*.

He was wearing sandals and a brown caftan that could have passed for a cassock, a small polished wood-and-silver crucifix hanging on the front of it from a black silk cord. His shorn bald head was fringed with a halo of brown hair that matched his brown eyes. He had just finished shaving when he opened the door for Matthew; his face was littered with blood-stained scraps of toilet tissue. Matthew guessed he was in his late forties, but the bald head may have been misleading.

He offered Matthew a cup of coffee, which Matthew was immediately sorry he'd accepted; it tasted as if it had been laced with strychnine. Sitting in the snug, warm rectory lined with bookshelves containing theological works in dusty leather covers, a fire blazing in the small fireplace, the rain slithering along stained-glass windows, Father Ambrose told him what had happened on the morning of January thirtieth.

Rain.

The sound of rain drilling the cedar shakes on the rectory roof, awakening him long before dawn. In his narrow bed in his narrow cubicle, he listens to the sound of the rain and hopes it will end before tomorrow; attendance on Sundays always drops off when the weather is bad.

A gray dawn palely lights the small stained-glass window in his room.

He hears shouting.

Voices raised in shrill, shrieking anger.

He thinks at first—the shouting is so loud—he thinks it is coming from just outside his window, on the lawn someplace, or perhaps on the beach, teenagers sometimes drink beer on the beach and get rowdy. He stumbles out of bed in the near-gloom, slips into his sandals, throws on a Burberry raincoat over his undershorts—he sleeps only in boxer undershorts—and goes out into the rectory proper, the room in which they are now sitting, moves directly to the front door, and throws it open to the howling storm.

He squints through the driving rain.

There is no one on the lawn.

No one on the beach, either.

But the voices persist, rising in renewed anger, drifting on the strong wind, slashing through the slashing rain.

The voices are coming from the Parrish house.

He knows a homosexual lives in that house. Sometimes, in fact, the midnight parties there get a bit loud. But this is something else again, this is not revelry he is hearing, this is *rage*. A rage as cold as the rain, he shivers at the sound of it. He cannot discern what the voices are saying, the words are tumbled on the wind, a jumble of accusation and denial, but even without a grasp of their meaning he can sense impending explosion in their force, and suddenly he crosses himself and mutters, "God save us." For he knows with an immediate and frightening certainty that rage such as this can only terminate in violence greater than the violence of words alone.

Words.

Unintelligible on the wind, carried brokenly on the driving rain. Words pregnant with the threat of imminent horror.

And then a single understandable word.

Sharp. Clear. Unmistakable.

Knifing through the wind and the rain.

No!

And a scream.

A terrifying scream.

The fire suddenly crackled and spit. New wood.

Father Ambrose shook his head.

Matthew watched him.

And now the rectory sitting room was silent except for a low steady hiss from the fireplace and the steady pelting of the rain on the cedar-shingle roof.

"Did you hear just that one scream?" Matthew asked. "Following the word 'No'?"

"Just that one scream."

Ralph Parrish had told Matthew he'd awakened to the sound of voices arguing, his brother screaming. And then he'd heard his brother—

"Did you hear anyone shouting, 'I don't *have* them, I don't know where they are'?"

"The only word I could make out was the word 'No.' The other words . . ."

He shook his head again.

"Father Ambrose . . . you said when the voices awakened you . . ."

"No, the rain woke me up."

"But later you heard these voices arguing . . ."

"Yes."

". . . and went to the rectory door and looked out at the lawn . . ."

"Yes."

"And then looked out at the beach, is that right?"

"Yes."

"I'm assuming you could see the beach from the rectory door."

"Oh, yes."

"And there was no one on the lawn, and no one on the beach."

"No one."

"Was there anyone on the beach *after* you heard the scream? Did you see anyone running away from the Parrish house?"

"I don't think I checked the beach again. Not after I heard the scream."

"What *did* you do?"

"I closed the rectory door. It was raining very hard. I was getting wet."

"You closed the rectory door . . ."

"Yes."

"And then what?"

"I locked it."

"Why did you lock it?"

"I was frightened."

"But you didn't call the police."

"No."

"You were frightened, but you didn't call the police."

"No."

"Why not? You had just heard a violent argument, you had just heard a scream, you say you were frightened . . . but you didn't call the police."

"No."

"Why not?"

"I didn't want attention drawn to St. Benedict's."

"In what way would attention . . . ?"

"There are homosexuals in my congregation, Mr. Hope. Our

choir, our entire Music Department has a very high gay population. If there was some kind of trouble in the Parrish house up the beach, I didn't want it reflecting on the law-abiding homosexuals in my parish."

"So you remained silent."

"Yes."

"Until when? When *did* you go to the police?"

"I didn't."

"You didn't? I was informed yesterday that the State Attorney intends calling you as a witness."

"I was visited on Thursday by a detective from the Sheriff's Department. He was making what he called a routine canvass of the neighborhood. I couldn't very well lie to him about what I'd heard on the morning of the murder."

"Did he ask you specifically about what you'd heard on the morning of . . . ?"

"No, his questions were general. He wanted to know if I'd seen or heard anything out of the ordinary."

"On the morning of the murder?"

"Yes, and in the twenty-four hours preceding the murder."

"*Had* you seen or heard anything out of the . . . ?"

"The argument. I told him about the argument. And the scream."

"I meant in the twenty-four hours preceding the murder."

"No. Nothing out of the ordinary."

"You didn't see anyone wearing black, did you?" Matthew asked. "Anywhere in the vicinity of the Parrish house?"

Father Ambrose looked up at him.

Matthew knew that look.

Recognition.

Gold.

"Did you?"

"Why do you ask?"

"*Did* you see someone in black . . . ?"
"No," Father Ambrose said.

He watched the Karmann Ghia pulling out of the driveway, watched it as it disappeared into the falling rain. And then he watched only the rain, and wondered why he had not told Matthew Hope about the couple he'd married on the day before the murder.

Just passing through, the dark-haired man had said.

It looks like such a pretty old church, the little redhead had said.

Good a place as any to get married, the dark-haired man had said.

Bright sunny day, possibly the last one Calusa would see this winter. Sat out on the lawn behind the rectory. Chatting.

Dressed almost entirely in black.

Black jacket and trousers. Dark blue T-shirt, could've passed for black. Black loafers, no socks. The sleeve of the jacket was torn just above the right elbow. Tall white man in his forties, with a scruffy three-day growth of beard, looking tattered and travel-worn as he sat in the sunshine asking his innocent-sounding questions. Took off his jacket, it was that hot in the sun. The little redhead with him couldn't have been older than twenty, twenty-one. Long rust-colored hair, blue eyes, freckled face. Wearing faded blue jeans, pale blue T-shirt, silver-studded belt, sandals. Both of them exceedingly nervous.

Well, they were always a bit nervous, making a commitment like this made them nervous. So they always asked a lot of questions. Or commented on how pretty the church was—it *was* an extraordinarily beautiful church, a medieval sort of jewel settled snugly in the sand, facing sunsets that set it aglow with a light that seemed God-inspired. The stained-glass windows *were*, in fact, medieval. Crafted by sixteenth-century artisans, they had been transported from a little village in Italy, the gift of a Whisper Key parishioner who'd made a fortune in aluminum siding back in his native Cleveland. The mahogany pews had been fashioned right here in Calusa, but they'd been stained and waxed and burnished over the years since the church was built to create a patina that seemed centuries old. So, yes, the church provided conversational fodder for young people—and sometimes older ones as well—who were nervous because they were there to bind themselves irrevocably, one to the other, in the eyes of God. Which is exactly how many of them put it. In the eyes of God. Or in God's eyes. Variations on a theme. Seeking God's blessing.

The questions they asked had very little to do with the ceremony they were seeking. They wanted to know about the weather in Calusa, those who were passing through, those who had spotted this perfectly beautiful little medieval sort of jewel of a church settled snugly in the sand. Was it always this hot here? Or this rainy? Or this cold? Or this windy? Or this lovely? Or they wanted to know where they could enjoy a good celebratory dinner tonight, was there a very nice romantic place anywhere in town, you know, candlelight and wine, where they could seriously and in solitude reflect upon the enormously serious step they'd taken and toast their future together, was there such a place in town? Father Ambrose usually sent them to the Orchid Room at the Adler Hotel.

So yes, there were always the questions, always the comments, always the brittle chatter to cover the nervousness.

This *was* an enormous step for a couple to be taking.

This *was* commitment.

This *was* a solemn ceremony performed in the eyes of God.

He had married them at four o'clock on the afternoon of January twenty-ninth.

The day before the murder.

Married them in the little chapel off the rectory.

Both of them on their knees before the altar.

The one in black and the little redhead.

"Dear friends in Christ," he'd said. "As you know, you are about to enter into a union which is most sacred and most serious, a union which was established by God himself. And because God himself is its author, marriage is of its very nature a holy institution, requiring of those who enter into it a complete and unreserved giving of self. This union, then, is most serious because it will bind you together for life in a relationship so close and so intimate that it will profoundly influence your whole future.

"That future, with its hopes and disappointments, its successes and its failures, its pleasures and its pains, its joys and its sorrows, is hidden from your eyes. You know that these elements are mingled in every life and are to be expected in your own. And so, not knowing what is before you, you take each other for better or for worse, for richer or for poorer, in sickness and health, until death . . ."

They were alone in the chapel, the three of them.

No one there to object to the union.

Late-afternoon sunshine streaming through the stained-glass windows.

Father Ambrose looked down at the one in black.

"Do you, Arthur Nelson Hurley, take this person as your wedded spouse to live together in the state of holy matrimony, to love, honor and cherish in health, sickness, prosperity and adversity, forsaking all others so long as you both shall live?"

"I do," he said.

Father Ambrose looked down at the little redhead.

"Do you, William Harold Walker . . . ?"

You had to change the ceremony for them, of course.

Had to delete any words that might imply or even suggest that the act was a legally binding one. You also had to cut out all the words applying to gender, although some of them insisted you referred to one of them as "man" and the other as "wife," rather than both as the androgynous "spouse."

Over the years, though, Father Ambrose had evolved a ceremony that seemed to work for the participants. He thought of himself as one of the participants. Never mind Rome, the hell with Rome. Rome didn't know what he was doing down here in this remote little corner of Florida, and he guessed they never would find out—not from him, anyway. The way Father Ambrose looked at it, if two men wanted to get married, then by God he would marry them. Two women, the same thing. Two alligators, two snakes, two warthogs, two chickens, two of any of the creatures the good Lord had made, if they wanted to get married, Father Ambrose would offer them the comfort of the holy sacrament and the hell with Rome.

He was fond of telling any homosexuals who found their way to St. Benedict's the joke about the Catholic priest, did they know the joke? Well, this pair of homosexuals wants to get married, and they go first to a rabbi who says no, he won't marry them, and then to a Protestant minister who says no, he won't marry them, and finally to a Catholic priest who says, "*Sure*, I'll marry you, what do *they* know about true love?"

The joke usually put his customers at ease, they were always very nervous when they arrived, and self-conscious, as if they were attempting to do something ridiculous and might therefore become the objects of laughter or even scorn. The joke, of course, implied that the Catholic priest was himself homosexual, a not far-fetched surmise, but that was neither here nor there, since Father Ambrose was as straight as an arrow and always had been. His one and only sexual experience had, in fact, been with a girl. A long time ago, before his mother decided he had a calling to the priestly vocation. And yes, thank you, he'd enjoyed it, but his love for God was all-consuming, and he had not for a single moment looked back with longing on that afternoon of utter bliss he'd shared with fifteen-year-old Molly Pierson on the roof of a Chicago tenement, long, long ago. Occasionally, though, he wondered if Molly herself had ever married.

Never a week went by, even in the off-season, that someone didn't knock on the rectory door and ask for Father Ambrose. Usually a pair of men. Now and then women. Women didn't seem to need the church's blessing, he didn't know why. Maybe women didn't need *anyone's* blessing, maybe they knew they were God's chosen and didn't have to do a damn thing to prove it.

Knock, knock on the rectory door, Hello, we were just passing by, saw this lovely church, thought it might be a good place to get married. They'd heard about him, of course, the baldheaded priest who was willing to marry gays, his name was common currency in the homosexual communities of most American cities. He supposed sooner or later Rome *would* find out. Hell with Rome. Until then . . .

The looks on their faces when he said the words "And may God bless your union."

Beatific.

The joy he himself felt, knowing he was bringing such pleasure, his anointed thumb making the sign of the cross first on one forehead and then the other, *And may God bless your union.*

Joy.

Exaltation.

But those two . . .

The one in black and the little redhead . . .

They had left him with a curious feeling of unease. He had felt for a fleeting instant that perhaps they hadn't been homosexual *at all,* that perhaps the entire exercise had been a mockery. But for what purpose and to what end?

And then he remembered the questions they'd asked. While they were still sitting on the lawn chatting. Before he'd performed the ceremony.

Questions that had seemed pointed.

Well, not at first.

Merely inquiring at first about the availability of beachfront property here in Calusa.

Now that we're about to take the big step, time to think about really settling down someplace. Seems like a nice community here, Calusa does.

This from the one all in black.

Do you think there might still be any property left on the beach?

This from the little redhead, all bright-eyed and blushing.

And then zeroing in on the Parrish house.

How about the house next door, for example? Do you think it might be for sale? Do you know who owns it? Do you think he might be interested in selling it? Would you know the owner's name? How do you spell that last name? And it's Jonathan, you say? Jonathan Parrish? Does he live there alone?

All this from the one in black.

He tried to remember now everything he'd told them about Jonathan Parrish, tried to remember at which point they'd seemed to lose interest and stopped asking questions.

He wished it would stop raining.

The thought of them coming back in the rain frightened him.

The two men sitting with Warren Chambers could have been nothing but cops. Or rednecks. Or both. They were both. Warren guessed neither of them liked the idea of taking orders from a nigger, but the pay was good. The one with the blue eyes was called Charlie. The one with the brown eyes was called Nick. Aside from the color of their eyes, they could have been twins. Massive shoulders and chests, thick wrists and hamlike hands, Colonel Oliver North expressions on their faces: arrogant, surly, self-righteous, challenging, self-satisfied, and smug. Warren would rather have been working with a pair of alligators, but it was tough to find experienced surveillance help down here in the boonies. Four cops in all on a daily round-the-clock basis. Six-hour shifts. Charlie had worked the six A.M. to twelve noon this morning. Nick had just come off the noon-to-six P.M.

They were sitting in a bar called Curley's, off Route 41, near the South Dixie Mall. Warren was the only black man in the place. This was not unusual for Calusa, Florida, but Warren guessed Charlie and Nick were uncomfortable sitting here drinking with a nigger, even though he was paying for the drinks.

"We think somebody's casin' the house for a hit," Charlie said.

"Pretty much what we sep'ately come to conclude," Nick said.

They even *sounded* like twins.

"Have you talked to the other two?" Warren asked.

"Yeah, they ain't seen nothin' 'spicious. This is just today we got all this *ac*tivity."

"This car goin' by, two men in it."

"Driver dressed all in black."

"The other one with red hair."

"When was this?"

"On my shift," Charlie said, "the car first come by around ten o'clock, musta been."

"What kind of car?"

"Blue Honda Civic."

"Florida plates?"

"Uh-huh."

"Rental?"

"Nope. You gettin' ahead of me, Chambers. You want to hear what you payin' for or you want to run off at the mouth?"

Knock all your fucking pearly white teeth out of your mouth, Warren thought.

"Sure, go ahead," he said.

"Made a pass at the house, drove off in the rain, pulled in the church driveway down the road, made a U-turn in it, come on up past the house again. Made a slower pass this time, checkin' it out, casin' it real careful."

"This was about what time now? Ten after ten? Ten-fifteen?"

"In there."

"Did the car stop?"

"Nope. Just drifted on by, slow and easy, both of them all eyes."

"Where were you?"

"Inside the house."

He saw Warren's expression.

"Anything wrong with that?"

"Not if it doesn't bother you."

"It's where *I* been settin', too," Nick said. "On *my* shift."

"Fine."

"Anybody gives us static, we show the potsie, tell 'em Calusa P.D. planted us."

"Fine by me," Warren said.

"'Cause you looked a little troubled by it," Charlie said.

"No, no."

"I mean, you want us to see anybody comes in that house, best way to do it is to be *in*side the house our ownselves, ain't that right?"

"Seems like the best way to me," Warren said.

Break your fucking redneck nose in six places, he thought.

"So this was around ten, ten-fifteen," he said, "when the car made a second pass."

"Yeah," Charlie said. "In there."

"And you were where inside the house?"

"Upstairs bedroom. You get a good view of the road and also the beach if you change windows every now and then. On'y problem is there's no air conditioning, and it gets hot as hell up there."

"Even *with* this friggin' rain," Nick said.

Warren had noticed that redneck law-enforcement officers rarely used hard-core profanity. Redneck law-enforcement officers would shoot you as soon as look at you, but they always tiptoed politely around obscenity.

"When's the next time the car came by?" Warren asked.

"Around twenty of twelve," Charlie said. "Not only come *by*, but parked across the street."

"Sat there how long?" Warren asked.

"Still there when I come to relieve," Nick said. "Twelve noon."

"Uh–oh," Warren said.

"No, no," Nick said.

"I knew what was happenin'," Charlie said. "I was watchin' the whole action from the upstairs window."

Warren was still worried.

"We ain't amateurs," Charlie said, reading his face.

"I hope not," Warren said. "But what I see right now is two people casin' a house where one guy is staring down at them from an upstairs window and a second guy is about to walk in the front door."

"Nobody saw me at the window," Charlie said.

"And I spotted the car right off," Nick said. "I cruised on by, mindin' my own business."

"Did they keep sitting there?"

"All day long," Charlie said.

"And you're telling me they didn't know you were in that house?"

"That's what I'm telling you. Nobody made me."

"What'd *you* do, Nick? Keep driving back and forth till they made the car, too?"

"I tole you nobody made me," Charlie said angrily.

"Me, neither," Nick said. "I never even went *by* the house after that first pass. I parked up at Pelican Reef, walked up the beach, and went in the house by the back door. Relieved Charlie must've been about twenty to one."

"Was the Honda still parked there?"

"Still there."

"What time did it leave?"

"Bit after five o'clock."

"The two of them sat watching the house all that time, huh?"

"Watching it, yeah," Nick said.

"Fiddling with maps, like they were trying to figure out where in hell they were," Charlie said, "but watching the house."

"Why do you figure they watched it for such a long time?" Warren asked.

"Not 'cause they *made* either of us," Charlie said, "if that's what you're suggestin'."

"My guess is they were clockin' traffic," Nick said. "Tryna figger out who's goin' in and out of the house at what times. On'y the house is empty, so what they got was no traffic at all."

"Unless they spotted you going in from the beach side."

"No, they were in the *car* when Nick relieved me," Charlie said. "You beginnin' to irritate me, Chambers. You don't think we can do this friggin' sissy job, then get yourself somebody else. Ain't many people I know'd be willin' to sit in a empty house all day for a shitty ten bucks an hour."

"A shitty ten bucks, huh?" Warren said.

"I get fifteen when I supervise traffic up the country club," Charlie said. "When they havin' a dance up there."

"How many times a week do you do that?" Warren said.

"Well . . ."

"Well, my *ass*," Warren said. "You're getting sixty bucks a day here, seven days a week, which where I come from is four-twenty a week, which is probably more than you're making on the force. Moonlighting never paid so good, and you know it."

"Well, maybe that's true," Charlie said. "But that don't mean we have to take no shit about bein' made by two hippie assholes in a Honda. We ain't amateurs, Chambers. If you thought we was amateurs, you shouldn'ta hired us."

"Well, I did hire you."

"So then get off our backs, huh?" Nick said. "We doin' the job, man."

There was a long silence.

"You think we can maybe get another beer here?" Charlie said.

Warren signaled for the waitress to bring another round. The beers came some five minutes later. The waitress was a dark-haired girl wearing a very short mini. When she left the table, Charlie said, "Like to get me a little bit of that, man."

"Slide my hand right up that leg of hers," Nick said.

"Right under that skirt," Charlie said.

"Find somethin' *real* sweet under that skirt," Nick said, and licked his lips.

"Why'd you call them hippies?" Warren said.

"We talkin' pussy here, he's talkin' hippies," Charlie said, and shook his head. "Muss be somethin' wrong with the man."

Warren guessed he'd been accepted as one of the gang. A redneck didn't discuss white pussy with a black man unless he thought they were good ole buddies. Either that, or the black man was being set up for a kick in the balls. Warren didn't think this was the old Let's-Walk-the-Nigger-Round-the-Block ploy. He suspected his little lecture about the hourly wage had turned them around. Told them he knew he was paying top dollar and expected top-dollar work in return. Touched on their sense of pride. Maybe they weren't amateurs, after all.

"Why hippies?" he asked again.

"The one dressed in black looked like he'd been sleepin' in his clothes for a month," Charlie said. "Had a earring in his left ear. Long black hair. Forty years old, a total friggin' hippie asshole."

"Twenty years too late," Nick said, and shook his head.

"The other one, too," Charlie said. "Long red hair, wearin' clothes he picked outa some trash bin."

"Fine pair of friggin' hippie housebreakers," Nick said.

"You said they were clocking traffic," Warren said. "When do you figure they'll make their move?"

"Hey, he's askin' us our advice," Charlie said.

"I'll be damned," Nick said. "He's askin' the amateurs their advice."

But both of them were smiling.

"If they sat out there from eleven-thirty . . ."

"Eleven-forty," Charlie said.

"Eleven-forty till five o'clock . . ."

"Bit past five."

"Then chances are that's when they plan to hit, don't you think? Say between noon and five o'clock?"

"Well, maybe so," Charlie said.

He was still smiling.

"Between noon and five tomorrow, am I right?" Warren said.

"Could be," Nick said.

He was smiling, too.

"So what's funny?" Warren said.

"Well, what we figured . . ."

"This was before we knew they were gonna sit out there so long, but it still holds . . ."

"What we figured . . ."

"This was when I come in the back way to relieve Charlie, and we were both watchin' that Honda from the upstairs window . . ."

"Without nobody *makin'* us, Chambers, 'cause we were usin' the old Hole-in-the-Shade trick . . ."

"What we figured was if these two hippie assholes were watchin' that house there with such great interest . . ."

"Sittin' out there like they owned the friggin' street . . ."

"Not scared anybody was gonna see them payin' so much 'tention to the premises there . . ."

"Why, what we figured was maybe they'd be so engrossed in they *own* activity, they wouldn't notice nobody comin' up the street behind the car and checkin' out the license tag."

"So when I relieved Charlie here, what he done was walk up the beach to Pelican Reef, and then come back down the street and glom the tag on the car . . ."

"Wrote it down later," Charlie said.

"Checked it through Motor Vehicles, too," Nick said.

"Wouldn't you just know it?" Charlie said, grinning. "I come up with a name an' a address for the man owns that car."

"Registered in St. Pete," Nick said.

"Which means they're out-of-towners maybe staying in some motel down here . . ."

"Which means we got a shot at findin' 'em even if they *don't* bust into the Parrish house . . ."

"Unless they're sleepin' on the beach, which judgin' from the looks of them is a good possibility."

"What's his name?" Warren asked.

"Arthur Nelson Hurley," Charlie said, "Now whether that's the one all in black or the redheaded one, I couldn't tell you." His grin widened. "That's 'cause I'm juss a li'l ole amateur, you see."

"Let's call that li'l girl back here for some more beer," Nick said.

This is the man all tattered and torn that kissed the maiden all forlorn . . .

There were forty-nine hotels and two hundred and sixteen motels listed in the yellow pages of the Calusa telephone directory. On Monday morning, February 8, two people working for the law firm of Summerville & Hope divided the yellow pages between them and began calling all those hotels and motels.

Twenty-four-year-old Andrew Holmes, who'd been graduated from law school in January and who would be taking his bar exams late in July, worked from the motel list. Andrew had a Juris Doctor degree from the University of Michigan; Summerville & Hope was paying him forty thousand dollars a year to work as a so-called "legal assistant." Moreover, the firm had promised him an immediate raise to fifty thousand a year the moment he was accepted to the bar. If Andrew had chosen to work in New York City, he probably could have started at sixty, seventy thousand bucks. That was because he was an honor grad who'd also been editor of the *Law Review*. So here he was on a rainy Monday morning in Florida, repeatedly dialing a telephone and asking to speak to Arthur Nelson Hurley, please.

At her receptionist's desk in the lobby outside, Cynthia Huellen worked the shorter hotel list, interrupting herself only to answer incoming calls. From where Cynthia sat, her splendid legs crossed, she could see through the long lobby windows to the street outside. Rain drilled the sidewalks, ran in the gutters, flooded the roadways. She had never seen so much rain in her life. She had been born and raised in Calusa, and she was now twenty-five years old, and never in her life had she seen such steady, torrential, incessant, interminable, shitty rain. Cynthia was a sun person. Usually, there was not a day that went by that did not find Cynthia sunning on a beach or a boat. But her tan was beginning to fade. She noticed this as she reached for the phone. Looked at her hand holding the phone. The back of it. Her tan was most definitely fading. She consulted the hotel list again, and was beginning to dial the number for the Crescent Edge Beach Club on Sabal Key when an incoming-call light flashed on her panel. She tapped a button.

"Summerville and Hope, good morning," she said.

"Matthew Hope, please."

"May I say who's calling?"

"Hello?" Matthew said.

"Matthew?"

"Yes, Marcie."

"It's Marcie."

"Yes, how are you?"

Marcie Franklin, who—until the middle of last month, at least—had considered Matthew the neatest thing ever; Marcie was thirty-three years old, but she sometimes sounded like a teenager. She had sounded like a teenager when she'd breathlessly revealed that she had just met and fallen madly in love with a sixty-year-old humanities professor at New College in Sarasota, and that this was why, although she'd tremendously enjoyed her brief (December 24–January 13, but who was counting?) relationship with Matthew, she now felt they had to end it, okay?

Once upon a time, long ago—this past New Year's Eve, as a matter of fact—Marcie had told him she loved him.

He wasn't quite sure he'd believed her.

She had also told him he was devastatingly handsome.

That was nice of her, too.

At an even six feet tall and a hundred and eighty pounds, with dark hair and brown eyes, Matthew considered himself an average-looking man in a world more and more populated with spectacularly good-looking men. He went to Nautilus three times a week and most of the workout machines he used were set at ninety pounds. He was a B-level tennis player at best, with a lousy backhand and an even worse serve. He owned a nineteen-foot Grady-White bow-rider named *Kicks*, which he'd never once taken out into the Gulf. He was thirty-eight years old and slowing down, man, slowing down.

But in Marcie's eyes . . .

He'd been faster than a speeding bullet, able to leap tall buildings in a single bound . . .

In Marcie's eyes.

Marcie's emerald-green eyes.

A memory now.

Just as the voice on the phone was almost a memory.

"Matthew," she said, "the reason I'm calling, Jason doesn't know about you and me . . ."

"Jason?"

"My fiancé."

"Oh."

He was already her fiancé. Terrific.

"He doesn't know about us, the relationship we shared, and I was hoping, if you're going to be at the Poseidon Ball this Saturday night, that you won't reveal by word or gesture that you and I had known each other in anything more than a casual way. However briefly. Or, even, you know, *look* at me as if you knew me better than I would like Jason to think you knew me."

"Marcie, I certainly would never reveal to your fiancé that you and I had known each other intimately."

"Right. No lingering glances, Matthew, or covert touches, or . . ."

"I wouldn't even ask you to dance."

"I wish you wouldn't."

"I wouldn't."

"Good. I'm sorry, Matthew, but he's very jealous."

"I understand. Thank you for calling, Marcie."

"And don't come sit at our table to chat," Marcie said.

"Would I do that?"

"Because he's got antennae, Matthew."

"Is he a cockroach?" Matthew asked.

"I'm telling you he can detect signals."

"No sitting, no chatting, no looking, no touching, no dancing, I've got it," Matthew said. "I never knew you at all, right?"

"Well, you don't have to go *that* far, but . . ."

"Marcie . . . I won't be at the ball."

"What?"

"I won't be there, Marcie. You can relax."

"But you said . . ."

"No, Marcie. You have nothing to worry about. I'll be sitting home all by myself this Saturday night, all alone . . ."

"Oh, stop it, Matthew."

"Sipping martinis and staring out at the rain . . ."

"Goodbye, Matthew, I have to run."

"Goodbye, Marcie," he said, and hung up.

He sat scowling at the receiver, realizing all at once that he was still extremely angry with her for having dropped him so perfunctorily.

I love you, Matthew Hope, she had said.

New Year's Eve.
I love you, Matthew Hope.
Bullshit, he thought.

Leona Summerville walked and moved like a panther in heat.
Getting out of her Jaguar in the George Brothers parking lot, she exposed enough leg to attract the attention of four teenage boys trying to load a crated washing machine into the back of a pickup truck. One of the boys shouted, "Hey, Mama!" and another called, "What's your name, honey?"
Leona smiled.
As she was entering the revolving doors to the department store, a man came through from the other side, and then went around yet another time, following her back into the store. The man stood shaking his head in amazement, hands on his hips, watching Leona as she swiveled her way across the store toward the escalator. As Warren came through the doors, the man turned to him and said, "Mmmm-*mmmm*," and still shaking his head, left the store. Warren moved swiftly across the store, stepped onto the escalator while Leona was still on it, glanced upward, and then turned away in embarrassment when he realized he could see her panties under the short skirt she was wearing.
She got off the escalator on the second floor, and he followed her into the lingerie department—what George Brothers here in downtown Calusa called Intimate Apparel, this on a sign with a mauve background and avocado-green script lettering. Leona walked directly under the sign and past a female mannequin wearing a black bra, a black garter belt, a pair of black net stockings, and a pair of black panties cut high on the thigh and unfortunately showing the joining of the mannequin's legs and torso, which made her look like a reassembled double amputee.
Intimate Apparel.
A great many people had difficulty spelling the word "apparel."

You asked them to spell it without looking at it, they came up with the oddest combinations of p's and l's. Not Warren. "Apparel" was a word that had come up frequently while he was typing up reports for the St. Louis P.D.; superior officers always wanted to know what kind of damn *apparel* a person had been wearing.

Leona was wearing a pale blue denim miniskirt with a partially unzipped, big brass zipper on the left thigh. The skirt, together with high-heeled white sandals, gave her a long, barelegged, girlish look. A cutoff white T-shirt made her look like a woman with exuberant breasts and erect nipples, maybe because she wasn't wearing any bra under it.

Warren may have been wrong about the significance of sudden weight losses or new hair styles or public telephone calls, but he did not think he was wrong about a flimsy T-shirt and no bra on a lady as well put together as Leona Summerville. If this lady was *his* wife, he would not have let her out of the house dressed this way. Not even if he was with her. Not even if she was handcuffed to his left wrist.

If this lady was not having an affair, Warren would swim the Gulf of Mexico to Corpus Christi, Texas.

Warren was willing to swear a deposition this very moment that this woman was having an affair.

She was looking at a red garter belt now.

Across the store, Warren busied himself fingering the lace on the bottom of a half-slip.

And now she was looking at red net stockings.

Yessir, Warren thought. This lady—

And now she was looking at him.

His heart leaped into his throat.

Eyes meeting his.

Faintly quizzical expression on her face.

He turned away at once.

But she had made him.

Never in his goddamn life, *never!* Tailing hoods in St. Louis, guys who had radar could smell cops if they were anywhere within a mile's distance, *never!* And here, in a backwater little Florida town, he gets made by a housewife who's fucking around!

Jesus!

"Hello?"

"Yes, is this the Albemarle Motel?"

"It is."

Lizzie Borden had stayed at the Albemarle *Hotel* on her visit to London in the year 1890. Andrew Holmes knew such things.

"Is a Mr. Hurley staying with you?"

"Hurley?"

"Arthur Nelson Hurley."

"Second," the man on the other end said.

Andrew waited.

Corner of Piccadilly and Albemarle. He was tempted to ask the person at the other end of the line if he knew there'd once been an Albemarle Hotel in London.

"Nobody by that name registered here," the man said.

"Can you tell me if he might have been registered in the past few days?"

"No," the man said, and hung up.

There.

Sitting in the gray Ford.

Tall black man built like a basketball player, wearing dark glasses, chino slacks, and a tan cotton sweater with the sleeves shoved up to the elbows. The same man who'd been in the lingerie department. Left the moment she'd looked at him, but here he was again, waiting outside the store.

The rain had let up a little.

Without bothering to open her umbrella, Leona walked swiftly to the Jag, dodging puddles, unlocked the door on the driver's side, got in, let down the window, threw the umbrella onto the backseat and then started the car.

And listened.

Behind her, two lanes back and three cars over, she heard the Ford starting.

She backed the Jag out of her space, her eyes on the rearview mirror, and then turned into the lane leading to the parking-lot exit on Main Street. She looked into the mirror again. The gray Ford was just turning in behind her.

She made a right turn onto Main Street.

The Ford made a right turn behind her.

Okay, she thought, let's *really* check it out.

For the next ten minutes, she led the Ford through a series of lefts and rights through downtown Calusa, and then south on the Tamiami Trail all the way to Manakawa, and then back north to Calusa again. The Ford stayed behind her all the way.

She had read about rapists, even murderers, who followed their victims for days.

She wondered if she should stop the nearest police car, tell the officer she was being followed.

Oddly, she wasn't frightened.

She was only annoyed.

The dashboard clock read ten minutes to twelve.

She did not need this inconvenience.

She checked her own wristwatch.

She wondered if she should call, cancel.

Instead, she headed west on Bayou Boulevard, the Ford a discreet five cars behind her, and then pulled into the parking lot of the Bayou Professional Building. She looked into the rearview mirror. The Ford was still cruising, searching for a parking space.

It was raining hard again.

The dashboard clock read five minutes to twelve.

She checked her lipstick in the mirror. Freshened it. Blotted it. Tossed the Kleenex into the little plastic trash container.

Three minutes to twelve.

The Ford had found a space. The engine died.

She lighted a cigarette, sat smoking it, watching the clock.

Ground-level office door opening. Black umbrella and white skirts, little white cap, white pantyhose, flat white rubber-soled shoes. Running off into the rain. Little red Toyota. Flurry of skirts, car door slamming behind her. Engine starting. Car moving off. Gone.

Leona put out her cigarette.

The clock read five minutes past noon.

She leaned over the backseat for her umbrella, opened the door and the umbrella almost simultaneously, and stepped out into the rain, skirt riding high on her thighs, long legs flashing.

As she walked rapidly toward the building, she could feel the black man's eyes on her back.

"Mr. Hope?"

"Yes, Cindy?"

"It's your wife . . . your *former* wife . . . on six."

"Thank you. Any luck on those calls?"

"Not yet."

"Keep trying."

"I'm down to Magnolia."

"What?"

"The Magnolia Hotel."

"Oh. Good. Thank you."

He stabbed at the 6-button in the base of his phone.

"Hello, Susan," he said.

"Matthew, how are you?"

"Fine, thanks. And you?"

"Just fine. Will you be going to the Poseidon Ball this Saturday night?"

Good old Susan. Straight for the jugular.

"Why?" he said. "You want to tie my tie for me?"

"Thanks, I did that for too many years," Susan said.

"Or fasten my cufflinks?"

"That, too," she said.

"Why did you want to know, honey?"

"Did you just call me 'honey'?"

"No, *you* just called *me*, honey."

"Mat*thew* . . ."

Warningly. No time for nonsense. Important matters on her mind.

"Yes, honey, I called you 'honey,'" he said. "Force of habit. Forgive me."

"Well, please don't call me 'honey' at the ball, okay?"

"Wait, don't tell me," he said. "You'll be there with a very old cockroach and you don't want me to indicate by word or gesture that you and I ever shared the joys of . . ."

"Close but no cigar," Susan said. "He's twenty-three years old and he . . ."

"Susan, shame on you."

"Matthew, please don't let's . . ."

"Twenty-*three?*"

"Matthew . . ."

"Sorry. But twenty-*three?*"

"Yes, and a linebacker for the Tampa Bucs."

"Gee."

"Yes. He's six feet four inches tall, Matthew . . ."

"Golly."

"And he weighs two hundred and forty pounds . . ."

"Well, sure, a linebacker."

"And he's very *very* jealous."

"Ah."

"Which is why I called. I don't want any trouble Saturday night, Matthew . . ."

"Oh, neither do *I*!"

"So please don't ask me to dance . . ."

"I won't, I promise."

"Or chat with me . . ."

"Or sit with you, or even look at you. Got it, Susan."

"Matthew, this is not a joke. I'm truly concerned for your well-being."

"Then maybe I'll just stay home."

"Well, I wasn't about to suggest . . ."

"Skip the ball entirely."

"Matthew . . ."

"Stay home and sip martinis, stare out at the rain. Maybe you could join me. We could try out my new waterbed."

"You didn't *really* buy a waterbed, did you?"

"Come find out, Susan."

"Don't tempt me," she said, and hung up.

"I love you, too," he said to the dead phone, and put it back on the cradle. It buzzed while his hand was still on the receiver. He picked up again.

"Yes?"

"Mrs. Summerville on five," Cynthia said.

"For *me?*"

"That's who she asked for."

"All right, I'll take it."

He punched the 5-button.

"Hello, Leona."

"Matthew, I'm sorry to bother you, I know you must be busy . . ."

"Not at all. What is it?"

"I was wondering if I could see you later today."

There was a long silence on the line.

"Matthew?"

"Yes. What's wrong, Leona?"

"I'd rather not discuss it on the phone. I don't want to come to the office, either. I don't want Frank to know about this."

"What is it, Leona?"

He knew what it was. You don't get a call from a woman you've known all these years, your partner's wife, no less, asking to see you but not at the office because she didn't want her husband to know about the meeting. *Divorce* was what it was.

"Can you meet me at Marina Lou's?" she said.

"Sure."

"Five o'clock?"

"Sure."

"We'll talk then."

"All right, Leona."

"Thank you, Matthew," she said, and hung up.

He put the receiver back on the cradle.

He suddenly felt like crying.

The phone buzzed again.

He picked up the receiver.

"Yes?"

"Mr. Hope, this is Andrew."

"Yes, Andrew."

"We've got him, Mr. Hope."

The problem was manifold.

There was no way Matthew could go to the police with this. He could not call Morris Bloom to say he had a man in black staying at a motel here in Calusa, which was no crime, and this man in black had been watching the Parrish house most of the day Saturday, which was also no crime, and this man in black might be the man who'd run away from the Parrish house on the morning of the murder—which was also no crime unless this man in black had actually committed the murder before taking his little run up the beach.

Ho-ho-ho, Bloom would say.

So Matthew called Warren's office instead, and got his answering machine, and told the machine they'd located Arthur Nelson Hurley, and asked Warren to get back to him as soon as possible, the idea being that he and Warren—an experienced law-enforcement officer—would together visit the motel, thereby lessening the risk inherent in a confrontation with a possible murderer. Warren carried a pistol and he knew how to use it, witness the dead raccoon.

By two-fifteen, Matthew began to get itchy.

He did not want to lose Hurley.

Well, the possibility still existed that he might try breaking into the Parrish house, and they'd get him *that* way, violation of Section 810.08, Trespass in Structure or Conveyance, a second-degree misdemeanor. In which case Bloom could ask him all sorts of questions, including where he'd been at seven A.M. on the morning of January thirtieth.

But suppose Hurley never went back to that house again. Suppose he'd tipped to the fact that the house was under surveillance . . .

Well, they still had his address in St. Petersburg, the address supplied by Motor Vehicles. So they could track him down there, Matthew guessed, unless the man was a murderer who might be thinking of leaving the country the day after tomorrow.

Matthew did not want to go to that motel alone.

But he did.

The motel called itself the Calais Beach Castle, though it was twelve miles from the nearest beach.

Despite the continuing rain, the No Vacancy sign was on out front; snowbirds never looked at the weather reports for Florida, they only read them for Michigan or Indiana or Illinois or Ohio or Toronto. If it was snowing up there, they automatically figured the sun was shining down here. There were a dozen or so occupied units in the motel, all set back from the road, all with cars parked in front of them, all with window air-conditioners and little wooden front stoops. A tiny pool sat forlornly in the rain, an inflated rubber dragon floating in it.

The place had a Forties look about it.

Matthew figured it for a Mom-and-Pop dream gone sour—come on, Maude, let's move to Florida, buy ourselves a little motel down there, live like a king and queen, whattya say? Back then, you couldn't build hotels or motels on any of Calusa's beaches, the local zoning regulations were that strict. All the motels—some ten or twenty of them in all—were strung out on U.S. 41, the Tamiami Trail. The few infrequent souls who happened onto the Gulf Coast didn't mind driving the five, ten, fifteen miles to the beach, depending on location. The beaches were wild and virtually unpopulated in those days; you could swim naked and alone at high noon. The town itself was nothing more than a sleepy little fishing village.

All of that changed in the late Fifties, early Sixties, when Calusa and the West Coast of Florida got discovered. The minute the builders and contractors sniffed money on the prevailing winds, they set about convincing the politicians that tourism would be a good thing. So the zoning regulations changed and the hotels and motels began sprouting like mushrooms on the white sands. Goodbye to the aspirations of all those Mom-and-Pop motels along the Trail. Except for the very height of the season—like now, in February, in the rain—the motels on the mainland were empty, and you couldn't build a dream on vacant rooms.

Matthew got out of the Karmann Ghia, opened his umbrella, and walked over the muddy driveway to the office. A woman in her late thirties was behind the counter. A little black plastic plaque with the words IRENE McCAULEY, MGR., stamped onto it in white was on the counter alongside a clear plastic holder containing American Express application forms. A newspaper was spread open on the counter. Irene McCauley, if that's who she was, stood leaning over the newspaper, elbows on the counter, reading the newspaper. She looked up when Matthew came in. She watched him as he closed the umbrella.

"Is the sign busted again?" she asked.

"What?" he said.

"The 'No Vacancy' sign," she said. "It's sometimes on the blink. If you're looking for a room, we're booked solid through the rest of the month."

"Are you Miss McCauley?" he asked.

"*Mrs.* McCauley," she said.

Pity, he thought. She was an extremely good-looking woman. Solemn blue eyes. Shiny brown hair worn almost to her shoulders, bangs on her forehead. Black short shorts and a black halter top. Slender nose, generous mouth. Good breasts. Good legs, too, what he could see of them behind the counter. She realized he was checking her out. Raised her eyebrows. So? her expression said. Everything in the right places? He felt suddenly embarrassed.

"Mr. Hurley is expecting me," he said. He was lying. "Can you tell me what unit he's in?"

"Eleven," she said. "Next to the last one on your right."

"Thanks," he said, and opened the door, and opened his umbrella, and stepped out into the rain.

The approach he'd worked out was a simple one:

Mr. Hurley?

Yes?

Matthew Hope. I'm an attorney. Summerville and Hope. I'm representing Ralph Parrish, who's been charged with the murder of his brother, Jonathan Parrish.

Yes?

So far, so good, everything on the up and up.

Now came the change of pace.

Mr. Hurley, my client has given me your name as a witness to certain events that occurred on the morning of January thirtieth. Before we answer the State Attorney's demand for notice of alibi, I wonder if I could have a few words with you.

So, okay. Two possible reactions.

Yes, I *am* that person your client saw running off, and I *did* witness a murder, but I've been afraid to come forward. It wasn't your client who committed that murder, it was . . .

Who?

That was the first possible scenario.

Benevolent witness fingers the true murderer. In which case, all of Matthew's troubles would be things of the past, and so would Parrish's.

Second scenario.

The dangerous one.

I don't know what the fuck you're talking about.

In which case, Mr. Hurley, the possible man in black, was also the possible murderer.

What then?

Sorry to've bothered you, sir, and get the hell out of there before Hurley . . .

Before he what?

Matthew wished Warren Chambers and his gun were here at the Calais Beach Castle.

Head ducked, umbrella tilted against the driving rain like a black shield shunting enemy arrows, Matthew hurried across the courtyard, dodging puddles, leaping across rivulets, and in general doing a fairly good job of broken field running until he stepped shin-deep into a pothole brimming with cold brown water.

"Shit!" he said, and heard someone laugh behind him, and turned to see Irene McCauley standing just outside the office door, hands on her hips, legs fully revealed now and as long and as shapely as he'd suspected they were. Tight black shorts, loose black halter top, legs slightly spread in black backless high-heeled sandals—he suddenly realized what she reminded him of: the poster for *Damn Yankees*, when he was still a kid and the show was playing Chicago. Lola getting whatever Lola wanted by standing spread-legged in what looked like just her underwear and black high heels, give 'em the leg-and-crotch shot, Gwen.

"That's a real bad one," Irene said. "Catches a lot of people. I should have warned you."

"Better late than never," he said sourly.

His shoe, his sock, and part of his trouser leg were covered with mud. He looked down at them. He lifted the sodden trouser. Mud on his leg, too, above the sock. He put down his foot. Water squished in his loafer.

"Let me get you a towel," Irene said, and went back into the office.

He followed her there. He stood outside on the front step, under the umbrella, looking out at the rain, feeling stupid.

"Well, come on in," she said. "This isn't a priceless Persian rug."

It wasn't a priceless *any* kind of rug, for that matter. It was only green linoleum, worn through in spots, especially directly in front of the counter and in front of the sofa on the right-angle wall. The screen door clattered shut behind him. He had the sudden feeling—as he sat on the sofa and took off his loafer and his sock, as he accepted a clean white towel from this woman with the solemn blue eyes and the shiny brown hair—that he had lived through all of this before, had sat in a small room that smelled of wet garments and dry heat while the rain fell steadily outside.

"Thank you," he said.

Their eyes met.

"I should have warned you," she said again.

He began drying his leg, his foot.

"Let me wring out that sock for you," she said.

"No, really . . ."

"No trouble," she said, and picked it up from where it lay on the floor near his loafer, her hand in sudden closeup, fingernails painted a bright red, hand closing on the blue sock, she moved out of the frame, he raised his eyes. She opened the screen door, stood holding it open with her hip as she wrung out the sock.

Beyond her, rain swept the courtyard.

He had been here before, had lived through these moments before.

"I love rain," she said suddenly.

The screen door clattered shut again.

"Let me throw this over the heater," she said.

"I really have to see Mr. Hurley," he said.

"He won't be going anywhere in this rain," she said, and went behind the counter. He watched as she draped the sock over the protective guard of the electric heater. "I'll have to fill in that hole once the season's over," she said. "Come summer, it gets dead as a doornail down here, I'll have plenty of time to fix it."

The rain beat steadily on the roof.

A faint trace of steam was already rising from the blue sock.

"Better be careful it doesn't burn," she said.

And smiled.

"Are you just visiting Calusa?" she asked. "Or do you live here?"

"I live here."

Their eyes met again.

"Then maybe you can come help me fill in that hole," she said. "Come summer."

Silence.

Except for the rain.

A steamy, wet silence.

And the certain knowledge that he had been in this musty room before. The worn linoleum. The louvered windows. Even the calendar on the wall. The rain. Primarily the rain. Enclosing them. Containing them. Beating on the roof.

"Think you might like to do that?" she said.

"Your husband might want to take care of that," he said.

"Not likely," she said.

"No, huh?"

"Seeing as he's been dead for four years."

"I'm sorry," Matthew said.

"Not me."

Matthew smiled.

"How's my sock doing?" he asked.

"You seem in a big hurry to see this Hurley," Irene said.

"I don't want to miss him."

"Maybe you ought to consider what else you might be missing."

She went to the heater, touched the sock. "Still damp," she said.

"I'll have to wear it anyway," he said.

She shrugged, took the sock off the heater, and carried it to where he was sitting on the sofa.

"How long will you be with him?" she asked.

"I don't know."

"I'll be having a drink along around four," she said. "You're welcome to join me. If you're interested."

"I'm interested," he said. "But I have another appointment at five."

"Oh," she said.

She watched him as he put on the sock.

"You've got nice feet," she said.

"Thank you."

"I've got the ugliest feet in the world," she said, and fell silent.

He put on his shoe.

"I don't know your name," she said.

"Matthew Hope."

"How do you do, Matthew?"

She extended her hand.

He took it.

"Call me sometime," she said.

"I will," he said.

"Whenever," she said. "I'll be here."

"I will," he said again, and released her hand. He walked to the door, picked up his umbrella, searched for the release catch on it.

"Any other potholes out there?" he asked.

He was smiling.

"There's one just outside unit number ten, about five yards from the front door. Just skirt wide of it."

She was smiling, too.

"Thanks."

"Don't get lost now," she said.

"I won't," he said.

He snapped open the umbrella and stepped out into the rain. She came to the screen door and stood watching him as he started across the courtyard.

He resisted the temptation to show off for her, dash across the courtyard like a Marine storming a machine-gun nest, stomp heedlessly into the mud, bullets flying everywhere around him. Instead, he proceeded slowly and cautiously, not wanting to step into another tureen of muddy water, wanting only to talk to Hurley now, find out what Hurley had to say.

He approached unit number eleven.

The venetian blinds on the unit's windows were drawn.

He climbed the low wooden stoop, approached the door, and knocked on it.

"Who is it?" a woman's voice asked.

In the Computer Room of the Public Safety Building some five miles south and four blocks west, Officer Charles Macklin yanked several sheets of paper from the dot matrix printer. He had not three minutes earlier typed Arthur Nelson Hurley's name into the computer, and then the letters RS for "Record Search," and the letters AC for "A Capo" (the technician who'd devised this particular program was Italian), which called for a search as far back as the records went rather than a limited search going back say five, six, seven years, which would have been called for by typing in a numeral when the prompt appeared on the screen. At the next prompt, Charlie had typed in the letters FL for "Florida" instead of US for "Nationwide" because Charlie knew a state-by-state search had to tap into FBI files and that would have taken hours.

Charlie—although he was not at the moment sitting the Parrish house—was nonetheless still moonlighting because here he was doing work for Warren Chambers while collecting a salary from the Calusa P.D. Charlie could not figure out why he liked that nigger so much. He just knew that he wanted Chambers to bust whatever it was he was working on. In fact, he couldn't wait to tell Chambers that he'd run a routine check on Hurley and had fallen into what looked at first glance to be a whole big potful of shit.

Without bothering to tear off the detachable margin strips on the printout, Charlie began reading it. Hurley's record—a full page of printout—went back some twenty years, to when he was first arrested for assault. His most recent arrest had taken place eight years ago, in Tallahassee; he had been charged with aggravated battery and attempted murder because he'd attacked a man with a broken beer bottle and almost killed him.

Charlie let out a long, low whistle.

This is the maiden all forlorn that milked the cow with the crumpled horn . . .

The girl who opened the door to unit number eleven at the Calais Beach Castle could not have been older than nineteen. She was wearing baggy white shorts and a white smocklike blouse that hung loose over the shorts. The yoke neck of the blouse was embroidered with a yellow-and-blue floral design that matched the color of her long straight hair and her wide-set eyes. Matthew guessed from the size of her belly that she was at least six months pregnant.

"Yes?" she said.

"I'm looking for Mr. Hurley," Matthew said. "Arthur Nelson Hurley."

"Art isn't here just now," she said.

"Is he expected?"

"Tell me your name again?"

"Matthew Hope."

"Does Art know you?"

"No, he doesn't."

"You should've told me that before I opened the door. I wouldn't have opened the door for a stranger."

"If you'll let me in out of the rain," Matthew said, "perhaps we can . . ."

"Who is it, Hel?"

A young man's voice, coming from somewhere inside.

"Somebody named Matthew Hope," she called over her shoulder.

The young man suddenly appeared behind her. Twenty-two or -three years old, Matthew guessed, red hair and blue eyes, face covered with freckles. He was wearing faded blue jeans, a pale blue T-shirt, a silver-studded belt, and sandals.

"What do you want?" he asked.

"I'm an attorney," Matthew said. "I'd like to . . ."

"Did Grandma send you?" the girl asked suddenly, her eyes opening wide. "Why didn't you say so? Come on in."

"Thank you," Matthew said.

He closed his umbrella, shook it out while he was still standing in the doorway, and then stepped into the room and closed the door behind him.

He was thinking: Grandma.

There were two beds in the room, side by side. A couple of suitcases in the corner. A television set. An open door, bathroom beyond it. Nobody in the bathroom.

He wondered if he should tell them Grandma hadn't sent him.

"Are you Arthur Hurley?" he asked the young man.

"Nope. I'm Billy Walker."

"Is this your wife, Mr. Walker?"

"Nope."

"I'm Helen Abbott," the girl said. "I knew she'd come around eventually, Billy, didn't I tell you?"

"That's what you said, all right."

"But why'd she send you looking for *Art?*" she asked Matthew. "Art only talked to her on the phone."

"Well . . ." Matthew said.

"I mean, Art never had any *personal* contact with her. It was my father who went to see her the first time, just before Christmas. And then me, last month sometime."

"Uh-huh," Matthew said.

"I know you can't negotiate with my father, not while he's in the hospital. But can't you talk to *me*? I mean, *I'm* the granddaughter, not Art. What the hell does *Art* have to do with Grandma?"

Matthew didn't know what Art had to do with Grandma. He didn't even know what Art had to do with Helen, unless he was the one who'd knocked her up. He knew only that Arthur Nelson Hurley owned a car that had been parked across the street from the Parrish house on Saturday afternoon. Two men had been sitting in that car, casing the house. One of them forty years old and wearing black. The other one a young redhead. Billy Walker was a redhead in his early twenties. Matthew figured the one in black had been Arthur Nelson Hurley.

"Any idea when he'll be back?" he asked.

"I guess that's my answer, huh?" Helen said. "She wants you to talk to *him*. That really ticks me off. She makes out that fucking check, it better be in my name, I'll tell you that."

Matthew said nothing.

"Is she going to meet my price?" Helen asked.

Matthew still said nothing.

"You sure know how to take orders, don't you?" Helen said. "Grandma tells you talk to the *man*, you talk to the *man*."

There was the sound of an automobile outside.

Helen went to the door and opened it.

A blue Honda Civic was just nosing in through the rain, braking to a stop in front of the unit.

The door on the driver's side of the car opened. The man who stepped out of the car and came sprinting toward the cabin was at least forty years old. He was wearing not black, but green. Green polyester slacks and a green short-sleeved sports shirt. There was an earring in his left ear. The two cops sitting the Parrish house had mentioned that the one dressed in black had worn an earring in his left ear. He had worn his black hair long. He had looked like a total friggin' hippie asshole.

"That's Art," Helen said.

Arthur Nelson Hurley came into the room.

"Damn rain," he said, and looked at Matthew and said, "Who's this?"

"Grandma's lawyer," Helen said.

"Oh?"

He looked at Matthew more closely.

"He's got orders to talk only to you," Helen said.

"Who are you representing?" Hurley asked. "The old lady? Or both her and her daughter?"

"Well . . ."

"What I'm asking, does Helen's *mother* know you're here?"

"Well . . . no," Matthew said.

"Then whatever you've got to say is coming from the old lady, is that right? Elise has nothing to . . ."

"Well, no, I wouldn't say that, either."

"What would you say?"

Matthew noticed that he had a tattoo on his left forearm. A huge snake strangling some kind of small helpless animal.

"Mr. Hurley," he said, "as you know, I'm an attorney . . ."

"Right, Sophie Brechtmann's lawyer."

"Well . . . no."

"You're *not* Grandma's lawyer?" Helen said.

"No."

"Then who are you?"

"I'm representing a man named Ralph Parrish, who's been accused of . . ."

"Parrish!"

The name hissed into the room as if it were coming from the tattooed snake on Hurley's arm. Instead, it came from Billy's mouth, an electric-blue whisper that seemed to surprise even him. He looked immediately to Hurley in apology, both of them realizing in the same instant that Billy's repetition of the name had confirmed his recognition of it.

"Did you know Jonathan Parrish?" Matthew asked at once.

"What do you want here?" Hurley said.

"The State Attorney has made a demand for notice of alibi . . ."

"We never set foot inside that house!" Billy said.

"Were you anywhere near it on the morning of the murder?" Matthew said.

"Murder?" Billy said.

"What murder?" Hurley said.

"All we done . . ."

"Shut up, Billy. What murder? Who got murdered?"

"Jonathan Parrish."

"Oh, shit!" Billy said.

"When?"

"Last month. The thirtieth."

"Where?"

"His house on Whisper Key."

"Oh, Jesus, Art! We were watching a house where a man got . . ."

"I told you to shut up!"

"I knew them damn pictures would get us in trouble!"

"Did he tell you to shut up?" Helen said.

"This man comes here talking about the State Attorney . . ."

"What pictures?" Matthew said.

"Goodbye, Mr. Hope," Helen said.

White man gets made, it's easy for him. He changes his clothes, he puts on a fake mustache or a phony nose, he starts driving a different car, he's a whole new private investigator. Black man gets made, it's tough shit. He can change his clothes, his car, his nose, his fingerprints, there's one thing he *can't* change. His color. He's black. The person he's tailing turns around and sees this black man, it doesn't matter if he's wearing a blond wig and a dress now, he's still black and he's the man doing the tailing, he's the man who's been made, man, and there ain't a goddamn thing he can do about it.

Warren Chambers had been made.

The lady was on to him.

Driving into the parking lot of Marina Lou's, the sky and the bay and the rain as gray as his aging gray Ford, Warren watched Leona Summerville get out of her green Jag and all he could think was *I've been made*.

He had followed her home from her doctor's appointment at the Bayou Professional Building.

He had waited a discreet two blocks from her house on Peony Drive until she emerged again at four-thirty.

He had followed her here to Marina Lou's. She had driven as straight as an arrow, no ring-around-the-rosie this time, the lady was on to him for sure, the lady knew he was behind her.

She was handing her keys to the valet now.

She had changed her clothes for cocktail time, pale blue pleated skirt and blouse, pale blue low-heeled pumps. Was her lover waiting inside for her? Little cozy drink overlooking Calusa Bay? Her eyes swept the parking lot. There was a smile on her face. He knew that she knew he was sitting there watching her. How could he possibly tell Matthew Hope that he had blown the surveillance?

Leona Summerville was about to enter the building.

And then, as though some unseen and all-powerful being had summoned into Warren's presence the very object of his thoughts, Matthew Hope himself pulled up to the front door in his tan Karmann Ghia, and got out of the car.

"Leona!" he called.

She stopped. She turned. She smiled.

Matthew handed the valet his keys. Leona took his arm. Warren watched them as they went inside together.

Huh? he thought.

And suddenly wondered . . .

But no.

But why not?

Was it possible?

He hoped not.

He hated Byzantine plots.

Helen was weeping.

Hurley hated it when she cried.

He felt like hitting her when she cried, give her something to really cry about. At the same time, he felt like holding her, comforting her. He wondered if he loved her. These mixed feelings about her. Wanting to belt her, tell her to shut the fuck up, wanting to hold her at the same time. Feelings about what she was carrying inside her, too. His baby. Never felt like this in his life. Never. Wondered if it'd be a boy. Sort of hoped it'd be a girl. Boys had it tough in this world. Too many things out there waiting to fuck you up.

"Don't cry, baby, come on now," he said, and took her in his arms, and kissed her.

Billy was sitting on the other bed.

Helen kept sniffling and snuffling into a little handkerchief trimmed with lace.

"Please, baby, I hate to see you so forlorn this way," Hurley said, and kissed her again.

"It's just I think I may have blown it," Helen said, and dabbed at her eyes with the lace-trimmed handkerchief. "I may have told him too much. I thought he was Grandma's lawyer. He passed himself off as Grandma's lawyer."

"No, he didn't," Billy said. "The man never said he was your grandmother's lawyer. It was you who jumped to that conclusion."

"*Did* the man say he was Sophie's lawyer?" Hurley asked.

"I guess not, Art. Oh, Art, I'm so damn sorry," she said, and burst into fresh tears. "I should've realized he was here snooping."

"Now, now," Hurley said, holding her in his arms, patting her. "Now, now, darling. What kind of questions did he ask?"

"Questions?"

"You said he was here snooping."

"Well, he kept asking about you. Wanting to know when you were coming back."

"That's all? Then how do you figure he was snooping?"

"Well, he asked you . . ."

"I'm talking about *before*."

"Asked if you knew Jonathan Parrish . . ."

"*Before* I got here is what I'm talking about. What did he say *before* I got here?"

"I told you all he said, Art. Well, wait, he asked me if I was Billy's wife."

"Did you tell him you weren't?"

"Well, Billy told him his name, and I told him my name . . ."

"Terrific, he has everybody's name."

"He had yours *already*, Art," Billy said, and got up and walked to the television set. "Before he even came here, he had your name."

"Leave that off," Hurley said.

"Just 'cause you and me are married," Billy said, smiling, "don't mean you can give me orders, Art."

"I said leave it *off*," Hurley said, and turned again to Helen. "What'd you tell him about your grandma?"

"I said I'd gone . . ."

"Yes?"

"To see her."

"Did you tell him *why* you went to see her?"

"I'm sorry, Art. I know I should've been more careful. But I really thought he was Grandma's . . ."

"Did you mention *money*, Helen?"

She looked at him. Her eyes were beginning to brim again.

"Did you?"

"I think I . . . I . . . may have mentioned something about . . . about her meeting my price."

"You also mentioned her writing a check," Billy said.

"No, I never said . . ."

"You said you wanted the check made out in your name."

Hurley scowled.

"I'm sorry, Art," Helen said.

"That's all right, darling," he said. He was silent for several moments, thinking. Billy stood near the television set, wondering if it was okay for him to turn it on now. Helen sat on the bed with her legs crossed Indian fashion, watching Hurley, wondering if he was mad at her. He used to hit her a lot whenever he got angry. She knew he was a violent man. But he hadn't once touched her since she got pregnant.

"So," he said, "as I understand it, this lawyer knows you went to see your grandmother, and he knows you want money from her."

"Yes," Helen said.

"Does he know *why* you want this money?"

"No, I don't think so."

"Billy?"

"I don't think anything was said about the why of it."

"Or the amount?"

"No numbers were mentioned."

"Then he doesn't know we're looking for a million dollars, is that right?"

"Nothing would have given him that impression," Helen said.

"So . . . all he really knows is you went to see her about money," Hurley said. "And you're expecting a check."

"He also knows we're expecting *negotiation*," Billy said.

"How the fuck does he know *that?*" Hurley said.

"Because Helen . . ."

"Because I . . . I thought she sent him to negotiate with you. And I . . . I must've said something about it."

"He *also* knows their names," Billy said. "Which *you* gave him, hubby darling. Helen had nothing to do with that."

"Who said Helen had anything to do with it?"

"Case you were thinking of blaming her," Billy said. "You're the one told him everything. Gave him the old lady's name . . ."

"I thought he was her lawyer," Hurley said. "Helen said he . . ."

"Gave him the name on a silver platter, Sophie Brechtmann. Gave him the daughter's name, too."

"No," Hurley said, "I don't recall telling him . . ."

"Elise, you said."

"That's true, Art," Helen said. "You did tell him my mother's name."

"Practically drew a map for him," Billy said sourly.

"Well, we all make mistakes," Hurley said, and went to Helen and kissed the top of her head. "Who among us can cast the first stone?"

"*Me*," Billy said. "*I* didn't tell him a fucking thing."

"Who was it mentioned watching the house?" Hurley said. "Who was it mentioned the pictures?"

"Well, yeah, maybe I . . ."

"So, okay, we're *all* to blame. But what's done is done. The important thing now is to dope out our next move."

"Our next move is to get the hell out of here," Billy said.

"No, our next move is to find those pictures," Hurley said.

"He's right," Helen said. "Nothing's going to convince her till she sees those pictures of me and my mother."

"We're not even sure those pictures *exist*," Billy said.

"They exist, all right," Hurley said.

"Only because a nigger up north *thinks* she remembers . . ."

"She *does* remember."

"She'd remember the birth of Christ if you talked to her long enough."

"She was there when the pictures were taken," Helen said.

"We have to find those pictures," Hurley said.

"Go back to the Parrish house," Helen said.

"No way," Billy said.

"Get in that house and find those pictures," Hurley said.

"A *murder* was committed in that house!" Billy said. "Didn't you hear him?"

"The pictures are in that house," Helen said.

"Somewhere in that house," Hurley said.

"We show her those pictures, she'll see the beads," Helen said.

The rain had stopped.

A rainbow arced over Calusa Bay.

"Make a wish," Leona said.

They sat at a table for two near the plate-glass windows overlooking the marina dock and the bay. Sailboats alongside the dock clanged with the sound of the wind rushing through their shrouds. The sky was still gray, the clouds tearing off in long tattered sheets. Far beyond the rainbow, there was the faintest patch of blue in the western sky.

"Do people wish on rainbows?" Matthew said.

"I always do. Tell me what you'd like most in the world."

"If I tell you, then it won't come true," he said.

"Who's making the rules?" Leona asked.

"That's a time-honored rule. If you tell your wish . . ."

"Time-honored rules are made to be broken," Leona said. "Here's my wish. Are you ready?"

"You're tempting the fates."

"Fuck the fates," she said.

Matthew figured she'd already had too much to drink. Six

o'clock and on her second martini. Here for the past hour and still not a word about why she'd wanted to see him.

"I wish . . . I wish I could be happy," she said, and nodded curtly, and looked down into her glass.

"I thought you were," Matthew said.

"Happy? Did you?"

She looked up at him. She raised her glass, lifted it to the rainbow in a silent toast. And drank.

"Now you," she said.

"The rainbow's almost gone," he said.

"Before it goes."

"I might as well wish for the moon. If I say it out loud . . ."

"Hurry, it's going fast."

"*I* wish you could be happy, too," Matthew said, and drank quickly.

Leona looked at him in surprise.

He nodded.

She kept looking at him.

"Why?" she said.

"Because I don't want you to be *un*happy," he said, and shrugged.

"But I am."

"Apparently."

"Yes."

"Do you want to tell me why?"

She shook her head.

"Why are we here, Leona?"

She lifted her glass, drained it, and said, "Do you think we can get another one of these?"

"Let's talk first," he said.

Leona sighed.

Here it comes, he thought. Matthew, I want to divorce Frank.

"Matthew," she said, "I'm being followed."

The first thing he felt was relief.

And then he realized that Warren had blown the surveillance.

"Don't be ridiculous," he said.

"No, I'm sure about it," Leona said.

"Well . . . what do you mean? Have you *seen* someone?"

"I have."

"What does he look like?"

"He looks like a tall black man driving an old gray Ford."

Shit, Matthew thought.

"Why would anyone be following you?" he said.

Leona smiled.

"Maybe Frank thinks I'm having an affair," she said.

Now it comes, he thought. He's right, Matthew. I *am* having an affair.

He waited.

"Maybe Frank's put a private detective on me," she said.

Matthew said nothing.

"Catch me in flagrante delicto," she said.

He still said nothing.

"In the very act," she said. "Red-handed. From the Latin, 'while the crime is blazing.' Did you ever study Latin?"

"Yes," he said.

"Take pictures of me in some cheap motel," she said. "While the crime is blazing. *Now* may I have another one of these?" Without waiting for his reply, she signaled with her empty glass to the waiter. The waiter nodded and hurried to the bar. She turned back to Matthew and smiled again. "Has Frank said anything to you?" she asked. "About, you know, putting a detective on me?"

"No," he said, and immediately wondered why he was lying. Not five minutes ago, Leona had told him she was unhappy. So why not put it all on the table, get it out in the open, tell her the truth, tell her what Frank suspected and what Frank was doing about it.

No, he thought.

If she wants it on the table, she'll put it there herself.

"Do you think he would?" she asked. "Tell you? If he thought I was having an affair?"

"I don't know."

"Did you tell *him?* When you were having an affair with Agatha Hemmings? All those years ago?"

"No."

"*Do* men tell each other such things?"

"Some men. Not me."

"Some women do," she said, and looked toward the bar, where her drink was being mixed. "Not me. Anyway, I don't have any women friends," she said, almost to herself, and then turned back to Matthew. "I consider you a friend," she said gravely.

"Thank you," Matthew said, and nodded.

"Do you consider *me* a friend?"

"I do."

"Truly?"

"Truly."

"A good friend?"

"A very good friend."

Put it on the goddamn table, he thought. Get it out in the open, Leona! If you want to tell me about it, tell me!

"As a very good friend," she said, "would you want someone taking pictures of me? Through a motel window, Matthew?"

"Well . . ."

"Pictures of me naked," she said.

"Well . . ."

"My legs spread."

"Leona, I . . ."

"Some guy's head buried in my crotch," she said.

"Tanqueray martini on the rocks, a twist," the waiter said.

He looked very pale and very apologetic.

Leona looked up at him and smiled angelically. "Thank you," she said.

"Sir? Another one for you?"

"No, thanks," Matthew said.

The waiter hurried away from the table.

"I think I embarrassed him," Leona said.

"I think you embarrassed *me*, too," Matthew said.

"Oh, don't be a jackass," she said, and raised her glass. "Here's to rainbows," she said. "And to wishes."

He watched her as she drank.

"Why are you unhappy?" he asked.

Leona sighed deeply.

"Tell me," he said.

She sighed again.

"Maybe because I'm getting old," she said.

"Nonsense," he said. "What are you, Leona? Thirty-seven? Thirty-eight?"

"I'll be forty next month."

"You could pass for twenty-three."

"Ah, sweet-talker," she said, and reached across the table for his hands. "Dear, good friend," she said, "dear, dear friend," and smiled wanly. "Matthew?" she said.

"Yes, Leona."

"I'm not having an affair," she said.

She squeezed his hands.

She looked deeply into his eyes.

"If Frank should ask you . . ."

"Yes?"

"You just tell him I'm not, okay?"

"Uh-huh."

Trying to sound noncommittal.

"I am not having an affair, okay?"

"Uh-huh."

Still going for noncommittal.
"Good," she said, and smiled, and picked up her glass again.

Warren Chambers was unlocking the door to his condominium apartment when he heard the phone ringing. He threw open the door, left the key in the latch, ran into the living room and yanked the receiver from the cradle.
"Hello!" he said.
"Warren, it's Matthew."
"Yes, hello, Matthew."
Now I have to tell him, he thought.
Matthew, I've been made.
Also . . .
Matthew, I know you met with the suspect this afternoon.
Here's a possible scenario, Matthew.
Let's run it by as an exercise, okay?
Your partner suspects his wife is playing around. He asks you to put a private eye on her. You oblige. But it is you *yourself*, Matthew, who is diddling the lady. So you tell her you'll have to behave yourselves while the private eye is on the job. So you both lay low, you should pardon the expression, until the p.i. gives the lady a clean bill of health. Then, when Summerville is convinced his wife is true blue, you and the lady go back to fucking your brains out.
How does that sound, Matthew?
Not bad for a spur of the moment improv, huh?
And if you happen to be asked—as well you might be in the next two minutes—how come you were meeting your partner's luscious wife at Marina Lou's this afternoon, you can always say . . .
"Warren, you've been made."
Warren blinked.
"Warren, did you hear me? You've . . ."
"Yes, I know," Warren said. "But how do *you* know?"

"Leona told me."

Warren said nothing.

"I had a drink with her this afternoon."

Warren still said nothing.

"I want you to put someone else on her," Matthew said. "Right away."

"I'm very glad to hear you say that," Warren said.

"What?"

"It makes me very happy to know that you want to continue the surveillance."

"I don't know what you're talking about, Warren. Why *wouldn't* I want to continue?"

"I don't know, Matthew. But I'm sure there are many reasons in this world why people start investigations and then want them stopped."

"Warren, have you been drinking?"

"No, Matthew. Very definitely not. I'll start looking for someone right away. I don't have to tell you that the pickings are pretty slim in Calusa."

"I know that. Do your best."

"I will. Matthew . . . ?"

"Yes?"

"Does the name Wade Livingston mean anything to you?"

"Yes. He's a doctor. Why?"

"A gynecologist. Leona went to see him this afternoon."

"So?"

"So nothing," Warren said. "Maybe she's pregnant."

"Or maybe she went for her yearly checkup."

"Maybe. I tracked her home after the visit, waited around outside her house till around four-thirty, when she left for Marina Lou's."

"Then that *was* your car I spotted."

"Some private eye, huh?"

"Warren, I'm going to need whatever you can get me on the Brechtmann family."

"The beer people?"

"Yes."

"Okay. How soon?"

"I plan to go there tomorrow, if they'll see me."

"By 'they'?"

"Sophie or Elise, either one."

"I'll get to work right away. Anything else?"

"Yes. I went to see Arthur Hurley."

"I wish you hadn't done that, Matthew."

"Why?"

"He's got a record as long as my arm."

"How do you know?"

"One of my cop people ran him through the computer. How'd you find him?"

"By calling around. He's staying at the Calais Beach Castle with a young blonde named Helen Abbott, and a guy named Billy Walker. You might ask your cop people to run a few more computer . . ."

"I will."

"And let me know who'll be tailing Leona, okay?"

"*If* I find someone."

"Find someone, Warren."

"Someone *good* this time, huh?"

"You said it, not me."

"Matthew . . . ?"

"Yes?"

"You have no idea how glad I am that you're not . . ."

"Yes?"

"Never mind," Warren said. "Talk to you," he said, and hung up.

. . .

Soaping herself in the shower, her hands gliding over her belly and her breasts, Helen Abbott wondered if they weren't all just kidding themselves. Never mind truth, never mind justice, truth and justice had nothing whatever to do with a million dollars.

She believed her father had told her the truth, and if there was any justice at all in this world, then the Brechtmann family would realize she deserved everything she was asking. But where was it written? That truth had to be rewarded? Or that justice would triumph?

All those years.

Her father keeping the secret.

Until he suddenly decided he'd kept it too damn long.

Told her all about it then.

And went to see her grandmother.

Came back empty-handed.

This was just before Christmas. By then, she'd known Art for almost six months. Met him in July. Him and Billy sitting in a St. Pete bar where her and another girl had gone. Odd-looking pair, Art a good twenty years older than Billy, looked more like his father than his good old buddy. Turned out they'd met each other in prison. Used to be cellmates at Union C.I., up in Raiford.

This excited her a little.

Art being a convict. Well, an *ex*-convict. Told her him and Billy had just got out that very week. Told her he'd been locked up for attacking a man with a broken beer bottle. Almost killed him, he told her.

This excited her, too.

The sense of violence about him.

Said he hadn't had a woman for too long a time. Asked if she'd like to help him change that sad predicament. Turned out Billy and her girlfriend were hitting it off, too. The four of them went back to her place, smoked a little dope, drank some wine, ended up in bed, her and Art in the queen-sized bed in the bedroom, Billy and Wanda on the hideaway bed in the living room.

After her father got beat up and sent to the hospital, she told Art all about him having gone to see the Brechtmanns.

"No shit?" he said. "The beer people? I drink their beer all the time. That's terrific beer, Brechtmann's. Why'd he go see them?"

She told him why.

Art listened very carefully.

"There can be a lot of money in this," he said.

And kept listening.

And then he explained that her father had made a mistake, approaching the family on a wing and a prayer, it was no wonder they'd told him to fuck off. What Helen had to do, she had to go back to that house, but this time she had to have cards she could play, here's my hand, this ain't bullshit, my dears, this is *true* and you *know* it's true, and I think I'm worth a million fucking bucks! So how about it?

She went to the house in January.

Art had found out about the pictures by then and she thought it'd be enough to just mention them. Without actually having them in her hand. Just tell them she *knew* all about the pictures. Knew all about the beads.

She was scared to death when she got there.

Big old house on the Gulf, iron gates surrounding it, she'd announced herself to the security guard, told the man she was Helen Abbott, here to see either Sophie or Elise Brechtmann. Fine high wind blowing that day, this was just last month, around the end of the month, her long blonde hair dancing on the wind, her palms sweating.

Gate man pressed a button on the intercom.

"Yes, Karl?"

A woman's voice on the speaker.

"Mrs. Brechtmann, I've got a girl here wants to see either you or your daughter, her name's Helen Abbott."

A silence.

Then her grandmother's voice on the speaker again.

"Show her in."

And Helen knew in that instant that her father had told her the truth.

6

This is the cow with the crumpled horn that tossed the dog . . .

They were drinking coffee and eating bagels in a Sabal Key joint called The Miami Deli. It was eight o'clock on Tuesday morning, the ninth day of February—and the sun was shining. This was akin to a religious miracle. Everyone in the place was grinning at the February sunshine that streamed in through the windows facing the beach road. Convertible automobiles with their tops down flashed by in the February sunshine outside. It was like Florida again.

The woman sitting with Warren Chambers was twenty-six years old, a tall, slender, suntanned blonde with frizzied hair and dark brown eyes. She was wearing a white T-shirt, cutoff blue jeans, and sandals. She looked like a beach bum. But she was a private eye. Her name was Toots Kiley.

"Where'd you learn your trade?" Warren asked her.

"From Otto Samalson. And May Hennessy."

"Who's May?"

"Chinese woman used to work for him. She went back to China after he got killed. Did you know Otto?"

"Only by reputation."

"One of the best," Toots said.

"How about you?"

"I'm pretty good," she said, and shrugged. "Otto taught me a lot."

"How long were you with him?"

"Six years. Started working for him when I came down from Illinois."

"And quit when?"

"Got *fired*, you mean."

"When?"

"Two years ago."

"Why?"

"You know why, or you wouldn't be asking."

There was a long silence at the table. Warren picked up his cup, sipped at the coffee.

"Who nicknamed you Toots?" he asked.

"It's not a nickname," she said.

"That's your *real* name? Toots?"

"Toots, yeah."

"Your parents named you *Toots?*"

"My father did."

"How come?"

"He loves the harmonica."

Warren looked at her.

"He named me after Toots Thielemans, best harmonica player in the world. Listen, I was lucky. He could've named me Borah."

"Is that another harmonica player? Borah?"

"You mean you never heard of Borah Minevitch?"

"Never."

"Borah Minevitch and the Harmonica Rascals?"

"Sorry."

"Boy," Toots said, and shook her head.

"How do you feel about that? People calling you Toots."

"That's my name. Toots."

"It's a good thing you're not a feminist," Warren said.

"Who says I'm not?"

"I mean . . . if Gloria Steinem happened to be around when somebody called you Toots . . ."

"Well, fuck Gloria Steinem, I don't like *her* name, either. Tell me about the job, okay?"

"First tell me you're clean," Warren said.

"Why? Do I look like I'm not?"

"You look suntanned and healthy. But that doesn't preclude coke."

"I like that word. Preclude. Did you make it up?"

"How do you like the other word? Coke."

"I used to like it just fine. I still think of it every now and then. But the thought passes. I'm clean, Mr. Chambers."

"How long has it been?"

"Almost two years. Since right after Otto fired me."

"And now you're clean."

"Now I'm clean."

"Are you sure? Because if you're still on cocaine, I wish you'd tell me."

"I am not on cocaine. Or to put it yet another way, I do not do coke no more. I am clean. K–L–double E, clean. What do you need, Mr. Chambers? A sworn affidavit? You've got my word. I like to think it's still worth something."

"There was a time when it wasn't."

"That was then, this is now," she said, and sighed heavily. "Mr. Chambers, are you here to offer me a job, or are we going to piss around all morning?"

"Call me Warren," he said, and smiled.

"What's the job, Warren?"

"Are you still licensed?"

"Class A. Paid the hundred-dollar renewal fee last June. What's the job?"

"Matrimonial surveillance. Man wants to know if his wife's playing around."

"How come you're not handling it yourself?"

"I got made," Warren said.

"Oh my."

"Yeah."

"Shame on you," she said. "Who's the client?"

"Man named Frank Summerville. Partner in a law firm I do work for."

"And the lady?"

"Leona Summerville."

"When do I start?"

"Do you have a car?"

"A very good car."

"What kind?"

"The nondescript kind."

"Best kind there is."

"Otto used to drive a faded blue Buick Century."

"I drive a faded gray Ford."

"Mine's a faded green Chevy," Toots said.

Warren took an envelope from his inside jacket pocket. He put it on the table, tapped it with his hand, and said, "The lady's address and phone number. Case you need to use it for whatever nefarious purpose."

Toots smiled as if she already had in mind a possible use for Leona Summerville's phone number.

"Five pictures of her," Warren said, "one in color, the rest black-and-white. A phone number where you can reach me, and a drop box you can use, all right here in the envelope."

"The drop box is in the envelope?" Toots asked, deadpan.

"No, wise guy, the drop box is at Mail Boxes, Etc., on Lucy's

Circle. The *key's* in the envelope. Aren't you going to ask how much the job pays?"

"I'm assuming I'll get what Otto paid me."

"And what's that?"

"Fifty an hour."

"Nice try."

"It's what Otto paid me," Toots said, and shrugged innocently.

"Bullshit," Warren said.

Toots shrugged again.

"So how much *are* you paying?" she asked.

"One-sixty for an eight-hour day."

"Nice try."

"Hey, come on, that's twenty dollars an hour."

"I know how to divide, thanks. Thanks for the coffee, too," Toots said, and stood up. "It was nice meeting you."

"Sit down," Warren said.

"Why? So you can buy a reformed user for coolie wages? No way, Mr. Chambers."

"We're back to Mr. Chambers, huh?"

"Only because you're fucking me around."

"Sit down, okay?"

She sat.

"How does twenty-five an hour sound?" he said.

"Forty sounds better," she said.

"Toots," he said, "we both know the going rate."

"I guess we do."

"The going rate is thirty-five an hour."

"That's right. So why'd you offer me twenty?"

"Because if you're still doing coke, you'd have grabbed it."

"Which means you didn't believe me, right?"

"Not when you asked for fifty. Fifty sounded like somebody figuring how much dope that kind of money would buy."

"No, fifty was to show you I wasn't desperate for the job."

"Are you desperate?"
"Yes."
He looked at her.
"I am," she said.
He kept looking at her.
"I need the job," she said. "You want to give me twenty, that's fine, I'll take it. But that doesn't mean I'm doing dope."
"I'll give you thirty-five," he said. "Plus expenses. The going rate."
"Thank you," she said, and nodded.
"You want some more coffee?" he asked.
"No, I want to get to work," she said, and picked up the envelope.

The security guard at the gate weighed at least two hundred and fifty pounds. He was wearing a brown uniform, and there was a very large pistol in a holster at his waist.
"Yes?" he said to Matthew.
The unadorned word bordered on rudeness.
The man had jug ears, a little black mustache, black hair trimmed close to his head, and brown eyes spaced too closely together. Except for his size, he bore an unfortunate resemblance to Adolf Hitler. The few words he'd spoken had been delivered without a trace of a redneck accent. Matthew figured him for imported talent.
"I have an eleven o'clock appointment with Mrs. Brechtmann," he said.
"Your name?"
"Matthew Hope."
The guard pressed a button on the intercom.
"Mrs. Brechtmann?"
"Yes, Karl?"

"Man named Matthew Hope to see you. Says he has an eleven o'clock appointment."

Says he has an appointment.

"Show him in."

"Yes, m'am."

He hit another button. The gate began sliding open.

"Follow the road straight back," he said. "Park on the right."

Morrie Bloom had once told Matthew that a cop was trained to think of all lawbreakers as bad guys. The good guys versus the bad guys. Ask any cop. The trouble with this sort of thinking, however, was that it left no room for differentiating between a man who'd illegally parked his car and a man committing a murder. This was what caused too many cops to behave like storm troopers when they approached a man who had exceeded the speed limit by two miles an hour. The man had broken the law. Hence the man was a bad guy. Hence he could expect the same treatment afforded a rapist. Argue with the cop, try to tell him he didn't have to behave this way with an honest citizen, and he'd slap you in handcuffs for resisting arrest, and then toss you into the backseat of his car like a plastic bag of garbage.

It took one highway patrolman thirty seconds to destroy the television, motion picture, and book image of the law enforcer as a sympathetic hero.

Thirty seconds.

Morrie said cops should think about that every now and then.

It had taken Karl Hitler here thirty seconds to raise the hackles on Matthew's neck, and he was only a security guard.

Matthew nodded icily, put the Ghia in gear, and drove through the open gate and up the road. In the rearview mirror, he could see Karl standing in the middle of the road, hands on his hips, staring at the car as it moved away from the gate.

The level road wound leisurely through stands of pine and palm.

Sunshine glanced off the polished tan hood of the car.

There was the sound of muffled waves nudging an unseen shore, and then the unmistakable aroma of salt and sea wafted through the open windows.

Florida.

Matthew smiled.

And eased the car around another bend in the road.

The Brechtmann house came suddenly into view.

It sat in majestic splendor some fifty feet back from a magnificent vista of the Gulf, the waters on this clear sunny day shading from an emerald green in the shallows to a cobalt blue in the deep beyond. Most of the sand on the southern end of Fatback Key had been washed away in last September's hurricane, but the Brechtmann beach had been spared, seeming proof that the rich only got richer. According to Warren's report, the Spanish-style mansion had been standing on this very spot since sometime around the turn of the century, when Jacob Brechtmann—then twenty-eight years old—carried his seventeen-year-old bride, Charlotte, to Calusa, where he gifted her with the house and erected a new brewery somewhat smaller than the one he already owned in Brooklyn.

The house had withstood at least five hundred hurricanes since it had been built, and it was still here, a seemingly permanent monument to Jacob Brechtmann's moneymaking prowess and his expansionist bent.

Matthew parked the Ghia, got out of the car, and walked to the front door.

Leona supposed she still loved that about him, his dedication to the law. Tell Frank he could no longer practice law, and he would cease to exist. The law was his life. In his study here at home, bookshelves lined three of the walls. They contained rows and rows of books concerning the law. There were windows set above the topmost shelves, creating a clerestory effect. Sunlight slanted through the windows. Dust motes from a Charles Dickens novel lazily floated on the air. Leona could imagine a bewigged British barrister sitting behind Frank's massive desk, pondering a brief, Big Ben tolling a quarter past the hour. Eleven-fifteen. Tooled black leather set into the desk's richly burnished mahogany top. A brass lamp with a green glass shade. A lawyer's room. Her husband's room at home. She felt like an intruder.

She went to the bookshelves, searching.

Last year's Florida Statutes.

He had brought them home from the office when the new ones arrived.

They would have to do.

She pulled the index volume from the shelf, began leafing through it, found the page she wanted, ran her finger down it:

GUARDIANS AND WARDS . . .

GUARDS . . .

GUEST GAMES . . .

GUIDE MERIDIAN . . .

GULF COUNTY . . .

GUNPOWDER . . .

GUNS . . .

See: WEAPONS AND FIREARMS

She kept flipping through pages:

MUNICIPALITIES . . .

PROBATE CODE . . .

RACING . . .

SCHOOLS . . .

SWAMPLANDS . . .

WILDLIFE . . .

Oops, too far.

She began leafing backward.

WEIGHTS AND MEASURES . . .

WEATHER MODIFICATION . . .

WEAPONS AND FIREARMS

Good.

The index directed her to Chapter 790. She took down the volume marked CHAPTERS 561–960. She sat behind Frank's desk again and turned on the lamp with the green globe. Light spilled onto the tooled-leather top. She opened the book.

At first she thought she might have difficulty.

Subsection 790.05 read: "Whoever shall carry around with him, or have in his manual possession, in any county of this state, any pistol, electric weapon or device, or Winchester rifle or other repeating rifle without having a license . . ."

Damn it, she would need a license!

". . . from the county commissioners of the respective counties of this state shall be guilty of a misdemeanor of the second degree."

Damn it!

How was that possible?

In the state of *Florida?*

She continued reading.

And under subsection 790.25—Lawful ownership, possession, and use of firearms and other weapons—she found:

"EXCEPTIONS—The provisions of ss. 790.05 and 790.06 shall not apply in the following instances and, despite said sections, it shall be lawful for the following persons to own, possess, and lawfully use firearms and other weapons, ammunition, and supplies for lawful purposes . . ."

Leona held her breath.

Under the long list of persons excepted from the licensing sections, she found at last:

"A person possessing arms at his home or place of business."

Which she guessed made it legal for just about anybody in the state of Florida to own a gun.

And in case the section had not made its point, it finally concluded with the words:

"CONSTRUCTION—This act shall be liberally construed to carry out the declaration of policy herein and in favor of the constitutional right to keep and bear arms for lawful purposes. This act shall be supplemental and additional to the existing rights to bear arms now guaranteed by law and decision of the courts of Florida, and nothing herein shall impair or diminish any of such rights. This act shall supersede any law, ordinance, or regulation in conflict herewith."

The hypocrisy of the law astonished Leona.

But it also delighted her.

Because now she knew she could go into a gun shop without a license and buy a perfectly legal lethal weapon.

Sophie Brechtmann was a fat lady with a hearing aid that wasn't working. She took the button out of her ear, shook it. She shook the battery case. She put the button back in her ear, adjusted the volume control.

"There's something wrong with it," she explained to Matthew. "You'll simply have to speak very loud."

She must have been a blonde in her youth. There were still the faintest of blond streaks in her otherwise gray hair. She must have been pretty, too. Never beautiful, but perhaps pretty in a *gemütlich* sort of way. Never slender, but perhaps not as fat as she was now, pleasantly plump perhaps, even *zaftig*. Perhaps there still resided within this cow of a woman the attractive young girl who had won the heart of Franz Brechtmann more than half a century ago. Perhaps. If so, it was nothing more than a shadow now, or—more accurately—a shade, a ghost. Only the piercing blue eyes seemed youthful. The rest—the corpulent body in the severe black dress, the bloated arms and legs, the pasty, puffed face, the hard line of her mouth—seemed to have been old always.

He searched those eyes.

Helen Abbott's eyes exactly.

"So," she said. "What's this about, Mr. Hope? On the phone, you said I might have information that could help your client. A murder case, you said."

"Yes, ma'am."

They were sitting in a sun-washed alcove off the larger living room, the room's French doors open to the beach and the overwhelming view of the Gulf. The day was magnificent. A day for celebration. But Sophie Brechtmann was dressed in the raiments of mourning.

"I must tell you at once," she said, "that I do not admire men who defend criminals."

"My client . . ."

"Especially murderers," she said.

"I would not have taken the case if I thought my client was guilty," Matthew said.

"I imagine all criminal lawyers say that," Sophie said.

"Perhaps they do. I happen to mean it."

"Perhaps you do," Sophie said drily. "I'll give you fifteen minutes to tell me what you didn't tell me on the phone."

"We're trying to find a person my client saw on the morning of the murder."

"What?"

"A person my client saw . . ."

"Yes, what about him?"

"He may be the murderer . . ."

"Unless your client is."

"No, my client isn't," Matthew said gently. "But even if this person *isn't* the murderer . . ."

"What?"

"I said if the person my client saw *isn't* the murderer . . ."

"Yes, yes, get on with it," Sophie said.

"The possibility exists that he may have *witnessed* the murder. We would like very much to find . . ."

"What do *I* have to do with this?" Sophie said, and looked at her watch. "You've got twelve minutes. And speak up, you're fading. My horn's on the fritz, I told you that."

"I thought I was shouting," Matthew said.

"What?"

"I said I thought I was *shouting!*"

"Yes, well, you are," Sophie said.

"Mrs. Brechtmann," he said, "tell me about your granddaughter and her friends."

"Oh, I see," Sophie said, and shook her head. "The little bitch has surfaced again, is that it?"

"Are we talking about . . . ?"

"We're talking about Helen Abbott," Sophie said. "What the hell does *she* have to do with your client?"

"Mrs. Brechtmann, two of your granddaughter's friends were . . ."

"I *have* no granddaughter," Sophie said.

Matthew looked at her.

"Helen Abbott told me . . ."

"Helen Abbott is a liar and a fortune hunter," Sophie said. "And so is her father."

"Her father's in the hospital," Matthew said. "Did you know that?"

"No, but I'm happy to hear it," Sophie said.

"In any event, Helen Abbott has two friends . . ."

"The little bitch."

". . . named Billy Walker and Arthur Hurley . . ."

"Yes, I spoke to Hurley on the telephone."

"That's exactly what she said."

"Did she tell you what the conversation was about?"

"I gather it had something to do with money. She said something about your meeting her price . . ."

"Fat chance of that!"

". . . your writing a check . . ."

"I'd rot in hell first! Helen Abbott's claim is an entire falsehood!"

"What *is* her claim, Mrs. Brechtmann?"

"Why, that she's my granddaughter."

"And you say she isn't?"

"Of *course* she isn't! I have only one child, Mr. Hope, my daughter, Elise. Elise has never married and she's certainly never had any children."

"Then why would Helen Abbott . . . ?"

"Mr. Hope, I really don't choose to go into a matter that for the past month and more has brought extreme discomfort to me and my daughter." She looked at her watch. "You still have nine minutes. You told me on the phone that I might be able to help your client. The meter's ticking. Speak."

"Did you or your daughter know anyone named Jonathan Parrish?"

"Parrish? No."

"Do you have any idea why Arthur Hurley and his friend would have been watching the Parrish house?"

"No. My only contact with Hurley was on the telephone."

"Billy Walker made reference to some pictures. Would you . . . ?"

"Pictures?"

"Yes."

"What sort of pictures? Paintings? Photographs?"

"I have no idea. I'm asking you."

"What about them?"

"He said he knew they would bring trouble."

"The pictures?"

"Yes. Do you know what he meant?"

"No. Pictures? No."

"Mrs. Brechtmann . . ."

"You've got seven minutes."

"But who's counting?" Matthew said, and smiled.

"I am," Sophie said.

"Mrs. Brechtmann, I know you don't want to talk about Helen Abbott, but . . ."

"That's right, I don't."

"I appreciate that. But I already know that her father came to see you sometime in December, just before Christmas . . ."

"That's true."

"And Helen herself came here last month sometime."

"Yes, the little bitch."

"And I really would appreciate it if you could tell me something about those visits . . ."

"No."

". . . because I'm defending an innocent man who . . ."

"I said no."

". . . may go to the electric chair if I can't prove . . ."

"Mr. Hope, I admire your tenacity, but . . ."

"Mrs. Brechtmann, if those visits are even *remotely* connected with the case I'm handling . . ."

"I don't see how they can be."

"Please," Matthew said.

She looked at him.

"Can you please spare me the time?" he said.

She looked at her watch.

"Five minutes is all you've got left," she said.

Matthew smiled.

"You're on," he said.

"This was just before Christmas," she said. "Last year. Just before Christmas . . ."

The man introduces himself as Charles Abbott. He tells the security guard at the gate that he wishes to see Sophie Brechtmann on a matter of some urgency. Sophie remembers the name out of the distant past, twenty or more years ago, the young chauffeur employed by her husband. British, as she recalls. Handsome young man. She vaguely remembers blond hair and blue eyes. She asks Karl to send him up to the house.

Charles Abbott comes into the living room. The room overlooks the sea. The sun is shining on this nineteenth day of December. It does not feel like the holiday season here in Calusa. It never does. Sophie can still remember Christmases in New York. The snow. The biting cold. Here in Calusa, although the room is dressed for Christmas—a huge tree in the corner, a wreath on the wall opposite the fireplace, evergreen garlands draping the banisters that lead to the upper stories of the house—one is aware only of the sunshine and the sea. No, this is not Christmas. Not for Sophie, and perhaps not for Abbott, either, who spent the first eighteen years of his life in England.

He has changed over the past . . *how* long has it been?

He reminds her that he left his employment here nineteen years ago. Well, just a tad more than nineteen years ago. Nineteen years and four months, to be exact, doesn't she remember? He smiles when he says this. Sophie feels suddenly uncomfortable.

He is, she supposes, in his late forties now, still handsome in a shabby sort of way. But advancing age has not been kind to him. He is far too thin. His hair is not quite as brilliantly blond as it was in his youth. His blue eyes seem faded. He has grown a sloppy mustache, and it tilts rakishly under his nose when he smiles. The smile continues to make Sophie uneasy. Why is he smiling this way? What does this former employee want here in the Brechtmann house?

He tells her he is here about his daughter.

Helen.

Sophie politely says, "I didn't know you had a daughter, Charles."

"Come off it," he says.

She looks at him.

"I beg your pardon," she says.

"How's Elise these days?" he asks.

The informal use of her daughter's first name irritates Sophie further. She is reaching for the intercom button when Abbott says, "I want a million dollars, Mrs. Brechtmann."

She blinks at him in astonishment.

"To keep quiet about little Golden Girl's baby," he says.

"I don't know what you're talking about," Sophie says.

"You know what I'm talking about," Abbott says. "I'm talking about Elise's *baby!* I'm talking about Helen, who's your *granddaughter,* Mrs. Brechtmann. I want a million *bucks,* Mrs. Brechtmann!"

"Yes, I heard you," Sophie says.

"No, I don't think you did," Abbott says. "You want to keep your Beautiful Beer beautiful, Mrs. Brechtmann? Or do you want all those beer guzzlers out there to know your darling Golden Girl got herself pregnant by the chauffeur?"

"This is absurd," Sophie says, and immediately presses the intercom button.

"Yes, Mrs. Brechtmann?"

Karl's voice.

"Karl, come to the house at once!"

Matthew waited.

Sophie Brechtmann was silent now.

Outside the living room, the sea sparkled in the sunshine.

"There was no substance at all to his claim," she said. "It was something he'd pulled out of thin air. Elise was a child when he started working here, only sixteen or seventeen when he left, can you *imagine* the nerve of the man? To concoct such a ridiculous story? To come back with a clumsy blackmail attempt after all those years? I had Karl toss him out like the scurrilous dog he was."

"But that wasn't the end of it," Matthew said.

"No. The daughter came to see me. His daughter. His little bitch, Helen. A chip off the old block."

"In what way?"

"Tried to milk me, same as her father did."

"This was last month sometime?"

"Yes."

"Would you remember the exact date?"

"Yes. The twenty-eighth. A Thursday."

Two days before the Parrish murder, Matthew thought.

There is a fire going in the living room when Helen Abbott enters. Sophie has let her into the house more out of curiosity than anything else. She wants to see what this brazen little bitch looks like. What she looks like is her father. Blond hair and blue eyes. The image of her father exactly. Tears fill the baby blues.

"Oh, Grandma," she says, and falls to her knees before Sophie. She clutches at Sophie's black skirts. She is playing *Anastasia* in a road-show production, but Sophie has already met and tossed the dog who masterminded this little scheme, and she is no more receptive to his conniving daughter than she was to him.

"I love you, Grandma," she says, sobbing.

"You don't even *know* me!" Sophie says.

"I *want* to know you. You and my mother both. Please let me know . . ."

"You have no mother here."

"Grandma, please . . ."

"Nor a grandmother, either."

"I don't care about the money . . ."

"Then why are you here?"

"The money was Dad's idea. All I want . . ."

"You want the same thing he wanted, you little thief."

"I promise you . . ."

"You can promise me you'll never come here again . . ."

"Grandma . . ."

"Because next time I won't let you in, do you hear me?"

"I want to see my mother."

"Liar, liar!"

"I can *prove* she's my mother!"

"You can prove no such thing."

"I'll *have* proof. The next time I come . . ."

"There'll be no next time."

"The minute I have proof . . ."

"Leave me. Now."

"I want my *share!*" Helen shouts.

"Ah," Sophie says, and nods. "I see."

"Yes, damn it! I want what's mine!"

"Yes, show me your true colors, thief. The money was *Dad's* idea," she says, mimicking her. "All *I* want . . ."

"I want a million goddamn dollars, you old cow!" Helen shouts. "You'd better get out your checkbook. Because the next time I come here . . ."

"Shall I have you thrown out, the way I had your . . . ?"

"You'll be hearing from me," Helen says, and turns her back and flounces out of the room.

Silence.

Matthew waited.

The silence lengthened.

Out on the water, a sailboat came suddenly into view. Red and blue sails. Spinnaker out. Matthew wished for a fleeting instant that he was out there on that boat. Wind in his hair. Everything clean and fresh out there. Here in this house . . .

"The next thing was the phone call from Arthur Hurley," Sophie said. "Same song. Said they had proof. Said they wanted a million dollars. I hung up."

"And that's the last you've heard of them?"

"Well, of *course.* The claim is entirely specious. *They* know it, and what's more, they know *I* know it."

Sophie Brechtmann looked at her watch.

"Your time is up," she said. "Good day, Mr. Hope."

7

This is the dog that worried the cat . . .

Warren Chambers came to the office at a few minutes before nine on Wednesday morning. Matthew had just ordered coffee and a cheese Danish from the deli on Heron. He buzzed Cynthia and asked her to make that *two* orders.

Warren got straight to the point.

"I hired a woman named Toots Kiley," he said, "used to work for Otto Samalson. She's very good. Or at least *was.* She hasn't been working for a while."

"How come?"

"She was doing cocaine."

"Terrific," Matthew said.

"I think she's clean now. I hope so, anyway. Matthew, this town ain't overrun with fantastic investigators, believe me."

"I know."

"So let's take a chance. If she doesn't work out, I'll absorb the loss, okay?"

"No, we're in this together."

"Thank you, but . . ."

"No buts."

"We'll argue it later, okay? Meanwhile, I'm hoping she'll be all right. She worked with Otto when he broke that tax-shelter scam Gabel and Ward were running, do you remember that one?"

"No."

"Three, four years ago. Otto's client was a guy named Louis Horwitch . . ."

"Oh, yeah. A cattle thing, wasn't it?"

"Close. It was oil wells."

"Right."

"Anyway, Otto and Toots worked that case together."

"What's her real name?"

"That's it. Toots."

"Really?"

"Yeah." Warren shrugged. "So let's see what happens, okay? As for the Brechtmann family," he said, and reached into his jacket pocket just as the buzzer on Matthew's desk sounded. He pressed a toggle.

"Yes?"

"Deli man's here."

"Send him in, Cynthia."

The man from the deli came in with a paper bag containing two plastic cups of coffee, two cheese Danish, four packets of sugar, two plastic spoons, two plastic knives, and three paper napkins. Matthew paid and tipped him. The man said, "Thanks," and went out.

"We shouldn't be eating cheese," Warren said, biting into the Danish. "Very high cholesterol level."

"What'd you get on the Brechtmanns?" Matthew asked.

"Not much. Have you ever noticed what a Mickey Mouse library we have here in Calusa?" He wiped his hands on one of the paper napkins, reached into his jacket pocket again, and took out several folded lined yellow pages. He handed the top page to Matthew. "That's the family tree," he said. "For reference. I've only taken it back four generations. And I've only followed the branch that ended up here in Calusa."

Matthew took the lined sheet of paper. He bit into his Danish. He sipped at his coffee. He looked at the handwritten page:

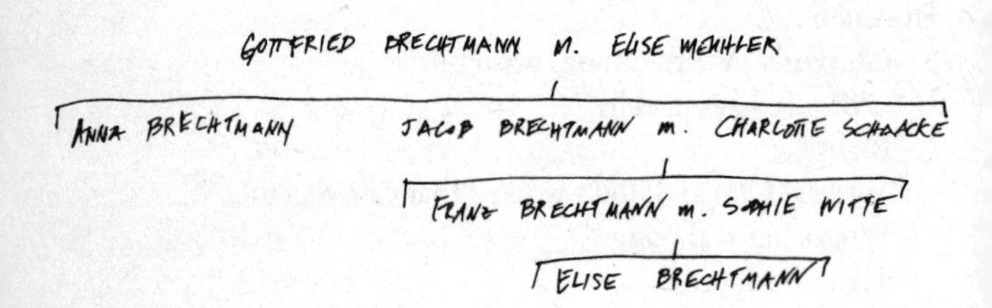

"Gottfried Brechtmann was a brewer in Munich," Warren said. "He married Elise Meuhler, daughter of a local banker, and had two children by her—Anna and Jacob. Jacob's the one who interests us. He's the one who came to America."

"When?"

"Turn of the century. 1901, to be exact. Came here with his wife, Charlotte—alleged to be a great beauty and something of a man-eater. Started the American branch of the Brechtmann Brewing Company."

"Here in Calusa?"

"No, no. Brooklyn, New York. That was the first one. There are nine of them now, including the one here. I'll get into that later, Matthew. Let's concentrate on the family right now."

"Okay."

"In the year 1905, Jacob and Charlotte came to Calusa for a winter vacation. They both fell in love with the place and built a house here the following year, when their son Franz was born. The house is still here, Matthew, on Fatback Key."

"I've been there."

"It must be a beauty."

"It is."

"Okay, this is now 1906. The Brechtmanns move into their new house and Jacob begins construction on a second brewery. Here in Calusa. Twenty-seven years later, there are *four* breweries and Brechtmann is the twelfth largest brewer in America. At a swank party in Palm Beach, handsome young Franz meets an eighteen-year-old beauty newly arrived from Nazi Germany. Her name is Sophie Witte . . . are you following me, Matthew?"

"I'm following."

"Okay, we are now down to Franz Brechtmann marrying Sophie Witte."

"When was that?"

"1933."

"And when was Elise born?"

"February of '52. Sophie was thirty-seven years old."

"Little late for childbearing."

"Indeed. But she gave birth to a beautiful little girl nonetheless. So beautiful, in fact, that her proud father promptly named her after his grandmother, and then a few years later brought out a new beer with a label bearing a reasonable facsimile of his then two-year-old darling. Does the name Golden Girl mean anything to you? How about the slogan 'The Beautiful Beer'? You've got it, Matthew. This is the beer that catapulted Brechtmann from number twelve into one of the biggest breweries in America. It's a shame old Jake wasn't alive when his granddaughter was born. He'd have been proud of her beer-selling potential."

"Fill me in on the company," Matthew said.

According to Warren, the Brechtmann Brewing Company now owned breweries in nine states. The original Brooklyn brewery packaged five million bottles and nine million cans of beer a day. The Calusa brewery—smallest of all the Brechtmann breweries, although it sat on two hundred and fifty acres of land off the Tamiami Trail—itself shipped close to two million barrels a year. In addition, the company brewed non-beer beverages, and it owned yeast plants, malting plants, metal-container plants, and several agricultural facilities where it grew and processed the corn and barley essential to the brewing of beer.

Again according to Warren, the company's gross sales for the last fiscal year were five and a half billion dollars, a 7.6 percent increase over the year before. Its net income was three hundred and sixty-four million dollars, a gain of forty-two million dollars over the previous year. Over the past eight years, Brechtmann's earnings per share had grown at an average annual compound rate of more than sixteen percent. The company founded by Jacob Brechtmann in the year 1901 had survived his death in 1945, and his son's death only five years ago. It continued to flourish under the leadership of Sophie Brechtmann, who at the age of seventy-three was now the company's single largest stockholder. The company's CEO was her daughter Elise, thirty-six years old now, whose little-girl face still adorned the label of the beer that had been named after her, the beer that had truly made the Brechtmann family fortune.

"Good work," Matthew said.

"It's a start," Warren said. "I want to do some more digging."

"For what?"

"Dirt," Warren said.

Matthew hated hospitals.

He had hated them ever since the death of Susan's mother. Fifty-six years old when she died. Never smoked a cigarette in her life, but her lungs were riddled with cancer. When the doctors performed the biopsy, they closed her up again at once, said there was nothing they could do for her.

It was Susan's brother who made the decision not to tell her she was dying.

Matthew had disliked him before then, but that was when he began hating him.

Because, you see . . . she was a marvelous woman who could have accepted the news, who would in fact have welcomed the opportunity to die with at least some measure of dignity. Instead . . . ah, Jesus.

He could remember going to the hospital one afternoon. His mother-in-law was propped against the pillows, her head turned to one side, where sunlight was streaming through the Venetian blinds. She had Susan's features and coloring exactly, the same dark eyes and chestnut hair, the full, pouting mouth showing age wrinkles around its edges now, the good jaw and neck, the skin sagging somewhat—she'd been a beauty in her day, and she looked beautiful still, though ravaged with disease and rapidly dying. She was weeping when Matthew came into the room. He sat beside the bed. He said, "Mom, what's the matter? What is it?"

She took his hand between hers. She said, "Matthew, please tell them I'm trying."

"Tell who, Mom?"

"The doctors."

"What do you mean?"

"They think I'm not trying. I really am, I really do want to get better. I just haven't got the strength, Matthew."

"I'll talk to them," he said.

He found one of the doctors in the corridor later that day. He asked him what he'd told her. The doctor said it had been the family's decision—

"*I'm* the goddamn family, too," Matthew said. "What did you tell her?"

"I was merely trying to reassure her, Mr. Hope."

"About what?"

"I told her she would get well. That if she tried hard enough . . ."

"That's a lie."

"It was the family's decision . . ."

"No matter *how* hard she tries, she's going to die."

"Mr. Hope, really, I feel you should discuss this with your brother-in-law. I was trying to help her maintain her spirit, that's all."

She died the following week.

She never knew she was dying.

Matthew suspected it came as a total surprise to her when she drew her last breath. He kept thinking of her that way; as dying in surprise. He'd loved her a lot, that woman. He still missed her. Perhaps she was one of the reasons he'd married Susan.

The smells of a hospital.

Cloyingly antiseptic.

The sounds.

Electronic monitors beeping. Address systems paging doctors urgently wanted. Nurses addressing patients in tones better suited for infants.

Charles Abbott was in a semiprivate room on the fourth floor of Calusa Memorial Hospital. The nurse at the desk in the corridor told Matthew that he had been there since the twenty-first day of December last year, a total of fifty-two days so far, which was a long time for anyone except a terminally ill patient to be in a hospital, but—

"He was in coma for almost a month," she said, and rolled her eyes. "You should've seen him when he got here."

Matthew didn't think he looked so hot now, either.

He lay in bed with casts on both arms and both legs, his face looking lumpy and discolored, his right eye half-closed. Across the room, the curtain was drawn around the other bed. From behind the curtain, Matthew could hear a man groaning.

Hospitals.

He introduced himself to Abbott and told him why he was there.

"*Who?*" Abbott said.

Trace of a British accent even in that single word.

"Jonathan Parrish," Matthew said.
"Never heard of him."
"Two people you know were watching his house."
"And what two people is that?"
"Billy Walker and Arthur Hurley."
"Don't know them, either," Abbott said.
"I think you do, sir," Matthew said. "They're here in Calusa with your daughter."
"All right, say I know them. What about it?"
"Why were they watching the Parrish house, can you tell me?"
"I have no idea."
"What does Jonathan Parrish have to do with Sophie Brechtmann?"
"Did *she* send you here?" Abbott said at once.
"No. As I told you, I'm representing a man charged with murder. I'm trying to . . ."
"Then how do you know her name? What do you want here, Mr. Hope?"
"I told you . . ."
"Or was it Elise who sent you?"
"I've never met Elise Brechtmann."
"But you *have* met Sophie, eh?"
"I have."
"Did she tell you how to find me?"
"No, your daughter did."
"What?"
"Indirectly. She told me you were hospitalized. I simply called every hospital in . . ."
"Did she tell you how *come* I'm in hospital?"
"No, sir."
"Because four men came at me with baseball bats."
"When was this, Mr. Abbott?"
"December twenty-first, two days after I went to see Sophie. Remarkable coincidence, what? They must've been following me.

I come out of this bar on Palmetto and suddenly they're all over me. Four of them. With baseball bats."

"Did you recognize any of them?"

"No. Four hired goons is all."

"Did you report this to the police?"

"Didn't *have* to report it. The cops came about the same time the ambulance did."

"Then the police know what happened to you."

"If you're thinking they'll ever catch those goons, forget it. Elise would've known better than to use local talent."

"Elise?"

"Sure. It had to be Elise who sent those gorillas after me. The old lady doesn't favor such tactics."

"Are you saying Elise Brechtmann hired four men to . . . ?"

"Is what I'm saying. I went to see Sophie on the nineteenth. Soon as I left, she must've talked to Elise. So Elise got worried, and bingo! On the twenty-first, I'm in the hospital with a fractured skull, a concussion, eight broken ribs, compound fractures of both arms and both legs, a broken nose, a broken collarbone and six missing teeth—all courtesy of little Golden Girl. You say you've never met her, eh?"

"Never."

"A beautiful woman, Elise. All those goddamn Aryan genes, I suppose. Sophie's a fat old lady now, but back when I was working on the estate, *she* was a good-looking woman, too. In her fifties at the time, but still taking good care of herself, swam thirty, forty laps a day, looked ten years younger than she was. Her hair was still blond, too, must've started going gray all at . . ."

"This was when?"

"I started driving for them back in '62. I was twenty-two years old, came here to Florida from California. I had good references, I used to work for some of the stars out there. Mr. Brechtmann hired me right off. Elise was still a little girl then. Ten years old when I started working there. Long blonde hair, green eyes—well, you've seen the Golden Girl Beer label, haven't you? Image of Elise. I haven't seen her since 1969, when Helen was born—but there was an article about the company in *Time* magazine last August, showed a picture of her with the blonde hair cut very short, almost like a man's, but still with those green cat eyes. Helen looks a lot the way her mother looked when she was a girl. Except for the eyes. Helen's eyes are blue. Well, so are mine. I guess blue is dominant over green, wouldn't you think? Moves like her mother, too. Same walk. Like a cat. Well, she's pregnant now, so it's difficult to tell, pregnant women waddle, don't they? But normally, she moves with a sort of jungle glide, do you know? Like a big cat on the hunt, stalking. Just like Elise. Something like that's inherited, I should think."

"You're saying that Elise is Helen's mother."

"Is what I'm saying."

"Sophie Brechtmann doesn't seem to think so."

"Is that what she told you?"

"That's what she told me."

"What a lying old biddy," Abbott said, and shook his bandaged head in amazement. "She knows damn well what happened. Why else would she have paid me all that money?"

The man behind the curtain groaned.

Abbott glanced at the curtain.

When he spoke again, his voice was almost a whisper.

"Half a million dollars," he said.

Matthew looked at him.

"I don't understand," he said.

"Paid me half a million dollars."

"I thought she'd refused to pay you anything at all. She told me . . ."

"That's right, she wouldn't give me a nickel when I went to see her 'round Christmastime, had her man throw me off the grounds, in fact. I'm talking about *then*. I'm talking about 1969, when Elise was pregnant and Sophie was frantic."

"Tell me about it," Matthew said.

"How can that help me?" Abbott said.

"How can it hurt you?" Matthew said.

Abbott looked at him.

"I'm trying to save a man's life," Matthew said.

"This has nothing to do with your client."

"Maybe it does. Let me hear it, okay?"

Abbott kept looking at him.

"Sure," he said at last, and shrugged. "Why the hell not?"

January of 1969.

In California, Governor Ronald Reagan asks the state legislature to drive criminal anarchists and latter-day Fascists off the campuses.

In Los Angeles, the trial of Bobby Kennedy's assassin begins.

In Paris, a Vietcong flag is placed on the steeple of Notre Dame.

And in Calusa, Florida, a girl who will not be seventeen until next month, a sixteen-year-old girl with long blonde hair and pale green eyes comes to the room over the garage on the Brechtmann estate and tells the Brechtmann chauffeur that she is pregnant with his child.

Legalized abortion in the United States is still four years away.

It is a bit past eleven o'clock at night.

Twenty-nine-year-old Charles Abbott is watching the news on television.

He is learning that Lyndon Baines Johnson has just sold the rights to his memoirs for one and a half million dollars.

Immediately he wonders how much the Brechtmanns will be willing to pay for *his* memoirs, Charles Abbott's memoirs.

He is willing to tell them—or *anyone*, for that matter—everything that happened in December of last year. Everything. Oh, such sweet memories.

Sixteen-year-old Elise coming to his room in the middle of the night.

Sixteen-year-old Elise in tears.

Sixteen-year-old Elise in his arms.

Never ask a beautiful young lady why she's in tears or why she's suddenly in your arms. He learned that in London. Never ask. Merely kiss away the tears and unbutton the blouse, and let those lovely breasts spill into your hands, and kiss the pink schoolgirl nipples and raise the skirt over pale white thighs and lower the white cotton knickers and let old John Peter find his own stiff way to where it's oh so warm and wet.

Now, at the end of January, the chicks have come home to roost, mate, the girl is here in tears again to tell you she's missed her period, the one due around the middle of the month, she is sure she's pregnant and she doesn't know what to do about it, she knows her parents will kill her.

"Now, now," Abbott tells her.

He is thinking of all the ways to spend the money he is going to get from the Brechtmann family.

He is thinking that what he has to sell is worth at least a hundred grand.

At least as much as it would be worth to any enterprising news magazine in the United States.

He can see the headlines now:

GOLDEN GIRL PREGNANT

BRECHTMANN CHAUFFEUR IS FATHER

What? The Golden Girl pregnant? Franz Brechtmann's darling little girl pregnant? The girl on the label of the Beautiful Beer? As pregnant as a common tart? The chauffeur the father, no less? Oh my my my my my, *quel scandale, quelle médisance!* Enough to make people stop drinking beer altogether!

He does not go to the family at once, suspecting the girl—being so young and all—has merely panicked. A single missed period needn't necessarily indicate pregnancy. He waits. And in February, when Elise tells him she has now missed *two* periods, they go together to her mother.

Sophie.

Calm, beautiful, sensible, slender Sophie.

"I fear the lass is in a family way," Abbott tells her.

Or words to that effect.

Sophie's blue eyes immediately dart to her daughter's belly; she does not seem to be showing yet.

"Is this true?" Sophie asks.

Elise nods.

"How could you have been so stupid?" her mother says.

Abbott clucks his tongue sympathetically.

Sophie's eyes meet his. Murder hangs electrically on the air between them. Abbott suddenly wonders if he's made a mistake coming to the mother. Perhaps the father would have been safer.

The Brechtmanns are Catholic; abortion is out of the question, even though surgeons' scalpels are available for a price in Denmark or the Virgin Islands. But even if they were willing to compromise their faith, there would be the danger of a leak, the original scandal escalating geometrically, the Brechtmann family taking their pregnant Golden Girl outside of the United States for an abortion that is illegal here. No. Abortion is not a viable option.

Elise must have the baby.

Can a suitable marriage be arranged with someone?

Elise has only just turned seventeen. Announce a sudden marriage and tongues would wag, and again there would be the danger of a greater scandal that could wreck the image of Golden Girl Beer. Taint the beer's image and the company will suffer tremendously. It is as simple as that.

Abbott is the easiest part of all this.

Merely pay him off and kiss him off.

Unless . . .

Mmmm.

Pay him *enough* and perhaps . . .

Why not?

Pay him for giving the baby a name. Pay him for taking the baby with him and disappearing from their lives forever.

"Tell me, Mr. Abbott, would that be worth half a million dollars to you?"

Half a million dollars is more than Abbott has ever dreamed of in his entire life. He does not even argue the price, fool that he is, fearful that Sophie will rescind the offer if he attempts to bargain with her.

In that same month of February 1969, Sophie tells her husband that she is taking Elise to Europe for the school break in March—"Some spring skiing in Zürs and Lecht, a little shopping in Paris and London." She prays her husband will not decide to join them. But she knows he will be occupied for the next several months with the construction of yet another brewery, his ninth, in Denver.

The European trip becomes an extended one.

In April, Sophie cables St. Mark's in Calusa to tell them that a tutor is helping Elise with her studies. The school is appalled. An absentee student? What kind of nonsense is this? But the Brechtmanns are rich and powerful, and nice customs curtsy to great kings, hmmm?

At the beginning of May, in a telephone conversation with her husband, Sophie tells him that they will probably stay abroad throughout the spring and summer; it gets so beastly hot in Florida, and anyway Franz is thoroughly occupied with the new brewery. When Franz says he thinks he may be able to get away for a week or so around the middle of the month, she almost panics. "Why, darling," she says, "that would be wonderful!" And is relieved beyond measure when he calls the following week to say there are problems in Denver and he won't be able to come over after all.

She gives a great deal of thought to logistics.

Should the baby be born in Europe or in the States?

If in Europe, the disappearing act will be complete.

But Abbott adamantly refuses to leave America. Sophie suspects there is a European past he has fled and is still fleeing, and she pursues the matter no further.

In June, Abbott meets the now visibly pregnant Elise in New York and takes her to an obstetrician-gynecologist highly recommended by a vague friend in London. Abbott tells him that he and his wife have just come from England, in fact, and need someone to look after Elise and to deliver her baby when the time comes. Abbott says he has no medical insurance in America as yet, but he'll pay the doctor in cash, in advance if the doctor so wishes. The doctor says, "No, no, don't be ridiculous, a personal check will do."

Two months later, Helen Abbott is born at Lenox Hill Hospital, on Seventy-seventh Street and Park Avenue.

"August of 1969," Abbott said. "Two days after Woodstock."

"Which would have made it . . . ?"

"The nineteenth."

"Were you there when she was born?" Matthew asked.

"Yes."

"Was Sophie Brechtmann?"

"No."

"You're saying Sophie was not present when her daughter gave . . . ?"

"She was in New York, yes, but she never came to the hospital. The seventeen-year-old girl I checked into Lenox Hill wasn't Elise *Brechtmann*, you see. She was Elise *Abbott*. My wife. Mrs. Charles Abbott."

"Then you're saying . . ."

"No."

"You're *not* saying . . . ?"

"I'm not saying Elise *is* or ever *was* my wife. Do you have any children, Mr. Hope?"

"I do."

"When your wife gave birth, did anyone ask to see your marriage certificate?"

"Well, no. But my wife's gynecologist knew she was . . ."

"Did she show *him* a marriage certificate?"

"No, I don't think so. I guess not."

"Well, the doctor we went to in New York never asked for one, either. We presented ourselves as married, and that was that. Mr. and Mrs. Charles Abbott. Period. Sophie had set up a checking account for us in New York. We paid all the doctor's fees from that account, all the hospital costs as well. The names printed on our checks were Charles Abbott/Elise Abbott. And when my daughter was born, the hospital records listed her as Helen Abbott."

"No trace of Elise Brechtmann anywhere along the line. How did you expect to prove . . . ?"

"I wasn't *thinking* of proving anything back then, Mr. Hope. I was doing what I'd been paid to do. See Elise through the birth, take the baby off her hands, move out of her life. That's just what I did. Went back to California. Raised Helen to be a fine young woman."

Matthew said nothing.

"And then it occurred to me that they'd cheated me all those years ago. That the secret was worth more than they'd paid me."

"So you came back to Calusa."

"Right you are. Just before Christmas. Showed up on Sophie's doorstep . . ."

"And asked her for a million bucks."

"And ended up in the hospital for my trouble. Because Elise must've got worried, you see. Must've thought Oh God, here he is, back again after all these years, here comes the same threat to the company. So she had me taken care of, sent a goon squad after me to help me change my tune."

He nodded bitterly.

"But I'm going to get that money, Mr. Hope, you mark my

words. Art Hurley went up to Lenox Hill looking for proof. And he found a nurse there who was working on the maternity ward when Helen was born. And now we have all the proof we need."

"What sort of proof?"

"Photographs. Lucy was there when they were taken."

"Lucy?"

"The nurse."

"Lucy what?"

"Strong. Lucy Strong."

"Photographs of what?"

"Elise and the baby. The baby lying on Elise's breast. Elise nursing the baby. The baby's hand on Elise's breast."

"Has Sophie Brechtmann seen these photographs?"

"Not yet."

"Why haven't you shown them to her?"

"Because we haven't *got* them yet."

"Who has them?"

"The man who took them."

"And who was that?"

"Someone named Jonathan Parrish," Abbott said.

Leona got out of the green Jag, locked the car behind her, and walked toward the front door of the shop. The plate-glass window was lettered with the words:

BOBBY'S GUN EXCHANGE
Guns Bought—Sold—Traded
All Shooting Accessories

She took a deep breath, reached for the doorknob, turned it, and entered the shop. A bell over the door tinkled. A man standing at the rear of the shop turned toward her. He did not look at all like the sort of person one would expect to find in a store selling guns. This was not your macho, suntanned gunslinger, oh, no. This was, instead, a chubby little man wearing chinos and a short-sleeved sports shirt, a wide toothy grin on his face as he turned toward the door.

There were guns everywhere Leona looked.

Rifles and shotguns on three walls of the shop. Handguns in cases along two of the walls. More handguns in a center case with an aisle on either side of it.

"Good afternoon, ma'am," the man said, moving behind the counter toward her. "I'm Bobby Newkes, this is my shop. May I help you choose a weapon?"

The word almost threw her. Weapon. Yes, she was here to buy a weapon. But naming it so openly seemed somehow to define without question its lethal properties. Weapon. She was surrounded in this shop by instruments of death.

"Yes, thank you," she said, and moved toward the counter.

"What sort of gun did you have in mind, ma'am?" Newkes asked.

She did not know how far she needed to go in order to present an image of a law-abiding citizen as defined by Florida's gun laws. Did she have to tell this man she planned to use the gun for target practice? Or hunting in the woods? She had looked at only last year's statutes; the most *recent* law made it possible for virtually anyone to carry even a *hidden* pistol. Not knowing this, she smiled nervously and said, "I really don't know. I've never owned a gun."

"Well, were you thinking of a rifle? Something like the Remington here on the wall? Or the Springfield?"

"No, actually . . ."

"A shotgun were you thinking of?"

"No. A smaller gun."

"Ah. A handgun."

"Yes. A handgun."

"Well, let's take a look in this case here," Newkes said, "all kinds of pistols in this case. What we've got here is Colts and Llamas, Rugers and Savages, Steyrs and Derringers . . ."

"Are those guns?"

"Yes, ma'am, the names of guns is what those are. Bernadellis and Crosmans, Smith and Wessons . . ."

"What's this gun here?" she asked. "This one."

She tapped her finger on the glass case.

"The one here in the bottom row?" Newkes said.

"No, just above. And to the left. Yes. That one."

"That one's what we call a snubbie, ma'am, because of the way the barrel is shaped. That model is an Iver Johnson Trailsman Snub, which a lot of women at twenty-five ounces find a bit heavy. There are lots of pistols have a lighter weight, you might find 'em more suitable to your needs. Did you just want to keep this in your home, ma'am? For protection? Or were you planning on carrying it about with you?"

"Just to keep at home," Leona said, and cleared her throat.

"Not a bad idea these days," Newkes said. "Here's a nice lightweight gun, this Llama here, their Airlite model. It's an automatic pistol, weighs only seventeen ounces, has a magazine capacity of nine shots. Or, you know, if you just plan to keep this in a drawer in your bedside table, weight possibly won't matter to you, and you've got a nice automatic here in the Walther P-38. Weighs twenty-seven and a half ounces, has a magazine capacity of eight shots. Beautiful gun. This gun right here."

"What's a magazine?" Leona asked.

"A magazine?" Newkes said, and blinked. "Well, it's this . . . well, let me show you."

He slid open the back of the case, reached into it, and took out the gun he'd just mentioned. "You see, there's this magazine, what we sometimes call a clip, it's this thing here in the handle of the gun . . ."

He pressed something or *did* something that caused a sort of drawer to slide out of the handle.

". . . with all these bullets in it. This is only on an automatic, mind you. Your revolvers don't have magazines, they load in the cylinder . . . well, you see this gun here in the case?"

"This one?"

"Yes, that's a thirty-two-caliber Smith and Wesson Terrier, a very nice gun by the way, you might want to consider it. Do you see that cylinder there?"

"Here?"

"You're pointin' right at it, that's it. That's where you load your bullets on a revolver. You put 'em in there one by one. With your automatic, you just slide the magazine in, and the job's finished. Revolvers or automatics, it's six of one, half a dozen of the other. I've had women whose preference runs to either. Solely a matter of taste."

"I still like the way this one looks," Leona said.

"The Iver Johnson. That's a nice weapon, ma'am, and it also comes in the thirty-two-caliber and the twenty-two long rifle, if that's . . ."

"No, I don't want a rifle."

"No, ma'am, I'm not talking about a rifle as such, I'm talking about the caliber of bullet, what we call a twenty-two long rifle. In that particular model, the gun has an eight-shot cylinder capacity."

"How many shots does it have in the model here?"

"This is the Sixty-six, this model, it's got a five-shot capacity."

"Mmm," Leona said.

"If you're thinking of a revolver, ma'am . . . you seem to be leaning toward a revolver . . ."

"Well, this *is* a nice-looking gun."

"Yes, ma'am, it is, and a fine gun, too. But I'll tell you what I really like in a revolver, and that's a gun here in the center case, ma'am, let me just come around the counter and show you."

He walked to the end of the counter closest to the door, came around it, and then moved into the aisle on the right-hand side of the center case. He took a ring of keys from his pocket, found the one he wanted, unlocked the case, and slid back a portion of the glass top.

"This here's a Colt Cobra," he said, taking the gun out of the case. "It's a part-aluminum version of the Detective Special. The difference is the Special weighs twenty-one ounces and the Cobra weighs only fifteen, which makes it nice for a woman to handle. It's got a six-shot capacity, and it also comes in a twenty-two-caliber model. You ever decide to do any game hunting sometime in the future, this is your ideal gun, 'cause it can be special-ordered with a five-inch barrel."

"It does look very nice," she said.

"It is nice, ma'am. Would you care to hold it?"

"Could I?"

"Certainly. It's not loaded, you don't have to worry."

"Are you sure?"

"Well, take a look for yourself," he said, and snapped out the cylinder. "Nothing in it, ma'am. Perfectly safe."

She took the gun in her hand.

The walnut stock felt cool to the touch. The barrel glinted under the overhead lights. She trained the gun on the front door. Her finger was inside the trigger guard. She tightened her finger on the trigger. There was a small *click*.

She could imagine herself using this gun.

Shooting this gun.

Killing someone with this gun.

"I'll take it," she said.

From where she sat hunched behind the wheel of the tired green Chevy, Toots Kiley saw her coming out of the gun shop with a package in her hands.

She turned the key in the ignition, starting the car before Leona had taken three steps from the front door.

On a tail, a suspect didn't pay much attention to a car starting before he'd climbed into his own car. But if he got into his car, and started it, and all of a sudden another car started up and began moving, this was likely to attract attention. Toots was playing it the way Otto had taught her. Spot your suspect, start your car, back out of your space, let her think you're on your way out. No way you could be following her, you simply had no interest in her at all. Until you picked her up again a few blocks down the line.

Otto knew everything there was to know about surveillance work.

He also knew everything there was to know about cocaine.

Come back when you've kicked it, he'd told Toots. I can't use you the way you are now.

She'd kicked it.

But meanwhile he'd got himself killed.

Toots drove to another part of the lot, made a turn, came circling back to where she'd been parked. Leona Summerville was taking a long time starting her car. Toots made yet another circle. On her third pass, Leona had finally got the Jag moving. Toots dropped in behind her.

She was wondering why Leona had purchased a gun.

This is the cat that killed the rat . . .

There were times when Warren Chambers felt that *everything* in Calusa was Mickey Mouse.

Take the morgue.

Not the morgue at Calusa's Good Samaritan Hospital, which Warren had never had the privilege of seeing, but the morgue at the *Calusa Herald-Tribune* where—at nine o'clock that Wednesday night—he and Toots Kiley tried to assemble some data on the Brechtmann family.

Now normally, if you ran a newspaper morgue the way it should be run, everything on any given topic was in a master file, with duplicates of individual stories in appropriate subfiles.

As, for example, take Warren Chambers.

There was not, in fact, a file on Warren—master or otherwise—in the *Herald-Tribune*'s morgue. But *if* there'd been such a file, it probably would have been labeled CHAMBERS, WARREN, and there'd be everything anyone ever wanted to know about him in that file—where he was born, what his parents' names were, where he'd lived, his various occupations over the years, and so on, right up to the present. A complete dossier on Warren Chambers. Anything about him that had ever appeared in the newspaper, right there in the master file.

But this primary source would also generate copies that filtered down into various other files. For example, if there was a story about Warren having worked for the St. Louis P.D., then a copy of that story would pop up in the file labeled ST. LOUIS and also the file labeled POLICE. The main file was like a smash-hit sitcom. It generated spinoffs. But you didn't have to look through all the spinoff files to understand what the initial programming had been. You just went back to the smash-hit CHAMBERS, WARREN file.

Well, in this Mickey Mouse morgue in the Mickey Mouse city of Calusa, Florida, there were no master files on anyone in the Brechtmann family.

Nothing.

Zilch.

Nothing on BRECHTMANN, JACOB, who'd opened the city's one and only brewery and built Calusa's most luxurious private dwelling.

Nothing on BRECHTMANN, CHARLOTTE, the great beauty Jake married and carried to Calusa.

Nothing on their son BRECHTMANN, FRANZ, who'd married Sophie.

Nothing on BRECHTMANN, SOPHIE, either.

Or BRECHTMANN, ELISE.

Who, according to Sophie Brechtmann, was the end of the Brechtmann line here in America, in that Elise was as yet unmarried and still childless.

But who, according to Abbott *père et fille*, was the mother of Helen Abbott, now the proper heiress to the Brechtmann fortune.

There was no file labeled ABBOTT, HELEN.

There *was* a file labeled SINATRA, FRANK.

Who did not live in the city of Calusa, Florida.

Warren shook his head. So did Toots. It was going to be a long night.

The man who'd let them into the morgue was a reporter Warren knew. He told Warren that if anyone asked them what they were doing there, they should say they were researching a story for Andy Marquez. That was the reporter's name. So now, at nine o'clock on a Tuesday night, with lightning flashes intermittently streaking the sky beyond the high windows, distant thunder indicating rain over Sarasota or yet farther north, Warren and Toots tried to get a handle on the newspaper's filing system because they knew for damn sure there *had* to be something on one of the most prominent families in Calusa.

"How about we look under 'Breweries'?" Toots said.

"Yeah," Warren said, and they went together to the "B" files. "Where'd she take you this afternoon?" he asked.

"To a gun shop," Toots said.

"What?"

"Yeah. Our lady bought a gun. At least circumstantially. She spent a half-hour, forty-five minutes in a place called Bobby's Gun Exchange, on the Trail and West Cedar. Came out carrying a wrapped package, I have to assume it was a gun."

"Why the hell would she buy a gun?"

"Maybe she plans to shoot somebody."

"God, I *hope* not," Warren said. "Nothing under 'Breweries.' What the hell kind of a newspaper *is* this?"

"Try under 'Beer,'" Toots said.

"Yeah," Warren said. "What time did you tuck her in?"

"I waited outside the house till her husband got home. At least, I *assume* it was her husband. He let himself in with a key."

"What was he driving?"

"Brown Mercedes."

"Yeah, Frank Summerville," Warren said.

There was nothing under BEER.

"Jesus," Warren said.

"Try 'Alcoholic Beverages,'" Toots said.

"This is worse than the Yellow Pages," Warren said.

They found a thick folder labeled ALCOHOLIC BEVERAGES.

"Bingo," Warren said, and carried the folder to a long table positioned between the windows and the filing cabinets. There were two green-shaded lights over the table. Lightning flashed outside. There was a rumble of thunder that sounded somewhat closer. The room felt cozy. They sat side by side and began leafing through the clippings in the folder.

There was no chronological order to the file.

"This is impossible," Warren said.

"Infuriating," Toots said.

They found a June 10, 1935, story about the formation of Alcoholics Anonymous in New York City.

They found a May 16, 1985, story about the Soviet Union cutting production of vodka, raising the drinking age from eighteen to twenty-one, and banning the sale of liquor before two P.M. on workdays.

They found an obviously misfiled story about the drug-overdose death of John Belushi on March 5, 1982.

They found an October 7, 1913, article about the death of the brewer Adolphus Busch.

There was a December 5, 1933, story about the jubilant *repeal* of the 18th Amendment.

And a January 16, 1920, article announcing the official *start* of National Prohibition.

And a November 23, 1921, piece about the Anti-Beer Bill, which made it illegal for doctors to prescribe beer for medicinal purposes.

And . . .

"I can't believe it!" Warren said.

A front-page story dated September 14, 1906.

The headline read:

BRECHTMANN BEER
OPENS CALUSA BREWERY

The subhead read:

JACOB BRECHTMANN DEDICATES
NEW FACILITY ON TAMIAMI TRAIL

The story told all about the new brewery on U.S. 41 and explained that it was not expected to raise local employment levels by very much since the actual brewing of beer was not a labor-intensive industry, and since management would still be operating out of the New York office. But the city of Calusa was nonetheless proud to have been chosen as the site of the first Brechtmann brewery outside of New York, and equally proud to welcome the Brechtmann family as neighbors. The article went on to describe the "beauteous European beauty Charlotte Brechtmann" and the "exquisite Spanish-style estate" the Brechtmanns had built on Fatback Key. It discreetly mentioned that Mrs. Brechtmann was expecting her first child in November.

There was nothing else about the Brechtmanns in the ALCOHOLIC BEVERAGES folder.

"Where do we go from here?" Warren asked.

"Try 'Births,'" Toots said.

There were eight folders labeled BIRTH ANNOUNCEMENTS.

Each of them was at least four inches thick.

"Please let them be chronological," Warren said.

They were.

They knew that the birth of Franz Brechtmann had been expected in November of 1906; the ALCOHOLIC BEVERAGES file had told them so. And there he was, the little darling, in an article clipped from the Society Page of the *Calusa Herald-Tribune* for November 19, 1906. Franz Eberhard Brechtmann, to be exact—named after Charlotte's father, or so the article reported.

"Now try 'Obituaries,'" Toots said.

There was a flash of lightning very close by, followed immediately by an enormous thunderclap and instant darkness.

"Shit," Warren said.

They waited in the darkness.

The lights came on again.

And immediately went off again.

"Shit," Warren said again.

In the darkness, they could hear the rain pelting the windowpanes. Another flash of lightning. More thunder.

"I hate Florida," Toots said.

They waited.

The lights came on again some three minutes later. It was still raining heavily. The green shades on the lights, the amber spill on the tabletop caused the room to appear protected, safe from the furious rain and the thunder and lightning. Somehow, it made them want to whisper.

Warren went to the uppermost "O" file and yanked open the drawer.

The drawer contained nothing but obituary notices.

As did the drawer below it.

And the one below that.

"We'll be here all night," Toots said.

"No, he died five years ago," Warren said.

"How do you know?"

"The library."

They found the notice of Franz Eberhard Brechtmann's death on the front page of the *Herald-Tribune* for April 19, 1983. The headline on the story was set in the same size type as the headline on the lead story about the bombing of the U.S. Embassy in

Beirut. The juxtaposition of the two headlines was perhaps unfortunate. Side by side, they read:

U.S. EMBASSY BOMBED BEER BARON DIES

Joined at the hip this way, the headlines made it sound as if Franz Eberhard Brechtmann had been killed in the attack. Instead, he had died in his own bed, of natural causes. If read yet another way, the combined headlines made it sound as if Brechtmann had been drunk when he died: Bombed Beer Baron Dies. Instead, he'd been cold sober, having retired early after a light dinner the night before.

The subheads, also printed side by side in the same-size type, were equally confusing. They read:

Suicide Attack Kills 40 Calusa Brewer was 77

"This is *some* newspaper," Warren said.

They turned to where the story was continued on the Obituary Page.

The article gave a summary of his life. Childhood in Calusa, schooling at Choate and later Harvard, frequent trips abroad with his beautiful wife, Sophie, and his daughter, Elise, who had been the inspiration for Brechtmann's best-selling Golden Girl Beer. A picture of the beer's label was implanted in the center of the column. Blonde, light-eyed kid, maybe three years old, smiling at all those beer drinkers out there. The story went on to mention the many years of guidance and support Brechtmann had given to the restoration of Calusa's art museum, the Ca D'Ped. It mentioned, too, his extraordinarily generous contributions to a wide variety of charitable causes. It quoted Jacob Brechtmann, the founder of the company, who in 1934—when his son took over as CEO—said, "I took it safely through Prohibition, my son can take it from here."

Franz Brechtmann had indeed taken it from there.

In 1934, when he was twenty-eight years old, and despite his father's bravado, the company had only barely survived the Volstead Act. In the years between then and 1981, when at the age of seventy-five he turned over the CEO post to his then twenty-nine-year-old daughter, Franz had built six more breweries and had taken the company to its leading position among the world's top beermakers. The article reported that this hadn't been a simple task. In 1941, when America entered the war against Germany, anti-German feeling had erupted all over the nation, and anything sounding even remotely German was virtually boycotted. The sales of the Brechtmann company's beers plummeted until well after the war. In fact, it was not until 1954, when Franz created the new beer inspired by his then two-year-old daughter, that the company's fortunes took an upswing. Since then, the only serious threat to its stability occurred five months ago, not long after Elise became CEO. It was then that internal problems led to charges and countercharges—

"Here it is," Warren said.

"Here's *what?*" Toots said.

"The dirt."

But that's *all* there was.

The paragraph merely ended with a seeming afterthought stating that everything was settled satisfactorily out of court and the company rose to even greater heights in the hierarchy of beermakers. The story concluded with the information that the deceased was survived by his wife, Sophie, and his daughter, Elise, and that services in Calusa would be private.

"Damn it," Warren said. "Where do we look *now?*"

"For what?" Toots said.

"For these internal problems and these charges and countercharges that were settled out of court."

"Let me think," Toots said.

Warren watched her thinking.

"How about 'Legal Notices?'" she said.

■ ■ ■

Matthew blinked at the bedside clock. Ten minutes to midnight. And the telephone was ringing. Joanna! Something had happened to his daughter up there in Vermont. The school's headmistress was calling to . . .

"Hello?"

"Matthew?"

A woman's voice.

"Yes?"

"It's Irene."

"Who?"

"McCauley."

"I'm sorry, who . . . ?"

"The motel," she said. "Irene McCauley."

"Oh. Oh, *hi!* Listen, I'm sorry I sounded so . . ."

"No, that's okay. You were probably asleep."

"Well, in fact, I was."

"Me, too. But then I woke up, and I thought I'd see if you were in the phone book. And you were."

"Yes."

"So here I am."

"So hello."

"Hello. I'm sorry I woke you up."

"No, hey, that's okay, really."

"How are you?"

"Fine. Just fine. And you?"

"Okay."

Silence. Then:

"I was hoping you'd call," she said.

"I was going to. But things started piling up, and I . . ."

"That's okay, I'm not one to stand on ceremony."

"So I see."

Another silence. Then:

"Shall I come over there?"

"What?" Matthew said.

"Do you want me to come over? I'd invite you here, but really, this place is a dump. Well, you saw it."

"Yes."

"Yes, you saw it? Or yes, it's a dump? Or yes, come on over."

"Yes, all three."

"Good," Irene said. "Give me directions."

Lying beside his wife Leona at a little before midnight, Frank wondered what she'd been doing in his study. There was nothing in there that could be of any possible use to a woman having an affair. No appointment calendar she could check to find out when he'd be where. No loose cash she could pilfer to buy lacy hooker underwear like the ones he'd found in her dresser. Nothing she could use. So why had she gone in there?

He knew she'd been in there sometime today.

But why?

He knew every inch of that study. The study was his cocoon. Came home from work sometimes to find the house empty, he'd mix himself a silver bullet and sit in the big padded leather chair in the study, sipping at the drink, listening to the palm fronds whispering outside the high windows, surrounded by the books he loved. The cleaning woman did the study every Thursday. She was due tomorrow, it was still only two minutes to midnight on the luminous bedside clock, still today, Wednesday, the tenth day of February. No cleaning lady in there today. But *someone* had gone in there while he was at the office. And since only two people lived in this house, and since *he* wasn't the one who'd been in there, it had to have been his darling wife, Leona.

He wondered why.

He did not know that she'd been in there twice today.

The first time had been to study the Florida Statutes.

The second time had been to hide the .22-caliber Colt Cobra she'd bought at Bobby's Gun Exchange.

Sitting the Parrish house was getting to be a pain in the ass.

Literally.

There wasn't a comfortable chair in the joint. Not a chair you could sit in and still see through the windows, anyway. There was a big comfortable easy chair downstairs, but you sank into it and couldn't see a thing, and also it was too heavy to lug all the way up here to the second floor of the house.

Officer Charles Macklin was ready to tell Warren Chambers to shove the job.

It was now a little past midnight, rain making the night look darker and colder than it actually was, rain drumming on the roof, rain lashing the windows, rain sweeping in sheets across the asphalt road on the entrance side of the house, rain pelting the beach on the deck side.

Charlie knew that rain kept the bad guys inside.

That was a fact of police work.

Nobody liked to work when it was raining, not even thieves.

You gave your average cheap thief a choice whether he wanted to do a job in good weather or when it was raining, he'd nine times out of ten pick the good weather. It only stood to reason. Who the hell wanted to get wet, thief or not? You come out of a house with a television set you just burgled, you got soaked before you could get it in the car. The television, too. Both of you got soaking wet. You come out of a liquor store you just held up, you're liable to slip on a wet sidewalk and break your leg before you even reach the car. You jump on a girl in the park, you're planning to rape her, it starts raining on your dick, you get your balls all wet, too, it wasn't worth the trouble. If you were any kind of thief whatever, it simply did not pay to work in the rain.

So what the hell was he doing here on a rainy night?

There wasn't nobody going to try breaking into this house on a rainy night, no matter *what* was hidden inside here.

Charlie didn't know that somebody was *already* inside here.

"I was really disappointed when you didn't call," Irene said.

She was curled up in one of Matthew's living-room chairs, legs tucked under her. Short black skirt, red scoop-necked blouse. Black high-heeled sandals, ankle-strapped. Red Lucite, art-deco earrings inlaid with sterling silver. Shiny brown hair combed sleek and straight to her shoulders, bangs running wild on her forehead. Blue eyes watching him.

"I'm sorry," he said. "I should have called, I know. It's just . . . I'm working a murder case, and things started . . . ."

"Oh my, murder," she said.

And smiled.

And sipped at her drink. Gin and bitters. Enough bitters to give it an orange color, she'd told him. On the rocks, please. He'd never known anyone in his life who'd drunk gin and bitters.

Rain streaked the sliding glass doors.

He had turned on the pool lights, and through the doors he could see rain riddling the surface of the water, pockmarking the blue. The palm trees swayed in the wind, rattling their fronds like dancers shaking maracas.

"Are you a cop?" she asked.

"No," he said. "A lawyer. I'm representing a man charged with murder."

"Do you enjoy murder cases?" she asked.

"This one, yes," he said.

"Why this one, in particular?"

"Maybe because it's so difficult," he said. "Keeps me on my toes."

"Difficult how?"

"Well . . . people telling contradictory stories, for example. It's hard to know who's telling the truth."

"About what?"

"About *anything*," he said. "Yes, she's your granddaughter, no, she's not. Yes, there's proof, but we haven't got it yet. Yes, there are pictures, but the dead man took them. Like that."

Irene blinked.

"Pictures?" she said.

"Baby pictures."

"Ahh, baby pictures," Irene said.

"Are the pictures inside the Parrish house? Were they really taken by . . . ?"

"Is there a church involved?"

"A church?"

"You said the parish house."

"*Jonathan* Parrish. The victim."

"Oh, is *that* the case?"

"That's the case."

"I read about it."

"Actually, a church *is* involved. St. Benedict's. Where the priest probably lied to me."

"About what?"

"About the man in black."

"Oh my," Irene said. "Missing baby pictures, and a lying priest, and a man in black and everything. Just like Agatha Christie."

"God forbid," Matthew said, and pulled a face.

"I have a good idea," Irene said, and put down her drink.

"What's that?" Matthew said.

"Why don't we turn out everything but the pool lights . . ."

"Okay," Matthew said.

". . . and then make love."

He looked at her.

"I don't have herpes or AIDS," she said.

"I don't, either," Matthew said.

"I haven't been to bed with any high-risk people," she said.

"Me neither."

"That I *know* of," she said. "I mean, I may get a call tomorrow from a hooker my late husband laid in San Francisco ten years ago, and she'll tell me she used to live with a homosexual guy that was involved with a bisexual girl that used to live with a lesbian junkie that just died of AIDS . . ."

"I know," Matthew said. "It gets to be 'The House That Jack Built,' doesn't it?"

"Yes," she said.

They were both silent for several moments. There was only the sound of the rain.

"So what do we do?" she said.

"What we did when we were seventeen."

"Won't that spoil it for you?"

"It didn't when I was seventeen."

"Then come kiss me," she said.

Under the green-shaded lights in the *Calusa Herald-Tribune*'s morgue, the rain slithering down the windowpanes, Warren and Toots found the first mention of the case in the file folder labeled LEGAL NOTICES. They tracked it from there to the front page of the paper for November 10, 1982. Like teenagers sharing a comic book, heads close together, they read the story:

Anthony Holden—Purchasing Agent for Agricultural Commodities in the Calusa Branch of the Brechtmann Brewing Company—had been summarily fired by Elise Brechtmann, the company's Chief Executive Officer since July of the preceding year. A reporter had called the brewery and asked Elise herself why she'd fired a man who'd been with them for twenty-two years.

"He stole a fortune from us," she said. "Anthony Holden is a crook."

Warren raised his eyebrows. So did Toots.

Elise Brechtmann had made an exceptionally reckless accusation at a time when caution might have been the byword: In the state of Florida, Grand Larceny was a first-degree felony punishable by a max of fifteen years.

Unfortunately, the newspaper had quoted her exactly.

And three days later *The New York Times* carried the same quote.

Little did Elise know that the Calusa P.D.'s White Collar Crime Division would decide after investigation that there was no evidence of criminal intent. Which meant that perhaps Anthony Holden was *not* a crook. Which, to Holden's way of thinking (and presumably his lawyer's as well) was good and sufficient reason to bring suit for libel.

"This is beginning to get good," Warren said.

It was just beginning to get good when the telephone rang.

Matthew picked up the receiver. The bedside clock read a quarter past one.

"Hello?" he said.

"Matthew, it's Warren."

"Hello, Warren," he said.

Beside him, Irene rolled over and reached for a package of cigarettes. A match flared in the darkness.

"I know it's late," Warren said.

"No, that's okay."

"But I thought you might want to get rolling on this first thing tomorrow morning."

"What've you got, Warren?"

"I don't know what the Brechtmann family has to do with all this, but you told me earlier today that Parrish is supposed to have taken some pictures of Elise and her baby . . ."

"According to Abbott . . ."

"Yes, I . . ."

". . . who may not be telling the truth."

"I realize that."

Irene let out a stream of smoke.

Matthew put his free hand on her naked thigh.

"But the Brechtmanns had a lot of trouble in 1982, which they agreed to settle out of court, and I'm wondering now why they don't just pay Abbott the two dollars and send him on his way."

"Abbott's asking for a million."

"In 1982, the tab was fifty-*seven* million," Warren said.

"Fill me in," Matthew said. His hand was still on Irene's thigh. She moved slightly, turning, making herself more accessible.

Warren told him about Elise Brechtmann firing Anthony Holden in November of 1982.

"Claimed he was stealing from the company. Exact quote: 'He stole a fortune from us. Anthony Holden is a crook.'"

"Wow," Matthew said.

"Wow," Irene whispered, but only because his hand had wandered higher on her thigh.

"Okay. A week later, Holden brings suit. You know where we found this, by the way?"

"Where?"

"In a file marked 'Libel,' can you believe it? Anyway, he asked for seven million dollars in compensatory damages. His salary with Brechtmann was stated as being two hundred thousand dollars a year plus stock options. He claimed that when Elise Brechtmann called him a crook, she caused the loss of future earnings potential."

"She probably did," Matthew said.

"He also claimed *fifty* million dollars in punitive damages."

"I'm not surprised," Matthew said. "Punitive damages are a sort of civil fine intended to discourage a defendant from doing the same thing all over again. To be meaningful, they have to be related to the wealth of the defendant."

"Right. Holden claimed that when it came to getting another job in the brewing industry, Elise had effectively *killed* him."

"Are those his words?"

"In a newspaper interview, yes. You want the exact quote?"

"Please."

"*Calusa Herald-Tribune*, November 18, 1982: 'Elise Brechtmann has killed me. In this business, or any other business, if you label a man a crook, he's dead.'"

"Which was the basis of his suit."

"Exactly."

"Which you say was settled out of court."

"Yes."

"For how much?"

"I don't know. Where do you think we should look next?"

"What?"

"They've got a funny filing system up here."

"Where are you?"

"At the *Herald-Trib*'s morgue. We looked under 'Settlements,' but all we got was a lot of stuff about the Calusa Indians and the first Spanish explorers. We looked under 'Claims' and 'Arbitration' and 'Disposition' and even 'Satisfaction.' There was only one clipping under 'Satisfaction.' A review of the Rolling Stones record."

"Why don't you call it quits, Warren? If you can get me an address for Holden . . ."

"I don't even know if he's still in Calusa. This was a long time ago."

"Give it a try, okay? If you find anything, you can call me at the office in the morning."

"Right."

"Good night, Warren," Matthew said, and put the receiver back on the cradle, and turned toward Irene.

"Are you always this busy?" she asked, and stubbed out her cigarette.

. . .

Leona lay awake in the dark, listening to Frank's gentle snoring beside her, wondering if the black man who'd been following her had been hired by Matthew. No sign of him today. Remarkable coincidence. Talk to your good friend Matthew over a few drinks on Monday, come Wednesday and the man following you has disappeared.

She hadn't expected that to be the result.

She'd asked to see Matthew only so that he'd soothe Frank's ruffled feathers if indeed there was any soothing to be done. Your wife having an affair? Don't be ridiculous, Frank. I can tell you on the highest authority that such a notion is absurd.

Couldn't have Frank suspecting anything.

Not now.

Couldn't afford a showdown.

Couldn't risk any sort of discussion about it, any confrontation, any attempt on his part to stop her from doing what she now knew she had to do.

The gun was hidden where he'd never dream of looking for it.

In his own lair. The counselor's den. Remove the copy of *Corbin on Contracts* from the shelf, and you'd find a .22-caliber Colt Cobra behind it.

If he found the gun, she would say she'd felt they needed protection. Too many burglaries in the neighborhood, too much dope moving across Florida from the East Coast, too many changes in the past several years, nothing the same anymore. See, Frank, here are the cartridges, right behind these volumes of *Black's Law Dictionary.* He would ask why she hadn't discussed this with him first, the purchase of a gun and bullets, so many bullets, and she would—but this was idiotic.

He would never find the gun.

The dust on those volumes was a quarter-inch thick, he hadn't once looked at them since his second year of law school.

He would never find it.

And after the deed was done—

If it were done when 'tis done,
Then 'twere well it were done quickly.

A handsome young English major named Salvatore Agnotti had played Macbeth to her Lady Macbeth at Hunter College in the fall of 1968. She was twenty years old then, and he was twenty-one. She could still remember . . .

Ahh, the innocence of those days.

"Was the hope drunk wherein you dress'd yourself?"

And both of them bursting into laughter. They could not get past that line for the longest time. Was the hope drunk wherein you dress'd yourself? She'd try it a dozen different ways. *Was* the hope drunk? Was the *hope* drunk? Was the hope *drunk?* Sal breaking apart almost the moment the words started from her mouth. She bursting into laughter not an instant later. Both of them giggling helplessly. Fat Professor Lydia Endicott, Speech and Dramatics, watching them patiently, "Come on, kids, let's do it, huh?"

And finally getting it right, oh, the *joy* of that wonderful speech, the venom in those lines!

"Was the hope drunk wherein you dress'd yourself? Hath it slept since? And wakes it now to look so green and pale at what it did so freely?"

Sal always flinched an instant before she delivered the next line. She began looking for the flinch as an unwritten cue.

"From this time *such* I account thy love!"

There was another stumbling block later on in the scene.

"I have given suck . . ."

And Sal would fall apart, and Leona would fall apart, and even Professor Endicott would begin laughing. In the empty auditorium the three of them giggled and giggled for five, ten, sometimes fifteen minutes at a time, *I have given suck,* and whap, both of them rolling around on the floor, and Professor Endicott falling out of her seat.

But later . . .

In performance . . .

Sal watching her with something close to awe on his face as she gave that part of the speech, as though truly frightened by the fearsome woman this college girl had become.

"I have given suck, and know how tender 'tis to love the babe that milks me. I would, while it was smiling in my face, have pluck'd the nipple from his boneless gums and dash'd the brains out . . . had I so sworn as you have done to this."

Jesus.

She had sworn to herself these twenty years later to do this thing she had to do.

"Bring forth men-children only," her Macbeth had told her all those years ago, "for thy undaunted mettle should compose nothing but males!"

Sal Agnotti. Sweet-faced Sal, trying to look regal and stern behind the fake beard, sweet, blue-eyed Sal, so young, so innocent.

Sometime soon . . . unless the situation changed dramatically tomorrow night . . .

Sometime soon . . . she would commit murder.

If she could summon up the strength, and the will, and the courage.

But screw your courage to the . . .

"Screw *your* courage!" Sal shouted the first time she said that line in rehearsal. Waiting in the bushes for her. Probably planned the ambush with fat professor Endicott, quaking there in her seat while Leona collapsed in helpless gales of laughter. After that, she could never get past the line without falling apart. Until, of course, it took. The line took, the words took, the meaning took, Shakespeare took, and she gave her fearful king the pep talk he needed: "But screw your courage to the sticking place, and we'll *not* fail!"

She could not afford to fail.

She'd be sitting there with a .22-caliber pistol in her fist, no one to whisper words of encouragement in her ear, no one there to give her a pep talk, just little Leona all by her lonesome with the gun pointed at his head or his heart, little Leona hoping she could somehow find the courage to squeeze the trigger.

She wondered where the sticking place was.

If only she knew where the sticking place was.

God help me, she thought, I'm about to commit murder.

Charlie heard something downstairs.

He turned immediately from the window.

He listened.

Someone moving around down there in the darkness.

He got out of his chair, eased the .38 out of its holster, and tiptoed toward the steps. A board squeaked under his weight. He stopped dead in his tracks, listening again. No change in the activity downstairs. Somebody still busy down there.

He started down the steps.

Faint light coming from the living room below.

No house lights on, had to be somebody with a flashlight. Maybe even a penlight, it was that dim.

Halfway down the stairs now.

Tense, the way he always got when something was about to go down. Tight feeling in his chest. Blood racing. Gun trembling just the tiniest bit in his right hand. Holding his breath, almost. Five steps down to the level below. Four now. Three. Two. One.

He stepped around the edge of the wall enclosing the stairwell, stepped into the living room itself, the kitchen on his right, scanned the room with his eyes and his gun hand, eyes sweeping, gun sweeping, past the bookcase and the rattan chairs and the sofa, settling on the figure all in black hunched over the desk against the far wall, penlight lying on the desk top, black-gloved hands going through papers and—

Sensing something.

Suddenly turning.

Looking straight at him.

And then reaching for something on the desktop.

"Freeze!" Charlie shouted.

Too late.

It came up off the desktop too quickly, gripped firmly in the gloved hand, the right hand, the barrel glinting for a moment as it passed the spray of illumination from the propped penlight, and then there was a flash of light from the muzzle and the shocking explosion of the gun and the instant searing pain in Charlie's shoulder and another muzzle flash and this time there was only the numbing pain of a nail being driven into his forehead and then nothing.

9

This is the rat that ate the malt . . .

Irene McCauley had just got out of the shower when the telephone rang early that Thursday morning. Matthew was standing behind her, drying her back. Her eyes met his in the mirror. He kissed the side of her neck, threw the towel onto the counter, and then went into the bedroom to pick up the receiver.

It was Morrie Bloom.

"Matthew," he said, "I have some police officers up here who tell me they were doing some work for Warren Chambers on this Parrish case. I've got to assume you authorized hiring them . . ."

"To sit the Parrish house, right, Morrie."

"The Parrish house is a crime scene, Matthew."

"*Was* a crime scene. My client owns that house."

"Who says?"

"The mortgage holder, First Federal of Calusa. Ralph Parrish owns the house, Morrie. Bought it for his brother to live in, but *he* owned it. The point is, we were in that house with the owner's permission."

"You and half the Calusa P.D."

"Only four cops, Morrie."

"One of whom is now dead," Bloom said.

"What?"

"You heard me. Charlie Macklin. Shot to death with a thirty-eight-caliber Smith and Wesson sometime last night. Body discovered this morning at six o'clock, when Nick Alston went to the house to relieve him."

Matthew said nothing.

"You with me?" Morrie said.

"I'm with you."

"Any ideas?"

"Yes. You might search that house from top to bottom for . . ."

"We already did that, Matthew. After the *first* murder."

"Did you find any baby pictures?"

"Any *what?*"

"Baby pictures. Pictures of a baby nursing at her mother's breast."

"We weren't looking for baby pictures, Matthew."

"Look for them now."

"It wasn't baby pictures that put two holes in Macklin."

"No, but it may have been someone *looking* for those pictures."

"What do you know that I don't know, Matthew?"

"Try the Calais Beach Castle, cabin number . . . hold it a minute, Morrie." He covered the mouthpiece. Irene was at the bathroom sink, wearing a pair of bikini panties now, studying Matthew's toothbrushes. "Is that crowd still in cabin number eleven?" he asked.

"The Hurley party?"

"Yes."

"They were last night. Okay to use one of these?"

"Sure," he said, and uncovered the mouthpiece. "We spotted two men watching the Parrish house," he told Bloom. "Their names are Arthur Hurley and Billy Walker. You might look them up. Cabin number eleven at the Calais Beach Castle on Forty-one. Hurley has a record."

"Thanks," Morrie said. "Why are you telling me this, Matthew?"

"Because if one of them killed Jonathan Parrish, my client can go home to Indiana."

"Right now I'm looking for who shot Charlie Macklin."

"It may be one and the same person."

"Maybe. Baby pictures, huh?"

"Baby pictures."

"I'll send some people to the house."

"Let me know what you find."

"Yeah," Bloom said, and hung up.

Irene was bent over the sink, brushing her teeth. Matthew went to her, put his arms around her waist, hugged her close. They looked at themselves in the mirror.

"We look alike," Irene said.

"We don't look alike at all."

"Yes, we do."

"Why don't we go back to bed?" Matthew said.

"Why don't we?" she said.

They were in bed again when the telephone rang.

Irene looked at him.

"You're busy *all* the time, aren't you?" she said.

Matthew picked up the receiver.

"Hello?" he said.

"Matthew, it's Warren. I've got an address for Anthony Holden. He runs a marina near the south bridge to Whisper, it's called Captain Hook's, don't ask me why. What else do you need?"

"Check with Lenox Hill Hospital in New York. I'm looking for anything on the birth of Helen Abbott in August of 1969."

"Spell that, will you?"

"Two B's, two T's. Parents are Charles and Elise Abbott. There was also a nurse named Lucy Strong working there when the baby was born. If you can find her, that would be helpful."

"Find her *where?*"

"In New York, I would guess."

"Matthew, this was nineteen years ago."

"I know. But give it a shot."

"What if I do find her?"

"You may be flying up there."

"Oh, goody, New York in February. Anything else?"

"Yes. Please don't call me for the next ten minutes," Matthew said, and hung up.

"Braggart," Irene said.

At ten minutes past eight that morning, the garage door to the house on Peony Drive swung up, and Frank Summerville backed a brown Mercedes Benz into the driveway. From where she sat parked diagonally across the street, Toots Kiley saw him reach up to the sun visor above his head. A remote control unit; the garage door swung down again. She started her car and drove off up the street. Five minutes later, she had circled the block and was parked again, in a different spot this time, near an undeveloped lot some five houses up from the Summerville house.

At eight-thirty sharp, Leona Summerville's green Jaguar appeared at the mouth of the driveway. Leona looked left and right, and then made a right turn onto Peony and an immediate left onto Hibiscus Way. Toots did not follow her.

Instead, she got out of her car and walked toward the Summerville house. She was wearing a smart brown business suit over a white blouse. Low-heeled walking shoes. Taupe pantyhose. She looked like a real-estate agent.

There were no cars in the driveway of the Summerville house. Toots walked directly to the front door and rang the bell.

She kept ringing the bell.

She was studying the lock.

No one answered the door.

She didn't think anyone would.

The lock was a Mickey Mouse spring-bolt lock. A credit card was palmed in her right hand. It took her two minutes to loid the door. Her back was to the street. She rang the bell again, and then, as if shouting to someone inside, said, "It's Martha Holloway!" and turned the doorknob and went in.

She locked the door from the inside.

She stood just inside the door, listening.

Not a sound.

This is known as Trespass, she thought. Chapter 810.08. Whoever, without being authorized, licensed, or invited, willfully enters or remains in any structure or conveyance. A misdemeanor of the second degree. Punishable by a term of imprisonment not exceeding sixty days.

I do not want to get caught inside here, she thought.

And immediately got to work.

There were three telephones in the house.

Toots planted a bug near each of the telephones.

One under the kitchen cabinet near the wall phone. Another behind the night table near the bedside phone. The third under the desk top near the study phone. The bugs she planted had nothing to do with the telephones. This was not a true wiretap that would record both ends of a phone conversation; she did not want to mess with taking the carbon mikes out of the phones and replacing them with her own mikes. Her bugs were small FM transmitters hooked into a voice-activated recording machine. If Leona made a phone call, they would pick up only her end of the conversation. They would also pick up any conversations that took place anywhere in the room. The battery-powered mikes had to be replaced every twenty-four hours. Which meant Toots had to risk coming in here again tomorrow morning. Which she'd have to do anyway. To listen to the tape and to decide whether she needed to record for another twenty-four hours. If there was anything useful on the tape, she'd simply pack her equipment and haul ass.

At five minutes to nine, while she was hiding her recorder on the top shelf of the bedroom closet, she heard a car in the driveway.

A rush of adrenaline, he's back!

Or she is!

One of them forgot something!

•

Captain Hook's Marina had a big billboard out front depicting a pirate who had a black patch instead of a right eye, and an iron hook instead of a right hand. Matthew's grandmother used to tell him that when she was a kid growing up in Chicago she went to the movies every Saturday and one of the silent serials they showed was something called *The Iron Claw*. The piano player would accompany the kids in a little vamp before each chapter began, and the kids would chant over and over again, "Dah-dah-dah-dah-*daht*, the I-Yun Claw! Dah-dah-dah-dah-*daht*, the I-Yun Claw!" Matthew could remember his grandmother saying, "Oh, Matthew, it was *soooo* scary." His kid sister Gloria thought it was disgusting, a person with an iron claw for a hand. Matthew thought it might be sort of neat; you could roast marshmallows on it. Gloria, who was in her pain-in-the-ass stage at the time, told Matthew that *he* was disgusting, too.

The marina billboard was visible as you came off the bridge from the mainland. This huge pirate with his iron hook. The lettering over his three-cornered hat. Captain Hook's Marina. You drove off the bridge and past a shopping mall that was built like a Cape Cod village transplanted to Florida—whoever had dreamed up *that* one—and then doubled back on a mostly dirt road that ran past the mall, paralleling the bridge, past the back side of the billboard, and then dead-ended at the marina.

Boats stacked under a shed with a tin roof. Boats in the water.

Most of them powerboats. A sign pointing to the marina office. Rickety docks with gasoline pumps on them. A ramshackle building with a smaller wooden sign that was a replica of the billboard announcing the marina. Beyond the main office the sky was gray with the promise of more rain. The water looked choppy. Matthew opened a screen door and stepped into a large cluttered room.

Boat keys hanging on a plywood board to his right. Little plastic float attached to each key. The float came apart; you kept your boat registration inside it. Virgin white line wound on spools. Unopened cartons containing portable toilets. Anchors of various sizes and shapes. Life preservers and throw rings. Cans of motor oil. Brass polish. Bottles of teak oil. Tools. Peaked caps, some blue, some white, some labeled "Captain," others labeled "First Mate." Flares. Charts. Boating shoes. A metal desk covered with papers, a wooden chair behind it. A calendar on the wall showed a blonde in cutoff jeans and nothing else, hanging to a sailboat's rigging. A big Evinrude engine was on the floor across the room, its parts scattered everywhere around it.

A young man in a grease-stained tank-top undershirt and blue jeans was squatting over the engine, a screwdriver in his hands. He looked up when Matthew came in.

"Help you?" he said.

"I'm looking for Anthony Holden," Matthew said.

The young man studied him suspiciously. Matthew—seersucker suit, white shirt, blue tie, black shoes, blue socks—looked out of place in a marina.

"In reference to?" he said.

Extremely tanned despite all the rain these past several weeks. Flinty blue eyes. Muscular arms and chest bulging in the tank-top shirt. Toothpick in his mouth.

"In reference to a lawsuit," Matthew said. "Where can I find him?"

"Somebody suing Tony?"

"No, this was a long time ago," Matthew said. He took a card out of his wallet. "Here's my card," he said. "You might want to give it to Mr. Holden, if you know where he is."

The young man took the card in his greasy right hand. He studied it. He turned it over to see if there was anything on the back of it.

"Hope, huh?" he said.

"Hope."

"Matthew, huh?"

"Matthew Hope."

"Are you famous or something?"

"Hardly."

"The name sounds familiar."

"It's a common name."

"I'll tell him you're here," the young man said, and went to a closed door at the far end of the large room.

He was gone for about five minutes.

When he came back, he said, "Go right on in."

"Thank you," Matthew said.

He went to the door, opened it, and stepped into a small office.

The man behind the desk weighed at least two hundred and fifty pounds. The man behind the desk had blond hair cut in the style of a Roman emperor, ringlets curling on his forehead and over his ears. The man behind the desk was wearing a shirt open to his waist. A gold medallion hung on his chest. The man behind the desk had rings on all his fingers. His fingernails were painted a screaming scarlet.

The man behind the desk was as gay as a tulip.

"Mrs. Summerville! It's me! Katie!"

On the shelf above Toots's head, the reels on the tape recorder began whirring, activated by the woman's voice.

Good, it works, she thought.

"Mrs. Summerville? Are you here?"

Silence.

The housekeeper, she thought.

Terrific.

She'll be here all day cleaning.

So how do I get out of this closet?

"Mr. Holden?" Matthew said.

Holden rose from behind his desk. Fifty-two or -three years old, big as a Buddha, he waddled toward Matthew, wide trousers flapping, sandals slapping on the wooden floor, pudgy hand extended, welcoming smile on his face.

"Mr. Hope," he said, "a pleasure."

Matthew took his hand. A moist, flabby handshake.

"Mr. Holden, I'm representing a man named Ralph Parrish, who's . . ."

"Yes, I know. I read all about it in the papers. Am I involved somehow?"

A flirtatiously impish look that managed to convey two separate reactions:

Me? Involved in a murder? How absurd!

But at the same time:

Me? Involved in a murder? How exciting!

"Are you?" Matthew asked.

"Well, I would hardly think so. Then again, here you are. And I have to wonder why."

"Mr. Holden, some six years ago . . ."

"Oh dear, *that*," Holden said, and waved it away with one pudgy hand.

"Your abrupt dismissal from the company . . ."

"Yes, yes," he said impatiently.

"Your subsequent suit for libel . . ."

"A*nd* defamation," Holden said.

"Which was settled out of court."

"Well, of course. For five hundred thou, enough to buy me a nice marina, thank you. *La Cerveza Grande* knew she was in trouble, making such absurd claims to the press. I'd have turned that brewery into a *parking* lot if she hadn't settled."

"By *La Cerveza Grande* . . ."

"The Big *Beer,* as our beloved CEO was familiarly known. Or, alternately, in straightforward English, the Blonde Bitch. Elise Brechtmann."

"Who fired you."

"Indeed."

"Why?"

"The real reason or the good reason?"

"Both, if you will."

"Why should I tell you *anything* at all?"

"You don't have to. But I can always ask for . . ."

"Yes, yes, depositions, how boring."

"They are."

"How well I know," Holden said, and sighed. "There were more damn depositions . . ." He sighed again. "She said I was stealing from the company. That was the *good* reason for firing me."

"Stealing what?"

"What does one steal, Mr. Hope? Paper clips? Rubber bands? Come now. *Money,* of course. Huge sums of money."

"How?"

"The brewing of beer doesn't take very many people, you know. Twenty men on the day shift, fifteen on the afternoon shift, and fifteen on the midnight shift. Plus two supervisors and a general foreman on each shift. Forty, forty-five people tops—to turn out two million barrels of beer annually. That is what one might call low overhead, hmmm? At least insofar as labor is concerned."

"I would say so, yes. What does that have to do with . . . ?"

"Management is something else. By the time I started working for Brechtmann, there were seven breweries all over the country, with local management teams for each brewery. I was purchasing agent down here. Which is what caused all the brouhaha. Would you like a beer?"

"Thank you, no."

"I'll have one, if you don't mind," Holden said, and moved to a refrigerator across the room. Trousers as wide as pajama bottoms, flapping as he walked. He opened the refrigerator door. "Developed a taste for it while I was working for Brechtmann. Comes in handy when one deals with rough trade," he said, and took a can out of the refrigerator. He closed the door, popped the can, tilted it to his mouth, drank. "I *adore* the foam," he said.

Matthew said nothing.

"Are you married?" Holden asked him.

"Divorced."

"Gay?"

"Straight."

"Pity," Holden said. "Where were we?"

"You were purchasing agent for . . ."

"Yes. And the purchasing agent in a brewery is responsible for purchasing the ingredients that go into making beer."

"Naturally."

"Of course. And the chief ingredients that go into making beer are malt, hops, and either rice or corn."

"Uh-huh," Matthew said.

"Do you know what malt is?"

"No."

"Or hops?"

"No."

"I didn't think so. Hardly anyone does. Hops are the dried ripe flowers of the hop plant, which is a sort of twining vine. They contain a bitter, aromatic oil. While I was working for Brechtmann, I bought my hops from Washington, Idaho, Oregon, even Poland and Czechoslovakia. It's the mixture of different hops in various quantities that give different beers their distinctive flavors. The recipe for Golden Girl Beer was a secret. I knew that secret because I knew which hops I was buying and in what quantities."

He stole the secret, Matthew thought. *That's* why she fired him. He stole the secret recipe and sold it to Anheuser-Busch or Pabst or Miller . . .

"I didn't steal the secret, if that's what you're thinking," Holden said. "I didn't steal *anything,* as a matter of fact."

"But Elise Brechtmann claimed you did."

"Well, of course!" Eyebrows rocketing onto his forehead. "What else would one expect from a bitch of her magnitude?"

"Claimed you stole huge sums of money from her, isn't that what you said?"

"Yes."

"How?"

"The malt."

"I'm sorry, what . . . ?"

"The crux of the matter. It was her claim, you see, that I was eating the company's malt—so to speak."

"I still don't know what malt is."

"Brewer's malt. Or barley malt, take your choice, they're both the same thing. Essential to the brewing process. Steeped from raw barley, I won't go into the details because they're too tiresome, really. Suffice it to say that without barley malt, there ain't no beer, Mr. Hope. So now we get to the basis of *La Cerveza Grande*'s charge."

"Which was?"

"Patience, Mr. Hope," Holden said, and sighed. He sipped at his beer. He looked at the can. "There was a time," he said, "when I detested the aroma of malt. Ah, well." He took another sip of beer. "When I was working for Brechtmann," he said, "we owned malthouses that supplied thirty percent of our malt needs. But thirty percent wasn't a hundred percent, and so I had to go to *outside* maltsters to buy the other seventy percent we needed. You have to understand how much malt we *used*, Mr. Hope, and how much it cost us."

"How much did you use?"

"To brew the two million barrels of beer we shipped each year, we needed sixty-three million pounds of malt."

"That is a lot of malt," Matthew said.

"Indeed," Holden said.

"And what did all that malt cost you?"

"Prices per bushel change all the time," Holden said. "But back in 1981 I'd say we were spending something like five million dollars annually for the malt we were getting from outside sources."

"Five million," Matthew said.

"Give or take." Holden smiled. "According to Elise, it was mostly *take*."

"How? She claimed you were stealing, but how?"

"Kickbacks."

"From whom?"

"The various maltsters I dealt with."

"How large a kickback?"

"Fifty cents a bushel."

"Is that a lot?"

"There are thirty-four pounds of malt in a bushel. You figure it out, Mr. Hope."

"No, you figure it out."

"We used sixty-three million pounds of malt a year. Divide that by thirty-four pounds per bushel, and you get one million, eight hundred and fifty thousand bushels, something close to that."

"At a fifty-cent kickback per bushel."

"So Elise claimed."

"That's a lot of money."

"I wish I had it," Holden said.

"What proof did she have for this claim?"

"None. Not a shred."

"Yet she fired you, and told the newspaper . . ."

"A crazy woman," Holden said, shaking his head.

"Why'd she fire you, Mr. Holden? You said there was a good reason and a real reason. What was the *real* reason?"

"You mean you didn't notice?" Holden said, and smiled. "I'm gay."

"She fired you because . . . ?"

"Because my lover happened to be a very good friend of hers."

"And who was that?"

"Jonathan Parrish."

"According to this, you've been a very bad boy," Bloom said.

He was sitting behind the desk in his office, tapping a copy of Arthur Hurley's rap sheet. Bloom's partner, Cooper Rawles, was sitting on the edge of the desk. Rawles was at least six feet two inches tall, and he weighed a possible two-forty. He had wide shoulders, a barrel chest, and massive hands. He did not look like a person to mess with. The man Arthur Hurley had attacked with a broken beer bottle eight years ago had been black. Cooper Rawles was black, too.

"That was then, and this is now," Hurley said.

"You're a good boy now, is that it?" Rawles said.

Hurley looked at him as if a cockroach had spoken.

"Answer me, Artie," Rawles said. "Are you a good boy now?"

"What am I doing here?" Hurley asked Bloom. "Are you charging me with something?"

"You want us to charge you with something?" Bloom asked.

"I want to know . . ."

"Give me something to charge him with, Coop," Bloom said.

"How about using obscenity to the police officer who . . . ?"

"He had no right arresting me in the . . ."

"Who says you were arrested?" Bloom asked. "All the officer did was ask you politely to come down here for some questioning."

"And that's not arresting me, huh? What do *you* call it? A field investigation?"

"No, it's not a . . ."

"I'm in *custody* is what I am. In which case, you better read me Miranda, and you better get a lawyer for me."

"You're not in custody," Bloom said.

"Good," Hurley said, and stood up. "In which case, I'll just run a . . ."

"Sit down," Rawles said.

"Why? Your friend here said I'm not . . ."

"Sit the fuck *down!*" Rawles said.

Hurley glared at him.

"I think you'd better sit down," Bloom said softly.

"What comes next?" Hurley said, sitting. "The rubber hose?"

"For a man who didn't do anything," Bloom said, "you certainly are defensive."

"Maybe I spent too much time in jail for things I didn't do," Hurley said.

"That's right," Rawles said. "Everybody in jail is innocent."

"Not everybody."

"Just you."

"A couple of times, that's right. A couple of times, I really *was* innocent. I didn't do a fucking thing, and there I was in jail."

"What a shame," Rawles said.

"Sure, it's supposed to be justice," Hurley said. "And I didn't do anything *now*, either."

"Nobody said you did anything," Bloom said. "We just want to talk to you."

"I guess you want to talk to Billy, too, huh? You dragged him in, too, I guess you want to talk to him. Where you got him? In the other room? Asking him the same questions you're asking me, checkin' our stories?"

"Have we asked you any questions yet?" Rawles said.

"No, but . . ."

"Then shut the fuck up."

"Why? Your partner just said I didn't do anything. In which case . . ."

"In which case, shut the fuck up," Rawles said.

"If I didn't do anything, what is it I'm supposed *not* to have done?"

"You're supposed not to have murdered a police officer," Bloom said.

"Oh, shit," Hurley said, "is *that* what you're trying to hang on me? Jesus, let me out of here."

"Sit down," Rawles said.

"Nossir, you better read me my rights right this fucking minute. This is a cop got killed, you better read me my rights and get me a lawyer. You better tell Billy, too. You better tell him a cop got boxed. Man, this is serious. This is very serious here."

"Sit down," Rawles said.

"Sit down," Bloom said.

"I didn't kill any fucking cop," Hurley said. "You think I'm an amateur?"

"Who said you killed a cop?"

"Am I hearing things then? I thought somebody said a police officer . . ."

"I said you *didn't* kill a police officer," Bloom said.

"Sure, bullshit," Hurley said.

"Why were you watching the Parrish house?" Rawles said.

"Oh, so that's it," Hurley said.

"You *were* watching the Parrish house, right?"

"That's right, and somebody was *in* that house, and I wasn't going in till they got *out*. So what is this? Was it a cop inside that house? Did a cop get killed inside that house?"

"You seem to know an awful lot about what was inside that house or not inside it," Bloom said.

"I know a plant when I see one, and this was a plant. I see a guy peeking around the window shade, I don't have to be a genius to know it's a plant. So it was a cop in there, huh? And he got cooled, right? Well, it wasn't me who did it. It wasn't Billy, either."

"Why were you watching the house?" Rawles asked.

Same question. When a thief didn't answer a question, there was a reason. Thieves were as good as movie stars at not answering questions. You asked a famous actress, "Is it true you'll be leaving *Dynasty* next year?" she answered, "The weather in Southern California is so beautiful." You asked a thief, "What are you doing with these burglars' tools in your hand?" he answered, "My mother has angina pectoris." Movie stars and thieves were identical in the way they handled questions they didn't want to answer. All a cop or a reporter could do was ask the same question all over again.

"Why were you watching the house?"

This time from Bloom.

Ask it often enough, maybe come Christmas you'd get a straight answer.

"First tell me was a cop killed inside there," Hurley said.

"Yes," Bloom said.

Rawles looked at him.

Bloom shrugged.

The shrug said, "Let's play it straight, see what we get from him."

Rawles grimaced.

The grimace said, "He's a fuckin' thief, we'll get lies from him no matter *how* we play it."

Hurley nodded.

"So I was right," he said. "A cop *did* get killed inside that house."

"Yes," Bloom said.

Rawles sighed and shook his head.

"When was this?" Hurley asked.

"All of a sudden *he's* the cop!" Rawles said angrily. "*He's* the one asking questions."

"It was last night," Bloom said.

"For Christ's sake, Morrie . . ."

"I was nowhere near the Parrish house last night," Hurley said.

"Then where were you?"

"Home in bed with my girlfriend. Who by the way is pregnant."

"We send lots of guys to jail who have pregnant girlfriends," Rawles said.

"No kidding?"

"In casc you expected us to break into tears or anything."

"No, I didn't expect *that*, don't worry."

"What's her name?" Bloom asked.

"Helen Abbott. Call her right this minute, go ahead. She's back at the motel, she doesn't know why you picked up me and Billy. Ask her where I was last night, whatever time the cop got killed, go ahead, ask her. Pick up the phone and ask her. She'll tell you I was home in bed with her."

"What time was this?"

"Was what?"

"That you were with her. From what time to what time?"

"All night."

"From what time to what time?"

"What time did the cop get killed?"

"Answer the fucking *question*," Rawles shouted.

"Listen, you," Hurley said, "I'm answering these questions voluntarily, you don't have to . . ."

"From what *time* to what *time?*" Rawles said.

"We got back from supper it must've been nine o'clock. We watched some television and went to sleep. Billy was in the same room, in the other bed. You ask him where we were all last night, he'll tell you. Ask them both. There wasn't any one of us anywhere near that Parrish house last night."

"What time did you go to breakfast this morning?" Bloom asked.

"Around eight o'clock."

"All three of you?"

"All three of us."

"Where'd you go?"

"Burger King."

"Why were you watching the Parrish house?"

Fourth time around.

"Helen's grandmother says she doesn't believe us," Hurley said.

Which was the same as saying "The weather in Southern California is so beautiful." Or "My mother has angina pectoris."

Both cops looked at him.

"Which is bullshit, of course," Hurley said.

"Just what I was thinking," Rawles said.

"I mean, her saying she doesn't believe us. She *knows* we're telling the truth."

"About what?"

"That Helen is her granddaughter. The point is, we need proof."

"Proof," Bloom said.

"Yeah."

"Of what?"

"That she's the granddaughter."

"Uh-huh."

"Which the baby pictures would prove," Hurley said.

"Uh-huh."

"We think maybe they're inside the Parrish house. Which is why we were watching the house. But we weren't going in there when we knew there was somebody *already* in there."

"*What* baby pictures?" Rawles asked.

"Helen's. Her pictures when she was a baby. With her mother, you know? Helen and her mother."

"Uh-huh."

"Pictures of them both together. So the grandmother can't say this girl nursing the baby isn't her daughter. Because she *is*. I mean, there's her picture, her *face*. Which means Helen is telling the truth. Which the grandmother knows anyway. But that's the proof we needed. The pictures. And we thought they were inside that house. Which is why we were watching the house."

"But you didn't go inside there, huh?" Bloom asked.

"No way," Hurley said. "With somebody sitting it? No way."

The cops looked at each other.

"What do you think?" Bloom asked.

"It's dumb enough to be true," Rawles said.

Vacuum cleaner going now.

The housekeeper was in the living room.

Toots's mind raced like sixty. Carpet here in the master bedroom, extending clear into the closet. Meant she'd be vacuuming in here, too. Maybe she wouldn't open the closet door. But suppose she did? Hang up something that came back from the cleaner's, put away a pair of shoes or a robe someone had left under a chair or draped over it, any number of reasons she might come into this closet and find a frizzied, twenty-six-year-old blonde wetting her pants. Had to get out of here before she came in. But how?

The telephone rang.

On the shelf above her head, there was a tiny *click*. The sound of the ringing phone had triggered the mechanism. The recorder reels began whirring. The vacuum cleaner suddenly stopped.

"Coming!" the housekeeper yelled to the phone.

Toots was out of the closet in a wink.

Slithering herself cautiously and minutely around the doorjamb, a snake or a roach couldn't have done it better, one eye and a nose showing, part of her chin maybe, housekeeper's fat ass swinging down the carpeted corridor toward the wall phone over the kitchen's passthrough counter. Toots stepped into the corridor. Housekeeper reaching for the phone. Don't turn this way, Toots thought, and tried to orient herself. Open door to a second bedroom across the hall, street side of the house. The garage would be . . .

"Hello?"

A glance toward the kitchen. Housekeeper leaning on the counter, big fat ass mooning the dining room.

"Yes, this is the Summerville residence."

The garage would be near the kitchen. No way to get to the garage without passing Brünnhilde.

"I'm sorry, Mrs. Summerville isn't here just now. May I take a message, please?"

Study across the hall was worthless. Dead end room, high windows.

"Yes, Mrs. Horowitz, I'll remind her. A meeting tonight, yes. Could you spell that, please?"

But maybe . . .

"The league to *what?*"

Run across the hall, pop into the study. Stay in there till Brünnhilde vacuumed her way up the corridor and into the master bedroom, then run like hell for the front door.

"Florida wildlife, yes, ma'am. The league to protect Florida wildlife, yes, ma'am, I've got it. And the meeting is tonight. Yes, ma'am. Mrs. Colman's house. Yes, ma'am. Eight o'clock. Yes, ma'am, I've written it all down. I'll leave the message right here by the phone in case she's not back by the time I leave. Yes, ma'am, thank you."

Click of the receiver being replaced on the hook.

The housekeeper came up the corridor and switched on the vacuum cleaner. She vacuumed her way past the study and the second bedroom and then vacuumed herself into the master bedroom.

And opened the closet door.

And vacuumed around the shoe racks there.

Toots Kiley was already across the hall in the study.

Two minutes later, she was out the front door and walking very quickly toward where she'd parked the Chevy.

"How're we supposed to get back to the motel?" Billy wanted to know.

"We take a bus," Hurley said.

"They got buses in this two-bit town?"

"I saw buses," Hurley said.

It was a long walk to U.S. 41. It was almost twelve noon, the day cloudy and uncertain, the temperature hovering around seventy degrees Fahrenheit, twenty-one centigrade.

"This means we zeroed out, you realize that?" Billy said.

"Yeah," Hurley said.

"I mean, we steered wide of the murder rap, but we both told them about the pictures . . ."

"Yeah."

"I mean we *had* to."

"I know."

"Otherwise why were we watching the house? To kill a fuckin' cop was inside there?"

"I know, I know."

"So we had to tell them about the pictures."

"Nobody's blaming you."

"Who's saying anybody's blaming me? I'm saying unless we told them about the pictures, they'd have been all over us about the dead cop. 'Cause they knew we were casing the Parrish house."

"Yeah. And you know where they got *that*, don't you?"

"Where?"

"From that fuckin' mouse-fart lawyer who came to the motel."

"Right, I didn't think of that. It had to be him."

"Of course it was him."

"But what I'm saying, we can forget all about those pictures now. 'Cause the cops'll go in there with a hundred guys, they'll toss everything in the house, they'll find the pictures. And without the pictures, the old lady'll keep telling us to fuck off, and that's that. The deal is blown, Artie, we're finished here in this shit town."

"Yeah," Hurley said.

But he was thinking they weren't *quite* finished.

The first thing he had to do was teach little Miss Helen Abbott with her big fuckin' belly not to be so quick about letting strange lawyers in and telling them the secrets of the universe. That was the first thing. Teach her what it meant to keep her mouth shut about important matters, knock out all her fuckin' *teeth* if that was the way to teach her.

The next thing to do was to locate Mr. Matthew Hope and let him know that you don't fuck with Arthur Hurley.

You don't go to the police and blab that Arthur Hurley was watching a house where a cop got killed, you don't fuck Arthur Hurley out of a million bucks because you got a big fuckin' lawyer mouth, you don't do that to Arthur Hurley, man.

You just don't.

10

This is the malt that lay in the house that Jack built . . .

Ralph Parrish did not like the way Calusa County was taking care of him.

The Indiana corn farmer had a lot of complaining to do about the jailhouse clothing he was wearing, and the jailhouse swill they were forcing him to eat, and the fact that he had to protect his ass day and night or he'd pretty soon be wearing dresses the way his dead faggot brother had. Those were Parrish's exact words: "My dead faggot brother."

Matthew was here at the county jail to ask Parrish about his dead brother and some of his friends. He had to wait until Parrish went through his roster of complaints, though, and then he had to wait further while Parrish told him he saw no reason for a law-abiding citizen to be kept behind bars without bail when no one had the slightest shred of evidence to prove he had committed a crime. Matthew explained that the State Attorney believed he had proof enough to convict Parrish for the crime of murder, fratricide no less, which a judge had considered heinous enough to cause him to deny bail. Parrish went on complaining for the next ten minutes. He was a man of the outdoors, used to the sun on his shoulders and back, used to working under an open sky. Confinement was taking its toll. Matthew listened patiently and sympathetically. Keeping the farmer under lock and key did, in fact, seem like cruel and unusual punishment. But someone had killed his brother. And the state believed he was the man.

"I hate this place," he said in conclusion.

"I know," Matthew said.

"Are we making any progress?"

"Maybe," Matthew said, and filled him in on the most recent developments.

"I *knew* he'd go back to that house!" Parrish said. "He's our man, Matthew. Find him and . . ."

"Yes, but that hasn't been too easy so far," Matthew said. "Does the name Arthur Hurley mean anything to you?"

"No. Who is he?"

"Someone who was watching your brother's house. Together with a man named Billy Walker. Ring a bell?"

"No."

"Do you know anything about these baby pictures Abbott mentioned?"

"No."

"Anything about his daughter, Helen? Or her alleged mother, Elise Brechtmann?"

"I've never heard of either of them."

"Brechtmann Beer? Golden Girl Beer?"

"I don't drink beer."

"Tell me, Mr. Parrish . . ."

"Call me Ralph."

"Ralph then. Why'd you buy the house here in Calusa?"

"I had plenty of money, my brother had nothing. I figured if I could help him . . ."

"No, that's not what I meant. Seven years ago, you bought the house down here. Why?"

"I just told you. My brother needed . . ."

"But why Calusa? Why not Key West, or Miami, or Palm . . ."

"Actually, my brother *did* spend some time in Key West, but he said it was a bit too fruity, even for him. He much preferred Calusa."

"When was that?"

"Key West? It must have been during the Sixties sometime. When young people were roaming all over the country. All over the world, in fact. In tattered blue jeans, but with thousands of dollars in American Express checks in their pockets."

"Was your brother one of those?"

"Yes. A plastic hippie."

"How old was he then?"

"Well, let me think. This had to have been 1968, 1969—he would've been twenty or so. Yes. Around twenty."

"When he went to Key West?"

"Yes. Well, all over Florida."

"Calusa?"

"Yes, Calusa."

"Was he gay at the time?"

"He was gay before he left Indiana."

"How long was he here in Calusa?"

"I have no idea. This must have been . . . well, let me see. I know he left home sometime in September, yes, it was the fall of 1968, and he wasn't home for Christmas, so I know he was still here in Florida someplace, and I think . . . just a minute now . . . yes, now I remember. I sent him a birthday card here in Calusa. His twenty-first birthday. He was renting a house on Fatback Key, I sent it to him there. Yes. I'm sure of that."

"When did he leave Calusa?"

"I don't know exactly. I know he was in Woodstock during the summer of '69, the big thing up there, the flower children thing, he sent me a card from Woodstock. And then he left for Europe sometime that fall, and he was there for almost a year, France, Italy, Greece, and then he went on to India . . ."

"When did he come back to the States?"

"In 1972."

"Back to Indiana?"

"No. San Francisco and Los Angeles and San Diego and some time in Mexico, he loved traveling. And then New York, he lived in New York for a long time. And then from there to Calusa."

"Which was when?"

"Well, when I bought the house on Whisper Key."

"For him to live in."

"Yes."

"In 1981."

"Yes."

"Did your brother ever mention a man named Anthony Holden?"

"No, I don't recall that name."

"He used to work for the Brechtmann brewery. He was the purchasing agent there in 1982. Holden. Anthony Holden."

"I'm sorry."

"This would have been a year after you purchased the house."

"Yes. But I really don't remember ever hearing of him."

"Did your brother ever mention *any* of his friends to you?"

"Well, yes, I suppose so. We corresponded regularly, and occasionally I came down here, or he'd come to Indiana . . ."

"Did you ever meet Anthony Holden down here?"

"No, not that I recall."

"But you did meet some of your brother's friends on the occasions when you were here."

"Yes."

"But none of them were Anthony Holden."

"No."
"And he never mentioned the name in any of his letters."
"Never. Not to my recollection."
"How about Elise Brechtmann?"
"No. I told you earlier . . ."
"Could she have been someone your brother met on his first visit to Florida?"
"I have no idea."
"Were you corresponding back then as well? In '68 and '69?"
"Not too often. In fact, it sometimes seemed as if Jonathan had dropped into a black hole. I wouldn't hear anything for months, and then suddenly I'd get a postcard from some like village in Iran . . ."
"But while he was here in Florida? Did he write to you then?"
"Occasionally."
"You knew where he was staying. In Calusa, I mean. You said you sent him a birthday card . . ."
"Yes."
"Had you written to him at that address before?"
"Yes, I think so."
"Did he write back?"
"I really don't remember."
"But in any case, if he did write back, he never mentioned anyone named Elise Brechtmann."
"Not to my knowledge. Matthew . . . my brother was homosexual from the time he was fifteen. I really don't think he'd be writing to me about a *girl*. He had no interest whatever in the opposite sex, believe me."
"A man named Anthony Holden seems to think Elise Brechtmann was one of your brother's friends."
Parrish was shaking his head.
"A very *good* friend, in fact."
He was still shaking his head.

"But you've never heard of her."

"Never."

Matthew sighed deeply.

Billy was packing.

Every now and then, he glanced over to where Helen lay on the floor against the wall, whimpering.

He wanted to get out of here very fast.

He wanted to get very far away from Calusa and Arthur Hurley and the woman who lay there bleeding against the wall.

Artie had taken the car, he'd have to call a taxi to take him to the airport. Get the hell out of here fast.

He threw a stack of undershorts into his valise and then looked over toward the wall again.

Her hand came up.

Grabbing for the wall.

And then trailed limply down the wall.

Blood followed her hand, streaking the wall.

When Matthew got back to the office at a little past two, Cynthia handed him a handful of messages. The only call he returned was the one from Morrie Bloom.

"Morrie," he said, "it's me."

"Hello, Matthew," Bloom said. "Two things. We questioned Hurley and his pal Walker, and we let them go. We had nothing to hold them on, and besides I really think they were telling the truth about not going inside that house."

"Okay."

"Second, I had a team of men going over every *inch* of that house since I spoke to you early this morning, and I mean going *over* it, Matthew. They just got back here a little while ago. They found some photographs in a shoebox in the upstairs bedroom but none of them are baby pictures, just Parrish and some of his playmates cavorting on the beach. So it looks like if somebody went in that house looking for baby pictures, then he found them, Matthew, 'cause they sure as hell ain't there anymore."

"Okay, Morrie, thank you."

"You got any other ideas?"

"Not at the moment. Are you helping me with my case, Morrie?"

"I am a seeker of justice and truth," Bloom said.

Matthew smiled.

"Me, too," he said.

"Keep in touch, okay?" Bloom said, and hung up.

Cynthia buzzed almost immediately.

"It's Warren," she said. "He's at the airport."

"What line?"

"Five."

Matthew punched the five-button.

"Yes, Warren?"

"Matthew, there's a two-thirteen I can catch to New York. That gives me eight minutes. I located a woman named Lucy Strong, she's black like me, Matthew, she loved my voice on the phone. I think she's in her fifties, it sounded like, and she was a nurse on the maternity ward when a woman named Elise Abbott was there in the summer of 'sixty-nine. She remembers a man taking pictures, but she didn't want to tell me anything else on the phone, even if I *am* black, because she's afraid she might get in trouble."

"What kind of trouble?"

"Matthew, it doesn't *matter* what kind of trouble, I've got six minutes to buy a ticket and get on that plane. Black people are always afraid of getting in some kind of trouble, that's the way Whitey trained us. Do I go to New York or not?"

"Go," Matthew said.

"I'll call you later," Warren said, and hung up.

■ ■ ■

"Billy," she said.
He looked toward the wall.
"Help me," she said.
He said nothing.
He went to the closet and took from the rack the only suit he owned, and he carried that to the valise without looking at Helen all crumpled against the wall. He folded the suit neatly into the valise, and then went back to the dresser to collect the two dress shirts he'd put in the top drawer.
"Billy?" she said.
He didn't answer her.
"Is he gone, Billy?"
He put the two dress shirts into the valise on top of his folded suit jacket. Button-down collars on those shirts, the kind Yuppies wore.
"Billy, you have to help me."
"I don't have to do nothin'," he said.
"Billy, please."
He went back to the dresser.
Checked all the drawers to make sure none of his stuff was still in them. Rummaged through Helen's panties and bras, a few of her sweaters and blouses, couldn't find anything belonging to him.
"Billy?"
"Shut up," he said.
"Billy . . . I'm bleeding real bad."
He closed the valise, snapped the locks shut.
"I have to get to a hospital," she said.
The telephone rang. He picked up the receiver.
"Hello?"
"Mr. Walker?"
The good-looking broad who ran the place.
"Yeah?"
"Your taxi's here, sir."
"I'll be right up, ask him to wait."

He put the phone back on the cradle.

"Billy?"

"Shut up," he said.

"Help me. Please."

Like fun, he thought.

"Billy?" she said.

Help you and that fucking lunatic'll come after *me!*

"Billy?" she said.

But he was already gone.

Names stenciled in black on the concrete curbing for each parking space.

FRANK SUMMERVILLE and alongside that MATTHEW HOPE.

A brown Mercedes Benz in the Summerville space.

Tan Karmann Ghia in the Hope space.

The blue Honda was parked across the street. Hurley sat behind the wheel, watching the building. Summerville and Hope. Law Offices. 333 Heron Street. At a little before two-thirty, Hurley saw him coming out of the building and walking toward the Ghia.

Good, he thought. Now we're in the open, Mr. Hope. Now we see where you're going and we take care of you, Mr. Hope, we dance you around the block, sweetheart, we take you *out*.

He nodded curtly and started the car.

First the police coming by shortly after she'd got back here this morning, driving off with the two men. Then both of them coming back in a taxi around twelve-thirty or thereabouts. Then the older one driving off in the Honda at a little past one. And now the young one going off in a taxi. Which left only the pregnant girl over there in the cabin.

Irene looked at the motel register again.

Mr. and Mrs. Arthur Hurley.

Mr. William Harold Walker.

Said he was the girl's brother.

In this business, you didn't ask too many questions. Not if you wanted to make a living. Rented them the cabin at the going rate for three, wouldn't have cared if they were planning a *circus* in there, two of them on a pregnant woman, one on top, one underneath, in this business it was Ask me no questions, I'll tell you no lies. Yes, sir, Mr. Hurley, I hope you and your wife and your brother-in-law enjoy the accommodations, you can get a good hearty breakfast in the diner across 41. Let them come, do what they had to do, and then let them go. No skin off Irene's nose. This was a business.

But—

Matthew Hope had been interested in these people.

This morning, when she was still at his house, he'd received a phone call from someone, and then he'd asked about the crowd in cabin number eleven, the Hurley party, and then he'd told whoever was on the other end of the line that Hurley and Walker had been spotted watching the Parrish house and that it might be a good idea to look them up, and oh, by the way, Hurley has a record.

And then he'd said one of them might have killed Jonathan Parrish, or words to that effect, and next thing you knew the cops were on her doorstep—well, not exactly the *very* next thing, since it had taken her and Matthew a little while to make love again. But soon after she'd got back to the motel, here came the cops, and off they went with both of them, one of whom had a record.

She wondered why the cops had let them go.

Especially the one with the record.

She wondered if she should call Matthew to tell him the cops had let them go.

A man with a record.

Tell Matthew they were *both* gone now. Hurley gone in the Honda, Walker off in a taxi. Carrying a suitcase. When he called the office, he said he needed a taxi. She asked him if he wanted any particular company. He said he didn't care, so long as they could get him to the airport. So William Walker was gone for sure, and only God knew where Arthur Hurley was, though she suspected he'd be back to pick up his pregnant wife if, in fact, she *was* his wife. Irene had once rented a cabin to a pregnant one-legged woman and her husband, supposedly, but it turned out they were a working girl and her pimp. The lady turned a trick an hour, regular cavalcade of cars pulling into the parking lot every hour on the hour. When the couple checked out a week later, they probably went to Lake Como, Italy, for a vacation. In this business you never knew what—

The telephone rang.

Irene glanced at the switchboard.

Unit number eleven.

"Office," she said, "good afternoon."

An odd sound on the other end of the line.

"Hello?" Irene said.

The sound again.

Wet. And gurgling.

"Mrs. Hurley?" Irene said. "Is that you?"

And then her voice.

A single word.

"Please."

The man who came through the door in the walnut-paneled wall behind the receptionist's desk smiled and extended his hand.

"Mr. Hope?" he said. "I'm Henry Curtis, Miss Brechtmann's secretary."

"Nice to meet you," Matthew said, and shook hands with him.

Curtis looked at the card Matthew had given the receptionist.

"Summerville and Hope," he said.

"Yes."

"You're an attorney."

"Yes, I am."

"Has someone found another snake in our beer?" Curtis asked, smiling.

Matthew wondered why he thought a snake in their beer was comical.

"Or a rusty nail? Or a nest of scorpions? Or a used condom?"

He glanced quickly toward the reception desk, where a gray-haired woman sat doing a crossword puzzle.

"We have a battery of attorneys who do nothing but defend the company against claims of foreign objects found floating in our beer. One of these days, someone's going to claim he spotted the Loch Ness monster in one of our bottles," Curtis said, and smiled again.

Matthew suddenly liked him.

"I know you have an appointment . . ." Curtis said.

"Yes. I spoke to Miss Brechtmann on the phone earlier to . . ."

"Yes, I know. But I'm afraid her meeting's running a little long. She asked me to make you comfortable while you wait."

"How long will she be, do you know?"

"Oh, it shouldn't take too long," Curtis said. "I thought I might show you through the brewery . . ."

"*That* long, huh?"

"Well, how*ever* long, it'll help pass the time. Unless you'd prefer reading back issues of trade journals."

"I don't think so."

"I didn't think you would. Mrs. Hoskins," he said, "we'll be walking through. Send someone to find us when Miss Brechtmann is free, would you?"

"Yes, Mr. Curtis," the woman said, and went back to her crossword puzzle.

▪ ▪ ▪

Irene opened the door with her passkey.

At first she didn't see anyone.

"Mrs. Hurley?" she said.

No answer.

"Mrs. Hurley, where . . . ?"

The phone was on a night table alongside the bed farthest from the door. The receiver was off the cradle. Irene walked quickly across the room and around the bed, and saw—

"Oh, Jesus," she said.

The girl was lying in a puddle of blood.

Irene stepped around her and picked up the telephone receiver.

AUTHORIZED PERSONNEL ONLY
BEYOND THIS POINT

Hurley read the sign and then walked right on past it and through the gate. Way to do it with signs, you ignored them completely. You didn't stop and read them carefully as if this was the first time you were here, you just took them in with a single glance and then ignored them. Of *course* you were authorized personnel, and you were going beyond this point and beyond any fucking point you felt like.

REMOVE ALL ARTICLES
FROM SHIRT POCKETS
WHILE WORKING AROUND
THE GRAIN UNLOADING AREA

Another sign. Red letters on a white background. Place was full of signs. He ignored this one, too, because he didn't plan to be working around the grain-unloading area or *any* damn area. All he planned to do was find Mr. Matthew Hope, who had disappeared inside here someplace. And when he found him—

NO SMOKING
IN THIS AREA

White letters on a red background this time. More damn signs in this place. He was walking through a large open outdoor space adjacent to the parking lot and separated from it by a cyclone fence with an open, unlocked gate in it. The parking lot had been full of signs advising that only employees of the Brechtmann Brewing Company could park here, but he'd ignored those signs, and then ignored the sign on the cyclone fence, and was now ignoring every sign in sight. All he wanted to do was walk past these railroad cars, and get inside where—

Jesus!

Matthew Hope himself coming out of the building and—

Hurley ducked behind the closest railroad car.

"This is where our grain comes in," Curtis said. "The malt and the corn. The cars you see out here each hold about two hundred thousand pounds. Hoses suck the grain up to the fifth floor, where it's crushed and then transported to the scale room where it's weighed. Right now, these cars are bringing in malt."

"From where?"

"The Midwest, mostly. Want to see how we brew the stuff?"

Matthew looked at his watch.

"Don't worry, they'll let us know when she's free," Curtis said.

Hurley waited until the door to the building had closed behind them. He walked out swiftly from behind the railroad car, up the concrete steps, opened the door, and caught sight of them just as they entered the elevator at the far end of the corridor. He watched the floor indicator. Two, three . . .

The needle stopped at four.

He pressed the button alongside the doors.
A sign on the doors read:

DANGER
GRAIN DUST
HAZARD
No Smoking, Matches,
or Open Lights

The stainless steel doors opened.
Same sign inside the elevator.
Made him feel like lighting a cigarette.
He pressed the button for the fifth floor.

"We store the malt here on the fourth floor," Curtis said. "These bins hold a hundred thousand pounds each."

"Uh-huh," Matthew said.

"Downstairs was the beginning, if you will. Where the malt came in. Beginning, middle, and end, right? Up here is a sort of intermission, the malt just lying here until the actual brewing process begins. Now we'll go downstairs again, and I'll show you the middle."

"The middle, uh-huh."

"The mashing and cooking."

"Uh-huh, mashing and cooking."

"To get the wort we need."

"The what?"

"The wort. W-O-R-T. It's this sugary sort of solution that we send to the brew kettles."

"Uh-huh."

"Come on, I'll show you."

. . .

Never get off at the same floor. Do that and you ran the risk of your man standing there staring you in the face when the elevator doors opened. Always go to the floor above, take the steps down—the way Hurley was doing now—open your door cautiously, take a peek around it, see what was happening. No surprises. Hurley hated surprises.

A huge, plastic numeral four, white on a black field, alongside the stainless-steel door. Same grain-hazard warning sign on the door. White on red. He put his ear to the door. Nothing but the thrumming of heavy machinery somewhere in the building. He took the knob in his hand. Twisted it slowly. Opened the door just a crack—

And saw them getting back into the elevator!

What?

Hurley hated surprises.

He kept the door cracked just a jot until the elevator doors closed behind them. He came out onto the floor. Just these huge metal bins. Not a soul anywhere in sight. Didn't anyone *work* here?

Indicator over the elevator. Dropping. Three, two . . .

And stopping on the first floor.

He went back to the staircase and started downstairs.

A glistening stainless-steel tank some twelve feet in diameter. Capping the tank, a domed copper top. The tank and its domed top resembled a diving bell that had mistakenly surfaced inside the building. Set into the copper top was a circular opening some three feet in diameter. A steel-rimmed, thick glass lid on hinges was folded back against the sloping side of the dome. The lid resembled an oversized porthole cover. The opening in the tank was protected by a steel safety guard in the shape of a cross, quartering the space into pie-shaped wedges so that no one but a very small midget could accidentally fall into the tank. Steam billowed up out of the tank.

"The temperature in there is something like a hundred and seventy degrees Fahrenheit," Curtis said.

He was wearing a yellow cloth cap with a pair of red Bs intertwined on its crown, the distinctive Brechtmann Brewing colophon. He had given Matthew a yellow paper cap with the same red colophon on it, in obedience to a sign that warned:

ATTENTION ALL EMPLOYEES
HATS BEYOND THIS POINT

Matthew felt like a jackass in the paper hat.

The room containing the mash tank was stiflingly hot.

Several control panels at the far end of the room were studded with switches and toggles and red lights and green lights and temperature valves—but no one seemed to be monitoring them. The room was empty except for Curtis and Matthew, who stood on the raised metal platform that ran alongside the tank. Matthew remembered Anthony Holden telling him there were only fifteen men on the afternoon shift. Divide those fifteen men by the five floors in the building . . .

"This safety guard lifts out," Curtis said, "if you'd like to take a peek inside here."

Matthew did not want to take a peek inside there.

But Curtis was already lifting out the heavy, cross-shaped guard. With some difficulty, he set it on its side on the floor of the platform, peeked into the tank himself, and then stepped back for Matthew to take a look.

"This batch we're brewing is Golden Girl," he said, "that's our premium beer. Which means it contains the highest percentage of the choicer two-row barley malt."

"As opposed to what?" Matthew said.

"Why, the *six*-row," Curtis said, sounding surprised. "There's a price difference of at least a dollar a bushel. We brew Golden Girl with more of the two-row. Our other beers have *some* of the two-row in them, but they're mostly six-row. The process is exactly the same, of course. Malt and water in the mash tank—which is what *this* is—and corn and water in the cooker over there."

Matthew looked over there. Another huge stainless-steel tank. No dome on this one. Only what looked like a shining copper conning tower. The entire room seemed nautical to him.

"We bring both to a boil," Curtis said, "and then pump the corn and water into the mash tank with the malt. Take a look inside here."

Matthew took a look inside. He saw a bubbling, boiling brownish solution. Rising steam hit his face. The smell was of hot beer. No, not quite beer. Primitive beer. Fetal beer. An overpowering aroma that made his nostrils and his throat feel congested. He remembered what Anthony Holden had told him: "There was a time when I detested the aroma of malt."

A stainless-steel door set between the two control panels at the far end of the platform opened. A man wearing a yellow hat with the intertwined B-B colophon on it stepped out onto the platform.

"Hank?" he said.

"Yes?" Curtis said.

"Telephone."

"Thank you." He turned to Matthew. "Back in a minute," he said.

Mathew nodded.

Curtis walked to the end of the platform. He followed the other man out, and closed the door behind him.

Matthew was alone in the room.

He took another peek into the mash tank.

Hope.

Standing alone near a big stainless-steel tank.

Just a glimpse of him through the partially open door.

Hurley opened the door wider.

Some kind of stench hit his nostrils. He winced.

There was no one in the room with Hope, this whole fucking *place* was deserted. The door was on floor level. All he had to do was walk past the big tank to the right of the door, and then across the room to where metal steps with a tubular steel railing painted yellow led up to the platform where Hope was standing near the other tank.

Leaning over the tank.

Looking into a hole in the tank's top.

Hurley stepped into the room. He moved swiftly but silently. Past the first tank, crossing to the steps, metal floor, metal steps, grabbed the yellow railing in his left hand, started climbing, six steps up to the platform, Hope still with his back to him.

He thought Here we go, counselor!

And shoved out at him with both hands.

The shove came as a total surprise.

Matthew brought his hands up at once, pushing out at the copper dome of the tank and then starting to turn, only to feel hands on his back again, shoving at him again, pushing him toward the three-foot wide opening in the tank and the boiling brown mixture of malt, corn, and water below him.

A bad situation can only get worse.

Morris Bloom's words.

The words of a streetwise cop who had seen it all and heard—

A hand clutched into the collar at the back of Matthew's jacket. A violent shove from behind. Matthew's forehead banged against the opening's rim. His dumb paper hat fell off his head and into the boiling brew below. Whoever was behind him was trying to lift him now, trying to force him through the opening into the tank.

Don't wait. Make your move, make it fast.

Bloom again.

Matthew clenched his right fist. Like the drive-arm on the wheel of a steam-powered locomotive, his right elbow shot back blindly and desperately--and connected with something soft. He heard an *ooof* sound, tried to twist away from the hands still forcing him toward the gaping opening in the tank, feet shuffling, feet behind him, heels against toes, steam enveloping his head, the sickening smell of fermenting malt. He raised his left foot some four inches off the platform, brought the heel down sharply, connected only with metal, raised it again, down again, and this time hammered home on something soft, and this time heard a yell of pain behind him, and felt an immediate loosening of the hands clutching his jacket.

He twisted away at once.

Hurley.

Arthur Nelson Hurley, rage and pain mingled on his face, murder in his eyes.

Go for the money.

Still Bloom.

Matthew brought up his knee. Not a moment's hesitation, not a single thought about the worst kind of pain he could think of inflicting on another man, brought up the knee fast and hard, smashing it into Hurley's groin. Hurley bellowed in pain, and then doubled over, clutching for his balls.

Put him away.

Bloom.

Matthew brought his knee up again. This time he was going for Hurley's chin. This time he felt bone connecting with bone, knee against jaw, felt something snapping and knew damn well it wasn't his knee. Hurley staggered back toward the edge of the platform. Matthew wielded his right arm like a mallet, swinging it in a wide arc, the fist smashing into Hurley's left ear, knocking him into the tubular steel railing. Once more, Matthew thought, and brought his left fist up from somewhere down near his knees, all the power of his shoulder and arm behind a searing uppercut that caught Hurley on his broken jaw and sent him stumbling backward screaming in pain toward the steps, and then down the steps, his head crashing repeatedly against metal as he tumbled to the bottom. Matthew came down the steps after him, breathing hard, fists still clenched. But Hurley was lying quite still on the metal floor below.

Matthew unclenched his fists.

The door between the control panels opened.

"Mr. Hope?"

Curtis standing up there on the platform in his ridiculous yellow hat with the tangled red Bs.

"I'm awfully sorry," he said. "Miss Brechtmann has gone for the day."

And then he noticed Hurley lying on the floor at Matthew's feet.

"Who's that?" he asked.

"Call the police," Matthew said.

Warren took a taxi from the airport. The driver, a white man, drove all over the Bronx for close to half an hour, told Warren he didn't know the Bronx too well. The fare came to sixty dollars and change. The driver looked at his palm when he realized Warren hadn't tipped him. And then looked up at Warren. And looked down at the palm again.

"Let me have a receipt," Warren said.

"Sure," the driver said, and ripped a small slip of paper from the meter. Scowling now, he handed it to Warren.

"Got a problem?" Warren said.

"Yeah, I got a problem," the driver said. "You're stiffing me is the problem I got."

"The problem *I've* got is the one I'm taking to the Hack Bureau," Warren said. "Your number's on the receipt here, and your name's on the card right there on the dash. Albert F. Esposito. I'm sure somebody'll be contacting you, Mr. Esposito."

"You're scaring me to death," the driver said.

"Does the F stand for Frank, Mr. Esposito?"

"The F stands for Fuck You."

"Have a nice day," Warren said, and got out of the cab.

Cold as hell up here.

Never again would he complain about the lousy weather in Florida.

Dark, too, Dark even when he got off the plane. In Calusa at that time, it would've been twilight. Sky over the ocean turning red and then purple and then blue-black and then black. Up here it had been black already, even blacker now, only seven-thirty and black as midnight. Dirty snow was piled on either side of the walkway leading through the development's maze of high-rise red-brick buildings. The snow made him feel colder. Looked like it was fixing to snow some more, too. He should have gone home for an overcoat before heading for the airport, but there weren't too many nonstop flights out of Calusa these days.

On the phone, Lucy Strong had given him her address.

Shivering in the lightweight sports jacket he was wearing, he looked for it now.

Here she came, strutting out of the house in a smart linen suit and high-heeled tan pumps, opening the door to the Jag parked in the driveway, checking the street as she did. Looking for Warren. Looking for a beat-up old Ford. Instead, here was little old Toots in a beat-up old Chevy parked a good hundred yards from the house on the opposite side of the street. Leona Summerville got into the Jag and started the engine. Toots did not start the Chevy until the Jag was off and running.

Heading for her eight o'clock wildlife meeting, thank you, Brünnhilde, you have a good strong voice that carries far, and you also run one hell of a vacuum cleaner. Tomorrow morning, when everybody went off to work or exercise or wherever the hell they'd be going, Toots would break into the house again to check the tape recorder. This time, however, she'd get there at a little after *nine*, which was when Brünnhilde had come in this morning, and she'd make damn sure Brünnhilde's car wasn't parked outside.

Tonight, she would follow Leona Summerville to Mrs. Colman's house, wherever that might be, and she would pray that Leona wouldn't lock the car while she was in there listening to plans on how to protect and preserve the rare Calusa Cooze.

Lucy Strong was quite impressed.

Man flying all the way up from Florida to talk to her.

She was a woman in her early fifties, looking a great deal younger—she told Warren—because she still led an active and rewarding life. Oh, yes. Still worked at Lenox Hill Hospital in Manhattan. Still worked on the maternity ward, *loved* babies, didn't Warren just *love* babies?

Warren did not love babies, but he didn't tell this to Lucy Strong.

He simply nodded and smiled.

He was wondering if it would start snowing again. He had already missed the last flight back to Calusa tonight, but he could still catch any one of several planes to Tampa. Provided Kennedy did not get snowed in. Warren hated snow. Snow was one of the reasons he'd left St. Louis. The other reason was St. Louis itself.

"So what is this all about?" Lucy asked. "This must be pretty important, a policeman flying all the way up from Miami."

"Calusa, ma'am," Warren said. "And I'm not a policeman."

"What are you then? FBI?"

"No, ma'am. Definitely *not* FBI." Not when impersonating a federal agent could get you three years in the slammer. "I'm a private investigator, ma'am. Doing research on a murder case for the attorney who's . . ."

"That's what made me think a policeman," she said. "When you told me this was a murder case. On the phone."

"Yes, ma'am, probably."

"Or an FBI agent," she said.

"Here's my card," he said, "I'm just a private detective."

"I see," she said, and took the card and looked at it and nodded, and then handed it back to him.

"Miss Strong," he said, "on the telephone you told me you were there in the summer of 1969 when . . ."

"Yes, at Lenox Hill . . ."

"Yes, when a woman named Elise Abbott gave birth to . . ."

"Well, I wasn't there the *moment* she gave birth."

"No, what I meant . . ."

"I was on the maternity ward, yes. She was one of my patients. Elise Abbott."

"This would have been in August of 1969."

"Yes."

"According to what I have, the baby was born on August nineteenth."

"Well, as I say, I wasn't there at the actual birth."

"But Elise Abbott *was* one of your patients."

"Oh, yes, I remember her very well. A beautiful young girl, but there was . . . such a . . . a sadness about her. I don't know what it was. So young, so beautiful, why should she have been so sad? And married to such a handsome young man! Both of them blond, her with green eyes, him with blue. He was a good deal older than she was, an Englishman, you know. Spoke the way the English do, funny, you know? His name was Roger, I think. Or Nigel. Something like that."

"How about Charles?"

"Charles? Well, yes, it could have been. Charles does sound English, doesn't it? Their prince is named Charles, isn't he?"

"Yes," Warren said.

"Charles Abbott," Lucy said, and nodded. "Yes, that sounds right."

"Was it Mr. Abbott who took those pictures we talked about on the phone?"

"Oh, no."

"You said a man had . . ."

"Yes, but not her husband. I thought it was her brother. The same coloring, you know. The blond hair and the blue eyes. Sometimes a woman will marry a man who looks just like her father or her brother, have you ever noticed that? I see a lot of it at the hospital. The girl's father'll come to visit, and he's a dead ringer for the husband. It's amazing."

"This man who took the pictures . . . are you saying he resembled Charles Abbott?"

"No, no. Just that they were both blond and blue-eyed."

"How old was he?"

"The one who took the pictures?"

"Yes."

"Young. Twenty? Twenty-one? Young."

"When was this?"

"A few days after the baby was born, I think. She was nursing the baby, I remember. Which I thought was a little odd, even if he *was* her brother. I mean, her breast exposed and all. Very casual about it. The baby lying on her breast, nursing. I just came in on them, just checking, you know, making sure everything was all right in the room, and there he was with the camera to his eye, taking pictures. Baby on her mother's breast, nursing, the cutest little thing, her little hand resting on the breast, the little bracelet on it. I told him to stop taking those pictures right that minute! I don't know how many he'd taken by then, but he was using a flash attachment, and I thought it might harm the baby's eyes or something. You can't be too careful when they're that young, you know. He was very nice about it, of course, a nice young man. He put the camera away, introduced himself, a perfect gentleman."

"What was his name?"

"Jonathan Parrish. Same as I told that other fellow who was up here last month."

"What other fellow?"

"Man named Arthur Hurley. He was very surprised to learn about those pictures."

"I'll bet he was," Warren said. "But you say the baby was wearing *jewelry*, huh?"

"No, no. Jewelry? What do you mean?"

"I thought you said she had . . ."

"Jewelry? How could a baby be wearing . . . ?"

"You said there was a bracelet . . ."

"Oh. Yes."

"On her . . ."

"Yes, her wrist. But that wasn't *jewelry*."

"A bracelet wasn't . . ."

"Not jewelry at all."

"Then what was it?"

"Identification."

"Identification?"

"Yes. The baby's name. Spelled out on the beads."

"Beads?"

"Yes. They used to string these little beads and put them on a baby's wrist."

"What kind of beads?"

"Little white beads with blue letters on them. Nowadays they use a plastic strip with the name on it. But back then, it was beads. Ask your mama. I'll bet she still has your baby beads."

"I'll bet she does," Warren said.

He was thinking he could not wait to tell this to Matthew.

The moment Toots saw Leona getting out of her car, she knew she wasn't going to lock it.

Most people—even down here in sunny Florida—if they parked the car in a parking lot outside a movie theater or a mall, or if they left it parked at the curb outside a restaurant or a store, they locked it. But rarely did they lock the car when they parked it outside the house of a friend or a relative. Parking outside these houses was cozy and safe. But if these people knew how many cars were stolen each year outside the safe, cozy house of a dear friend or a cherished relative they'd have locked the car fore and aft, top and bottom, and they'd have left a two-thousand-pound gorilla sitting behind the wheel growling.

Toots knew how to get into a locked car.

She even knew how to start one without a key.

But all that took time.

Besides which, she didn't particularly feel like getting busted for a car thief. A car thief could spend a lot of time in jail. Judges in the state of Florida did not look kindly upon car thieves because a great many expensive Cadillacs and Mercedes and BMWs and Jags were stolen to order down here and then shipped up north for redistribution hither and yon across these United States. Toots shuddered when she thought of some redneck trooper from the Sheriff's Department cruising on up and saying, "Excuse me, Miss, but why are you working on that window with a wire hanger?"

She was glad that Leona had left the door unlocked.

Glad when she saw Leona walking away from the car without so much as a backward glance or a fond fare-thee-well.

The name on the mailbox outside the house was COLMAN.

The time on Toots's dashboard clock was three minutes to eight.

The meeting of the League to Protect Florida Wildlife was scheduled to begin at eight o'clock.

Toots waited until a quarter past eight, and then she approached the green Jag, looked up and down the street, and swiftly opened the door on the driver's side.

She reached under the dash at once, and pulled the hood release lever.

She closed the car door, looked up and down the street again, walked to the front of the car, unsnapped the hood, and lifted it.

It took her three minutes to splice her wires into the car's electrical system.

It took another three minutes to run them back to the panel behind the dash and feed them through into the car.

Her heart was racing.

Gently she lowered the hood, pressed firmly down on it to lock it, and then got back into the car.

She fished under the dashboard for the ends of her wires.

She attached them to the tiny microphone and fastened it in place under the center of the dash.

Unlike the FM transmitters she had planted in the Summerville house, the bug she'd just planted would not require a battery change every day; the battery it used for its power was the car's own. In dense city traffic—which one sometimes ran into in Calusa at the height of the season—the effective transmitting range of the bug was a bit more than a block. On the open road, Toots could figure on at least a quarter of a mile.

She did not get a chance to test the equipment until a bit more than an hour later.

Leona Summerville left the meeting at nine thirty-seven by Toots's dashboard clock. When she got into the Jag, the receiver in Toots's car picked up the sound of the door closing. When she started the car, the receiver picked up this, too. Several seconds later, when Leona turned on her radio, Toots heard a disc jockey doing a commercial, his voice coming over sharp and clear. She smiled; the bug was working. She smiled again when the music began; the DJ was playing one of her favorite songs, the theme from *The Summer of* '42.

Leona seemed in a hurry to get someplace, driving far too fast for a residential neighborhood. Good, Toots thought. Let's get there. When the Jag hit U.S. 41, Toots closed in behind it. She dropped back a bit when Leona pulled into the parking lot at Southway Mall. Kept driving through the lot to the very end, and then swung around to the back of the E.C. Daniels department store. Toots eased up on the accelerator. The store's own lot back here. Not as well lighted as the main lot out front. Half a dozen of the store's huge delivery trucks angle-parked against the rear wall of the building. Near one of the trucks, parked in its shadow, a black Corvette.

Leona was parking her car.

Toots drove on by.

She caught just a glimpse of a man sitting at the wheel of the Corvette.

In the rearview mirror, she saw Leona running toward the Corvette, skirts flying.

She drove the Chevy around toward the front of the store, circled back, and picked up the Corvette just as it came around the side of the building. She did not close on it too quickly. Kept her distance. But she didn't want to lose it, either.

The Corvette nosed through the night like a submarine, running silent, running black, running fast.

Heading toward Sarasota.

Whenever oncoming headlights struck the car's windshield, Toots saw the silhouettes of two heads, one male, one female. The woman's head—Leona's—was turned in profile toward the man's.

Picking up speed now as the traffic thinned on the outskirts of the city.

Toots's dashboard clock read a quarter to ten.

Five minutes later, the Corvette pulled into a roadside motel called CaluSara, presumably because it was midway between Calusa and Sarasota. Toots drove right on by. Kept driving for half a mile, made a left turn into a hot-dog joint, moved out onto 41 again, and approached the motel from the opposite direction. Made a cautious left turn into the motel parking lot. The black Corvette was parked outside room 27. Nobody in the car now.

Toots drove past it.

There was an MD plate on it.

Toots memorized the number.

She drove all the way to the far end of the lot, and then turned the car so that it was facing 41.

She wrote down the number.

Her dashboard clock read ten o'clock sharp.

At twenty minutes past ten, Leona and her doctor friend—else how come the MD plates?—came out of the room and walked swiftly to the Corvette.

Doors slammed.

The car started.

Toots followed them back to the E.C. Daniels parking lot, where Leona got into her own car and then drove directly home.

Toots wondered why Leona—with the alibi of a wildlife meeting tucked safely in her bonnet—had squandered the night on a quickie.

This is the house that Jack built . . .

Warren was appalled.

"You did *what?*" he said into the telephone.

Toots told him again about the bugs she'd planted in the Summerville house and in Leona's car. She seemed very proud of herself.

"You are not to go back inside that house again," Warren said.

"I have to go back in. The recorder . . ."

"I don't care if the recorder rots and rusts on that shelf, you are not to go back inside that house again, do you understand me?"

There was a long silence on the line.

"Grunt once if you heard me," Warren said.

He was very tired. He would never be able to understand why a snowstorm in Denver could cause departure delays in New York. It simply did not make sense to him. If an airplane got snowed in out there in Colorado, why should that affect a flight going from New York to Tampa? Did the airline have only one plane? Did they use that same plane for all their flights? In which case, snow in the

Rockies would naturally cause a three-hour delay on the Eastern seaboard.

Warren had got to Tampa at two in the morning.

It had taken the taxi another hour and a half to get him to Calusa.

At a quarter to four, he called Matthew, waking him up to tell him what he had learned from Lucy Strong. Matthew was pleased that Warren had called him in the wee small hours of the morning. He thanked Warren profusely. Warren then called Toots, who did *not* like being awakened at ten minutes to four in the morning. Maybe that was why she immediately told him she'd broken into the Summerville house and planted a few hundred bugs inside there.

He waited.

"Toots?" he said.

"Yeah."

Petulantly.

"Did you hear what I said?"

"I thought you'd be pleased," she said.

"No, I am not pleased," he said. "You are not to go back in there for those tapes."

"Those tapes might tell us who the doctor is. Save us the trouble of . . ."

"What doctor?"

"She got in a car with MD plates last night. A black Corvette. They drove to a motel called CaluSara, spent almost a half-hour in there together."

"MD plates, huh?"

"Yeah."

"Did you get the number?"

"Of course."

"Let me have it. I'll ask one of my cop friends to run it past Motor Vehicles. Did you check the motel register?"

"How could I do that?"

"I'll teach you sometime. Because maybe this doctor was Wade Livingston, hmm? Though I'm sure he wouldn't have registered under his own name."

"Who's Wade Livingston?"

"An OB-GYN with offices at the Bayou Professional Building, 837 West Bayou Boulevard. Leona visited him on Monday."

"He makes motel calls?" Toots said.

Warren chuckled.

"But today's Friday," he said. "And on . . ."

"The twelfth of February, in fact," Toots said.

"Correct. Lincoln's birthday, in fact."

"Very *early* on Lincoln's birthday, in fact," Toots said.

"In any event," Warren said, "on Fridays, the lady has a two o'clock aerobics class at The Body Works on Magnolia, two blocks west of the Cockatoo Restaurant on Forty-one. Please be there."

"I planned to be outside her house at eight."

"Fine."

"That was before I got a call at four in the morning."

Warren looked at his watch.

"It's only *five* to four," he said.

"Better yet," she said, and hung up.

At ten o'clock that Friday morning, Matthew went back to the Brechtmann house. A fine mist was rising from the water. The mist obscured the sky so that the house seemed rooted not on the ground but instead appeared a part of the mist itself, cloud-borne, ephemeral.

The security guard at the gate recognized Matthew.

Karl Hitler. Jug ears, a little black mustache, black hair trimmed close to his head, brown eyes spaced too closely together.

"Yes, sir," he said, "how can I help you?"

He made it sound sarcastic.

"Would you tell Miss Brechtmann that Matthew Hope is here to see her?"

"Why, certainly."

Still sounding sarcastic.

He pressed the button on his intercom.

"Yes?"

The old woman's voice. Sophie Brechtmann.

"Mrs. Brechtmann, there's a Matthew Hope here to see your daughter, ma'am."

"Miss Brechtmann has already left for the brewery," Sophie said.

"Mrs. Brechtmann?" Matthew said to the intercom.

Silence.

"Mrs. Brechtmann?" he said again.

"Yes, Mr. Hope?"

"Mrs. Brechtmann, I had an appointment with your daughter yesterday afternoon, but we . . ."

"My daughter's affairs are her own," Sophie said. "She is not here, Mr. Hope. She left for the brewery at a little past . . ."

"I called the brewery before coming here, Mrs. Brechtmann. They told me your daughter wasn't expected today."

Silence.

"Mrs. Brechtmann?"

"Yes?"

"I'd like to talk to your daughter."

"Good day, Mr. Hope."

And a click on the speaker.

"Beat it, pal," Karl said.

"I'll be back," Matthew said.

At twenty minutes to eleven that Friday morning, Leona placed a call from the telephone in the master bedroom. She did not know that there was an FM transmitter behind the night table not three feet from where she sat on the edge of the bed. The transmitter batteries were extremely weak by then, but there must have been at least enough power left to activate the tape recorder in the closet across the room; its reels began moving the moment she spoke.

"Dr. Livingston, please," she said.

A pause.

"Mrs. Summerville."

Another pause.

"Wade, it's me."

This sentence alone, in a court of law, would have been enough to convince a judge that Leona Summerville and Dr. Wade Livingston were intimately involved.

"Wade, have you given any further . . . ?"

A long silence. Then:

"I'm sorry, Wade, but . . ."

Another silence.

"Yes, Wade."

Silence.

"Wade, I have to see you again. I know, but . . . uh-huh. Uh-huh. But I have to talk to you. Uh-huh. Wade . . . uh-huh. Wade, I'll come by at noon. When your nurse goes to lunch. I'll be waiting outside for you. Wade, all you have to . . . Wade, please listen to me. After all this time, you can at least . . . no, Wade, please don't! If you hang up, I'll only call back. Listen to me, okay? Please listen to me. I'll be parked outside the office, all you have to do is walk to the . . . I just want to talk to you. Ten minutes. Can you spare me ten minutes? That's all I ask of you, ten minutes. Thank you, Wade. Thank you very much, darling. I'll see you at a little after twelve. Thank you. And Wade . . . ?"

Silence.

"Wade?"

More silence.

Leona put the receiver back on the cradle.

At eleven o'clock sharp that morning, an unmarked sedan belonging to the Calusa Police Department pulled up to the gate outside the Brechtmann mansion. Detective Morris Bloom was driving the automobile. Matthew Hope was sitting beside him.

The security guard looked at Bloom's shield.

"Tell Elise Brechtmann the police are here," he said.

Karl got on the pipe.

Sophie Brechtmann answered.

"Send the gentlemen in," she said.

Mother and daughter was waiting in the living room.

Charles Abbott had described Elise Brechtmann as a beautiful woman.

His description was almost on the money—but not quite.

A woman in her late thirties, Elise wore her blonde hair in a virtual crew cut that emphasized high cheekbones and intensely green, luminous eyes. Her full-lipped mouth seemed set in a perpetual pout that added a hint of turbulent sexuality to a face spoiled only by its subversive nose. Despite Elise's German ancestry, the nose could have been American Indian in origin, a trifle too large for her face, its cleaving tomahawk edge destroying the image of an otherwise pale and sudden beauty. It was, Matthew realized, the same nose that imparted a sense of obstinate strength to the face of her grandfather, Jacob Brechtmann, whose portrait glared down at them from the chimney wall.

"I'm sorry we missed each other yesterday," she said.

"Yes, so am I," Matthew said.

"Apparently," she said, and smiled. "But surely, Mr. Hope, a broken appointment needn't have prompted a call to the police."

Eyes twinkling. She was making a joke. But there was nothing funny about Matthew's visit here today.

"Miss Brechtmann," he said, "I wonder if you'd mind answering some questions for me and Detective Bloom."

"Does this have to do with the Parrish case? Mother told me you were here the other . . ."

"Yes, it has to do with the Parrish case," Matthew said. "Did you know him?"

"Who? Your client?"

"No. The victim. Jonathan Parrish."

"No."

"You did not know him," Matthew said.

"I did not know him."

Matthew looked at Bloom.

"Miss Brechtmann," Bloom said, "according to what Mr. Hope has told me, there seems reasonable cause to believe that you *did* know Jonathan Parrish."

"Oh?"

Pouting mouth forming the single word.

"Yes," Bloom said.

"And what has Mr. Hope told you?"

"Miss Brechtmann," Matthew said, "I spoke to a man named Anthony Holden . . . you *do* know Anthony Holden?"

"*That* rodent, yes, I know him."

"Who claims that the reason you fired him . . ."

"I fired him because he was a thief!"

"Not according to him."

"The man was a thief! He was getting kickbacks from our maltsters. He was *stealing*, Mr. Hope. Which is why I fired him."

"Did you have proof of this theft?"

"Of *course* I had proof!"

"Then why'd you settle out of court? If Holden *was* in fact a thief, then you hadn't libeled him when you *called* him a thief."

"Well, of course, don't you think I knew that? But what would a prolonged legal battle have done to the Brechtmann name? We're in the business of brewing beer, Mr. Hope, not manufacturing sensational headlines. I paid him off. And felt it was well worth it."

"You settled for five hundred thousand dollars, isn't that right?"

"Yes."

"Exactly what you paid Charles Abbott," Matthew said.

"Oh, my," Sophie said, "here's *that* scurvy dog again."

"I'm afraid so," Matthew said.

"Young man, you already *know* that I refused to give Mr. Abbott a penny!"

"Yes, you had him thrown out."

"Yes. So now you come here again, and you tell me . . ."

"I'm talking about 1969," Matthew said. "The money you gave him in 1969. Half a million dollars."

"Is that what he told you?" Elise said. "That we gave him . . . ?"

"Yes."

"He's a liar. Why would we have . . . ?"

"To get rid of him," Matthew said.

"Don't be absurd!"

"And to take the baby off your hands."

"What baby?"

"Your daughter," Matthew said. "Helen Abbott."

"I have no daughter," Elise said.

"Miss Brechtmann," Bloom said, "I have here . . ."

"Get out of here," Sophie said, "both of you. You have no right intruding on our privacy. You have no right coming here and . . ."

"Miss Brechtmann," Bloom said again, "I have here a warrant that authorizes me to . . ."

"A *what?*" Sophie said.

"A search warrant, ma'am. I'd appreciate it if your daughter read it. It authorizes . . ."

"She'll do no such thing," Sophie said. "What *you'll* do is leave this house at once."

"No, ma'am, I'm not about to do that," Bloom said, and shook the warrant at her. "This was signed by a magistrate of the Circuit Court, and it authorizes me to . . ."

"Then I know you won't mind if I call my lawyer," Sophie said, and reached for the phone.

"You can call the Attorney General if you like," Bloom said, "but that's not going to stop me from searching these premises."

"For *what?* What in hell do you *want* here, Mr. Bloom?"

"Two things," he said, and again offered the warrant to Elise. "If you'll just read this . . ."

"Don't touch that piece of paper!" Sophie shouted. "Get out of this house, Mr. Bloom! And take this shyster with you!"

"It's all right," Elise said suddenly.

Her voice sounded hollow. Her eyes looked vacant.

"Elise . . ." her mother said.

"Let me have the warrant."

"Elise!"

"Give it to me, please."

She held out her hand.

Bloom put the warrant into it.

She unfolded it, and began reading it silently.

She looked up.

"A thirty-eight-caliber Smith and Wesson revolver," she said.

"Yes, Miss. Which is the caliber and make of the pistol that killed a police officer named Charles Macklin on Wednesday night."

"And you think that pistol is in this house?"

"We think it may be here, yes."

"And these photographs?"

"Yes, Miss."

"You think they may be here as well?"

"Yes, Miss."

"Photographs of a baby and her mother, the warrant says."

Her voice caught on the word mother.

"Yes, Miss."

"Photographs of me and my baby, the warrant says."

"A little girl named Helen Abbott," Bloom said. "With baby beads on her wrist. Spelling out her name."

Elise looked at her mother.

"They know," she said.

There were tears in her eyes.

From the shelf in Frank's study, Leona removed the copy of *Corbin on Contracts*.

Behind it, just where she'd hidden it, was the .22-caliber Colt Cobra.

She took it in her hand, turned, and placed the gun on Frank's desk. She put the book back on the shelf. She knelt to where Frank kept his volumes of *Black's Law Dictionary*. She took down two volumes, and then removed the box of cartridges from the shelf, and placed this on the desk, too. She slid the volumes back into place on the shelf. A place for everything, and everything in its place. Aristotle. Or somebody.

She smiled.

And then she sat at the desk in Frank's swivel chair, and she loaded the gun the way the chubby little man in the gun shop had showed her. Bobby Newkes. Cute little man who knew all about things lethal. One cartridge at a time. Nice and easy. Squeeze off your shots, he'd told her. Don't *pull* the trigger, just *squeeeeeeeze* it gently.

She snapped the cylinder back into the gun.

And put the gun into her shoulder bag.

And looked at the clock on the wall.

Twenty minutes to twelve.

She took a deep breath and went out to her automobile.

▪ ▪ ▪

The women were explaining it all to Matthew and Bloom.

Trying to explain it all.

"After the call from Hurley," Sophie said, "I realized we were in trouble again. Abbott's visit to the house hadn't posed a serious threat. In fact, after his . . . accident, I didn't expect to hear further from him."

"But then Helen showed up," Elise said.

"Yes. Helen."

The two women looked at each other.

"I must admit . . ." Sophie said, and shook her head, and sighed.

"Yes," Elise said, and sighed, too.

"The resemblance," Sophie said.

"Yes."

"Your hair, your eyes."

"But blue."

"But your eyes exactly."

Both women sighed.

"We almost . . ."

"But you see, gentlemen . . ."

"If what we'd done back then was to have any meaning . . ."

"Protecting the name . . ."

"Making certain the name wouldn't be tainted . . ."

Sophie sighed again. "Giving away a . . . a granddaughter was . . . was not very easy," she said.

"A daughter," Elise said.

The word seemed to echo in the vaulting room.

"But, you see," Sophie said, "I knew that if my husband had learned of this . . . if we had not kept it from Franz, why . . . he would have killed them both. First that sniveling dog, Charles, and then Elise. Yes. I believe he would have killed his own daughter. For dishonoring the house."

"For bringing shame to the Brechtmann name."

"A name that stood for quality and wholesomeness."

Both women fell silent.

In that room, with the mist from the ocean crowding the French doors like a multitude of silent ghosts from the past, they seemed now to be wondering about the wisdom of what they'd done almost two decades ago—and what they'd been forced to do now, in order to protect that long-ago decision.

"We had to get them out of our lives," Sophie said. "Abbott and the baby both. To protect Elise . . . to protect the house . . ."

"The house?" Matthew said.

"Brechtmann Brewing," Sophie said.

Matthew nodded.

Sophie sighed again.

"And yet," she said, "when she returned, a grown woman, pregnant . . . oh, dear God, pregnant the way my daughter was pregnant so long ago . . ."

"Mother, please . . ."

". . . oh, dear God, calling me Grandma . . ."

Sophie covered her face with her hands.

"But you see," Elise said.

"Yes, yes, of course," Sophie said, as though her daughter were explaining it to her and not to Matthew and Bloom.

"If what we'd done *then* was to have any meaning now . . ."

"Yes," Sophie said, exhaling the word.

"If protecting the house had been important back then . . ."

"It was even more important now."

"How *could* we acknowledge her?"

"A bastard child?"

Sophie shook her head.

"I asked her to leave. I told her she had no mother here, no grandmother, either. I told her never to come here again. She said she had proof. I knew there was no proof. I sent her on her way."

The clock on the mantel was ticking.

Above the mantel, Jacob Brechtmann glared down from his portrait.

"And then Hurley called," Elise said.

"And told us he knew all about the pictures."

"Which is why I went to see Jonathan . . ."

Jonathan . . .

Jonathan . . .

It is not yet dawn on the morning of January thirtieth . . .

Elise does not yet know how she will handle this confrontation; it has been so many years, too many years. She is dressed for the rain: black slacks and black jersey top, a black raincoat and a black slouch hat that makes her look like Garbo. And because there is a chill accompanying the rain, she is also wearing black leather gloves.

She parks her car at Pelican Reef and begins walking up the beach toward his house. As she walks, she rehearses what she will say to him. She does not like having to go to him this way, begging a favor of him, especially after the way he treated her the last time, when all she was trying to do was protect him.

Because . . .

Because back then, even though Jonathan was what he was, there were still times when she succumbed to the dream of what might have been. If only. If only he weren't homosexual—but he was. If only he hadn't told her their relationship was hopeless—but he had. And then the self-pity: If only I'd never met him, if only I'd never gone to bed with him . . .

The rain encourages memories.

The whispering rush of the ocean against the shore prompts total recall.

Time has no meaning in the movie of her mind. When she can flip the switch either to fast forward or reverse, what possible meaning can time have? Choose any scene, choose any snippet, edit them in order or in reckless disarray. Seize each memory but only for a moment; most of the memories are painful. For Elise, time is meaningless except as it defines pain.

The movie is titled *My Life with Jonathan.*

A cheap little film.

Fade in on a luxurious Florida beach house.

Title over: NOVEMBER, 1968.

It is a gloriously balmy night. Japanese lanterns on the terrace, a band playing Beatles tunes. Elise is sixteen years old and attending the birthday party of her friend Marcia Nathanson, who has just turned seventeen.

The boy who comes walking out onto the terrace is the most beautiful thing she has ever seen in her life. Long blond hair and flashing blue eyes. A dancer's body, a dancer's moves. Barefooted. Wearing blue jeans and a white sweatshirt. The other boys at the party are wearing ties and jackets; Jonathan Parrish has dropped in from another planet.

Self-absorbed at sixteen, the curse of adolescence, Elise immediately thinks of him as an adjunct to herself, the perfect partner, the ideal mate, blond and blonde, pale and paler, together they will *dazzle!* She will capture this gorgeous alien male and keep him in a cage. She will tame this wild and splendid starman and make him her own. Confident of her own good looks, emboldened by her budding sexuality, she fastens herself like a succubus to this twenty-year-old stranger who has come not from another galaxy, as it turns out, but only from Indiana.

By the end of the night, she is lying in his arms on the beach.

He insists that she use only her mouth.

But she suspects nothing.

Two weeks later, in the house he is renting on Fatback Key, she persuades him to enter her, and surrenders her virginity to him.

Still suspecting nothing.

In the night, she whispers, "I love you."

And does not for a moment realize how these words trouble him.

My Life with Jonathan
A film by Elise Brechtmann
Starring, in order of appearance:
ELISE BRECHTMANN
JONATHAN PARRISH
And, in the role of Charles Abbott:
CHARLES ABBOTT

She goes to Abbott for the first time late in December. Deliberately seeks him out in his room over the garage. Goes to him in anger and in tears. Goes to him to get even. Because not an hour earlier, Jonathan Parrish has told her he is homosexual, he is gay, he is as queer as a turnip, he want nothing further to do with her. This entire episode with her—he calls it an *episode*, he calls what they shared together an *episode*—this entire episode was merely an experiment, something he still owed himself, something he still had to prove to himself. Prove? But prove what? Why, that girls . . . women . . . females cannot *satisfy* him.

So she is here in this room over the garage . . .

Title over: DECEMBER, 1968 . . .

. . . to make love to a stranger. In retribution for Jonathan's abrupt dismissal of her. Here in tears, here in anger and in shame, here to make love—no, not love. Certainly not *love.* Never again will sixteen-year-old Elise Brechtmann, star of this tedious little low-budget film, make love to any man. She is here to fuck and to be fucked. By the chauffeur. A man in her father's employ. A menial. She weeps into his shoulder as he claims her.

Fast forward.

Skip the boring months of her pregnancy and the frightening, painful delivery, cut to the goddamn chase. She has grown used to pain ever since Jonathan closed the door on their dream, the dream that still seeps unbidden into her mind, awake or asleep, these two beautiful people moving gracefully through life together, the dream that can never be, he can never be satisfied by a girl, a woman, a female, dig?

So she is understandably surprised (the camera moves in for a close shot of her utterly astonished face) when a few days after she gives birth, who should show up at the hospital but the Indiana Kid himself! Fresh from the recent festivities at Woodstock, he is sporting long blond hair and a long blond beard and feathers and beads, oh, how her girlish heart flutters!

He says he wants to take pictures of her and the baby.

He has taken at least a dozen of them when the nurse comes in and asks him to stop.

He kisses Elise on the cheek when he leaves an hour later.

A brotherly kiss.

He promises to send her prints of the pictures.

And is gone.

She is crying again. The pain, the pain.

He never sends the pictures.

She does not see him again until . . .

Title over: OCTOBER, 1981.

Twelve years later. Twelve long *years*, kiddies!

A montage of shots.

In the foreground, Jonathan Parrish on the Whisper Key beach. In the background, the house his brother has bought for him to live in. Jonathan Parrish is back in town, and up to his old tricks, moving into Calusa's growing gay community, discreetly to be sure, but not so discreetly as to hide his escapades from the all-seeing, all-knowing Elise Brechtmann, the writer, director, and star of this shabby little R-rated flick. Elise still nurtures the dream, you see, she still lives in the land of Might Have Been. It seems to her sometimes that her life is defined by loss. The loss of Jonathan, the loss of the baby, the loss of her father. Loss and pain, this is a three-handkerchief movie, folks.

When she discovers that Jonathan is having an affair with the blatant homosexual who is Brechtmann's purchasing agent, she decides to put an end to it at once. To protect Jonathan, you see. Because she knows what kind of a man Holden is, knows all about his unwholesome past, the hordes of younger men he's used and abused. She would, in fact, have fired him long ago were it not for a company policy initiated by her own father that guaranteed tenure to employees who'd been there for fifteen years or longer. But tenure does not apply to thieves. She concocts the story that he's been stealing from the company, goes so far as to falsify documents showing he's been receiving kickbacks, and is startled out of her wits (another close shot of her face, green eyes opened wide, mouth agape) when Holden sues for libel and defamation.

She learns later that the suit was suggested to Holden by Guess Who?

(Close shot of Jonathan Parrish, grinning into camera, pointing a prankish finger at himself. He is holding in his other hand a cane that looks remarkably like a phallus.)

She settles out of court.

She is beginning to hate Jonathan Parrish.

But now, she must deal with him yet another time.

On this cold rainy morning at the end of January . . .

It is, in fact, the thirtieth day of the month, but there are no titles, she does not need titles to remember the morning she put him out of her life forever . . .

Jonathan . . .

Jonathan . . .

She walks up the beach toward his house, dressed in somber black, black in mourning for her lost innocence, her lost love, her lost child, black against the falling gray of the rain and the gray of the sky.

He is at the kitchen counter when she comes in.

He does not look as if he has slept much the night before.

He is cutting a grapefruit in two with a chef's knife.

He explains that he had a dreadful argument with his brother. He tells her he feels rotten. He asks her if she wants half of this thing. She shakes her head no. Some coffee? No. Thank you.

He makes a comment which to her sounds faggoty but which probably isn't, something about it being a bit *early* for a social visit, isn't it, one eyebrow arched toward the clock on the wall, dawn breaks grayly on the horizon.

"I came for the pictures," she says.

"What pictures? What are you talking about?"

"The pictures you took of us. Me and the baby."

"God, that was *centuries* ago."

"Jonathan, I need them. Are they here?"

"Who remembers?"

"Do you have them?"

"Really, Elise . . ."

"Try to remember."

A look comes over his face. She has seen this look before. She knows exactly what this look means. It is a look compounded of opportunity and greed.

"How much are they worth to you?" he asks.

"You son of a bitch!" she says.

"Oh my, such language."

"You have them, don't you?"

Her voice rising.

"If I do, how much will you pay for them?"

"You son of a bitch bastard!"

Louder now.

"How much, Elise?"

"You fucking cocksucker *fag!*"

Shrieking the words.

And reaching for the knife on the countertop.

"No!" he shouts.

And screams.

Like a woman.

And then he shouts, "Put that down!"

She comes at him with the knife.

"I don't *have* them!" he shouts. "I don't know where they are!"

She does not believe him, she no longer cares *where* the fucking pictures are, she is consumed by rage. She knows only that this is the man who has caused her so much pain over so many years, the man who could never be satisfied by girls, women, females, *dig?* the man who not moments before has betrayed her yet another time. As she lunges toward him, her green eyes slitted, her lips skinned back over clenched white teeth, the knife in her hand becomes for her what he has always wanted and what she has never been able to give him. With all her might, she sticks it into him, glittering and stiff.

He screams.

And then he is silent.

All is silent.

She lets go of the knife. He sinks to the floor.

At first she thinks she is wet with his blood below.

But it is not his blood.

She runs off into the rain.

Toots was watching when she came out of the house at a quarter to twelve.

Leona was wearing black leotards and tights. Black pumps with a French heel. A black shoulder bag slung over one shoulder. Black Reeboks laced together and slung over the other shoulder. She tossed the Reeboks and the bag onto the front seat of the Jag and then got in herself.

Toots stayed a block and a half behind her.

Followed her up 41, turned when she did onto Bayou Boulevard.

Still with her when she parked the car in front of the Bayou Professional Building, 837 West Bayou Boulevard. Two-story, white clapboard building dead ahead. Doctors' shingles alongside doors in the wall. One of the shingles read WADE LIVINGSTON, M.D. Must be the place, Toots thought.

She waited.

In the Jag up ahead, Leona lighted a cigarette.

Toots's dashboard clock read three minutes to twelve.

Short nervous puffs of smoke came from the window on the driver's side of the Jag.

Hands on the clock straight up now.

One of the ground-level office doors opened. A nurse in white skirts, a little white cap, white pantyhose and flat white rubber-soled shoes came out and began walking toward a little red Toyota. She looked up at the sky, shrugged, got into the car, started it, and drove off.

Toots waited.

Leona tossed her cigarette out the window.

The door to the office opened again.

A tall dark-haired man wearing eyeglasses and a blue suit stepped out, checked the parking lot, spotted the green Jag, and walked toward it.

Dr. Livingston, Toots thought. I presume.

Livingston, if that's who he was, checked the lot again as he approached the Jag. He opened the door on the passenger side, got in immediately, and closed the door behind him.

"Let's get the hell away from here," he said.

Toots smiled.

The bug was working fine.

It was easy when there were only two poeple. Monitor a bug with four or five people in a room, you could go crazy trying to figure which voice was which. This one was simple. Only two people, one male, one female. *Vive la différence.*

"All right, Lee, what's the big urgency?"

Toots guessed he called her Lee. Term of endearment, she guessed. Lee.

"I hate it when you call me Lee."

Ooops.

"Oh, I'm sorry, I didn't realize . . ."

"My name is Leona."

"Yes, *Leona*, I *said* I was sorry."

Silence.

"So here we are, what's the big urgency?"

"I wanted to say goodbye properly."

"I thought that's what last night was all about. Saying goodbye properly. Leona, if you intend to . . ."

"No, I . . ."

". . . drag this thing out forever . . ."

"No. I know you want to end it."

"I've *already* ended it, Leona."

"Yes, I know. But I haven't. Not yet. Not properly."

"Where are we going?"

She was making a left turn into the parking lot of the Haley Municipal Arena. The big billboard out front advertised an automobile show coming next week. Trucks, Cars, Tractors.

"We can talk here."

"We can talk on the *road*, too. I don't see why . . ."

"I don't like to talk and drive at the same time."

Toots followed them in.

Several cars parked in the lot. Employees, Toots guessed. A yellow pickup truck with a golden retriever sitting behind the wheel. Man in coveralls walking diagonally across the lot toward the Motor Vehicles Bureau across the street from the arena.

Leona stopped the car.

Toots swung around the lot, drove all the way around the arena, and then parked facing the Jag, some three rows away from it. Risky, maybe, but she wanted to catch every word of this on tape, and if she pulled too close *behind* them, she might have attracted even more attention. A car parked in plain sight wouldn't be a suspicious car. She hoped.

"All right, let's talk." The doctor's voice again. "You said you wanted to talk, so let's . . ."

And a sudden silence.

Toots turned toward the recorder, thinking there'd been some kind of failure. The reels were still turning, the speaker switch was in the ON position.

"What's that, Leona?"

The man's voice. The doctor. Wade Livingston. Whoever the hell. Toots had heard voices like that before. A man trying to sound calm while he was on the thin boil of panic.

"What does it look like?"

Uh-oh, Toots thought.

"It looks like a gun, Leona, put it away right this minute."

Toughing it out. But the panic bubbling up now.

"No, I want to end this properly."

Holy shit, Toots thought, she's going to shoot him!

"You said you wanted to end it, Wade, so let's end it."

Toots was already halfway out of the car.

She ran straight for the driver's side. Neither of them saw her coming. The man, the doctor, Wade Livingston, whoever the hell, was fumbling to open the door on his side, and Leona was holding the gun in both hands now, the way she'd probably seen lady cops on television doing it, and Toots thought Oh, Jesus, don't shoot him, and grabbed the handle on the Jag's door and yanked it open, and though she'd never met the lady face to face, she yelled her first name, "Leona!" and then yelled, "Don't!" and then reached out for her shoulder and pulled her toward her, and hoped the gun wouldn't go off accidentally and put a big hole in the doctor's head.

"Toots Kiley," she said. "Give me the gun."

She held out her hand. The gun was shaking in Leona's fist.

"Give it to me, okay, Leona?"

On the other side of the car, Wade Livingston was backed against the door, watching in seeming fascination.

"Who are you?" Leona said.

"I told you. Toots Kiley. Let me have the piece, please."

Leona hesitated.

"Come on, Leona," Toots said. "There are better ways, believe me."

Leona looked into her eyes.

"I mean it," Toots said.

Leona kept looking into her eyes.

"Okay?" Toots said.

Leona nodded and handed her the gun.

"Good," Toots said. "Thank you."

"Are you a police officer?" the doctor said. "If so, I'd like to bring charges against . . ."

"You think your wife would like that?" Toots asked, taking a shot in the dark.

The doctor's face went pale.

"I didn't think so," Toots said.

The mist on the water was beginning to tear away in tatters. Matthew could almost see the horizon now. Elise sat beside her mother, drained by her bitter diatribe and her equally bitter confession of murder. She had equated her love for Jonathan Parrish with a film of dubious intent, and now she sat with her hands clasped between her mother's as if the frames of that film were flickering on the screen of her mind all over again.

"Miss Brechtmann," Bloom said, "I ask you now, did you go back to the Parrish house at any time after the day of the murder?"

A policeman's voice. Flat. Unemotional.

"I did."

"For what purpose, please?"

"To look for the photographs."

"Was there anyone in the house when you went there?"

"You know there was."

"Miss Brechtmann, could I now have the weapon and the photographs specified in the search warrant?"

"I'll show you where they are," she said, and rose, and slipped her hands from between her mother's, and then patted her mother's hands and said, "It's all right, Mama. Really."

She turned to where Matthew was standing beside Bloom.

The sun was almost coming through now.

The panes of glass on the French doors were almost alive with light.

"Nobody counted," she said, and smiled.

She was looking directly at Matthew. Perhaps because Bloom was a policeman from whom she felt she could expect no compassion. Perhaps because she included her mother among those who had not counted. Looking at Matthew, the smile on her face.

"Do you see?" she said.

"No, I'm sorry, I . . ."

"The baby was born in August," she said.

"Yes?"

The smile still on her face.

"I was with Abbott shortly after Christmas. The end of December. Do you see now?"

Her mother was staring at her.

Matthew already knew what she was saying. Matthew had already done the counting.

"The baby wasn't premature," Elise said.

"Elise, what are you . . . ?"

"I got pregnant in November, the baby was right on time."

"What?"

"The baby was Jonathan's."

Sophie Brechtmann brought her hand to her mouth.

"He never knew, isn't that rich? The night I went to tell him . . . well, you see, that was the night he chose to . . . to . . . to tell me it would never work, that was the night he said . . . goodbye." Elise shrugged. She was still smiling. "So I went to Abbott's shabby little room. In anger and in . . . in . . ."

"Elise," her mother said.

"Such a beautiful child we had," Elise said. "Jonathan and I."

"Elise, darling . . ."

"Such a beautiful family we could have been."

"Darling, darling . . ."

"Oh, Mama," she said, and burst into tears. "I'm so sorry, I'm so terribly sorry, please forgive me."

"Darling golden girl . . ."

Matthew watched them.

Mother and daughter.

This is the house that Jack built, he thought.

This is the end of the house that Jack built.

It was three o'clock in the afternoon.

Toots and Warren were in Matthew's office.

Toots was telling him all about how close Leona had come to shooting Dr. Wade Livingston. She was telling him there was no question but that Leona and the doctor had been intimately involved. No question, either, but that the affair was now over and done with.

"So what do we tell Frank?" Warren asked.

"I don't know yet. I want to think about it."

"I mean . . . it's over with, Matthew."

"I know."

"Well . . . let me know what kind of report you want."

"I will," Matthew said. "You both did a fine job. I hope we'll be working together again, Miss Kiley."

"Toots," she said.

"Toots, yes."

"You want to go have a beer or something?" Warren asked her.

"Love to," she said.

"Talk to you, Matthew," Warren said, and followed Toots out.

The phone began ringing. Matthew picked up.

"An Irene McCauley on five," Cynthia said.

He punched the button.

"Hello?"

The time was three-ten.

Irene was calling to tell him that Helen Abbott had died in the hospital last night.

"I tried to get you early this morning," she said, "but you were already gone. The son of a bitch did a real number on her, Matthew."

"Who?" Matthew said.

"Hurley. She named him before she died. The police are looking for him now."

"The police already *have* him," Matthew said. "I'll call over there, get them working on the same track."

"Matthew . . ."

"Yes."

"The baby's dead, too."

"I'm sorry," he said.

He was thinking that this was the *true* end of the house that Jack built.

At five o'clock that afternoon, he and Leona met again at Marina Lou's.

The first thing she said was, "I *told* you I wasn't having an affair, didn't I?"

"A technicality," Matthew said.

"No, Matthew, we'd already ended it."

"*He'd* already ended it."

She looked at him.

"How do you know that?"

"We have tapes. The bug saved you a lot of grief, Leona. If Toots hadn't heard that conversation . . ."

"I'd have shot him, yes."

"Probably."

"Most likely."

She sipped at her drink.

Second martini.

"You drink too much," he said.

"I know. Was it Frank who put the tail on me?"

"Yes."

"Then I ought to thank him."

"For what?"

"If Miss Kiley hadn't placed a bug in my car, I'd have shot and perhaps killed Dr. Wade Livingston. Miss Kiley was hired by Frank, ergo . . ."

"By Warren Chambers, actually. Who was hired by me. At Frank's suggestion."

"It still all goes back to Frank."

"Does it?"

"Well, if he's the one who . . ."

"You know what I mean, Leona. *Does* it go back to Frank?"

"Oh."

"What do you want me to tell him?"

Leona shrugged, lifted her glass, drained it, and signaled to the waiter for another one.

"No, Leona," Matthew said. "No more."

"Why not?"

"Because I'm your friend."

"I believe that, you know."

"What do I tell Frank?"

"Let *me* tell him," she said.

"All right, what will *you* tell him?"

"Everything."

"And then what?"

"I don't know. We'll have to see, won't we?"

"When did this thing with Livingston start?"

"Two months ago."

"That's not too bad."

"No, not too bad."

She was silent for a long time. Then she looked directly into Matthew's eyes and said, "I still love him, Matthew."

"Then either stop loving him or get out of the marriage," Matthew said.

"Okay."

Matthew sighed heavily.

"I'm sorry," she said.

"Yeah," he said, and sighed again.

"Really."

"Frank's going to ask my advice, you know. After you've talked to him, he's going to want my opinion. We're partners, Leona."

"And what will you tell him?"

"I'll tell him he ought to do everything in his power to keep you. Short of looking the other way while you fuck a stranger. That's what I'll tell him, Leona."

"Thank you," she said.

And suddenly she was crying.

Parrish was catching a nine o'clock plane to Indianapolis. He was packed and ready to go when Matthew went to see him at the hotel early that evening. Now that all charges had been dropped, he wanted to get the hell out of Calusa as soon as possible.

He took Matthew's hand.

"Thank you," he said.

And then, because Matthew had saved his life, and because he still hadn't the slightest idea what sort of man he was, he said, "If ever you're in Indiana, stop by. I'd be mighty happy to see you."

"I rarely get out that way," Matthew said, and smiled.

He was thinking You do your very best, you make it work at last, you make it all come together—and then there's nothing more to do but shake hands and say so long.

"I guess that means I won't be seeing you ever again," Parrish said.

"I guess that's what it means," Matthew said.

It sounded very much like goodbye.

This is the house that Jack built.

This is the malt that lay in the house that Jack built.

This is the rat that ate the malt that lay in the house that Jack built.

This is the cat that killed the rat that ate the malt that lay in the house that Jack built.

This is the dog that worried the cat that killed the rat that ate the malt that lay in the house that Jack built.

This is the cow with the crumpled horn that tossed the dog that worried the cat that killed the rat that ate the malt that lay in the house that Jack built.

This is the maiden all forlorn that milked the cow with the crumpled horn that tossed the dog that worried the cat that killed the rat that ate the malt that lay in the house that Jack built.

This is the man all tattered and torn that kissed the maiden all forlorn that milked the cow with the crumpled horn that tossed the dog that worried the cat that killed the rat that ate the malt that lay in the house that Jack built.

This is the priest all shaven and shorn that married the man all tattered and torn that kissed the maiden all forlorn that milked the cow with the crumpled horn that tossed the dog that worried the cat that killed the rat that ate the malt that lay in the house that Jack built.

This is the cock that crowed in the morn that waked the priest all shaven and shorn that married the man all tattered and torn that kissed the maiden all forlorn that milked the cow with the crumpled horn that tossed the dog that worried the cat that killed the rat that ate the malt that lay in the house that Jack built.

This is the farmer that sowed the corn that kept the cock that crowed in the morn that waked the priest all shaven and shorn that married the man all tattered and torn that kissed the maiden all forlorn that milked the cow with the crumpled horn that tossed the dog that worried the cat that killed the rat that ate the malt that lay in the house that Jack built.